WIDE IS THE HORIZON

By the Same Author

NOVELS

Scissors	17th Ed.	The Guests Arrive	17th Ed.
Sails of Sunset	14th Ed.	Volcano	12th Ed.
Little Mrs Manington	12th Ed.	Victoria Four-Thirty	26th Ed.
The Love Rack	12th Ed.	They Wanted to Live	13th Ed.
Sagusto	13th Ed.	One Small Candle	11th Ed.
David and Diana	13th Ed.	So Immortal a Flower	6th Ed.
Indiana Jane	8th Ed.	Eight for Eternity	8th Ed.
Pamela's Spring Song	12th Ed.	A Terrace in the Sun	6th Ed.
Havana Bound	11th Ed.	The Remarkable Young Man	4th Ed.
Bargain Basement	11th Ed.		
Spears Against Us	28th Ed.	Love is Like That	3rd Ed.
Pilgrim Cottage	19th Ed.	The Pilgrim Cottage Omnibus	

MISCELLANEOUS

Gone Rustic	13th Ed.	Diary of Russell Beresford	2nd Ed.
Gone Rambling	7th Ed.		
Gone Afield	5th Ed.	Half Way: an autobiography	18th Ed.
Gone Sunwards	5th Ed.	And So To Rome	3rd Ed.
And So To Bath	17th Ed.	One Year of Life	
And So To America	3rd Ed.	Portal to Paradise	4th Ed.
A Man Arose	2nd Ed.	Selected Poems	

WIDE IS THE HORIZON

by

CECIL ROBERTS

Illustrated by David Knight

HODDER AND STOUGHTON

*The characters in this book are entirely imaginary
and bear no relation to any living person*

Copyright © 1962 by

CECIL ROBERTS

First printed 1962

MADE AND PRINTED IN GREAT BRITAIN FOR
HODDER AND STOUGHTON LTD., LONDON, BY
HAZELL WATSON AND VINEY LTD., AYLESBURY AND SLOUGH

Wide is the horizon and free is the air,
　All heaven is over us, beneath us the grass,
Oh, let us ride gaily in sunshine, my fair,
　Too soon youth in the saddle and love's hour will pass.

David Knight

CHAPTER ONE

I

AMELIA MACREARY was a bright example of the saying, slightly altered in regard to sex, "You cannot keep a bright girl down." She was born with only two assets but both of them were priceless. She had beauty and she had brains. For a woman the greater of these is beauty, if the owner is possessed of the character to exploit it. There was plenty of character in the make-up of Amelia, a braw Scots lassie with a wealth of red hair, a peach-like complexion, and, most singular of all, very bright green eyes. In this manner she was notable from birth. She was not entered in Debrett's *Peerage, Baronetage and Knightage* but she was, by a fairy god-mother, entered

7

in the Book of Good Fortune. When she was a child she had gappy teeth. "She'll be lucky," said Aunt Emily, who read the tea-leaves. When her teeth closed up and became level, small and pearly, she was still lucky. To this same word she added a letter 'p' that helped the prophecy to come true; she was plucky.

She began simply enough, a girl born in a drab street that just succeeded in not being a Glasgow slum, in the year 1911. It took her twenty-three years to get out of it. She left school at fifteen, stood behind a counter at Woolworths, and went to night classes for shorthand and typewriting. She showed no disposition to waste her time with boys. One of a family of ten, she began to wonder, thus early, how she came to be in it. She looked upon them all as of the earth earthy, regarding her four brothers as louts, her three sisters as frumps. She had two sisters-in-law who were commonplace; they produced noisy brats.

Amelia flattered herself in being different. She carried an aura of breeding. She quickly learned shorthand and typewriting and at seventeen secured a position in an old established firm of whisky exporters with agencies abroad. Vivacious and striking with her red hair and green eyes, she never lacked suitors but as they all belonged to a class she was determined to escape from, she gave them no encouragement. She combined with her effortless physical distinction a lot of commonsense. She had an infectious laugh and natural elegant manners. To the envy of all her sisters she contrived to appear expensively dressed, at little expense. She read Vogue in the Public Library. She stunned the family by discovering a local branch of Elizabeth Arden and sank a large part of her earnings in acquiring its aids to enchantment. On such a splendid foundation the necessary aids were few.

Amelia always felt baffled by her surroundings. The Macreary family wore her down. She had to fight for every

8

refinement. They were good, honest and dreadfully dull. Every Sunday they filled a pew in the Presbyterian church at the end of the road. Two of her sisters were Sunday School teachers. Her father, a sidesman, employed as a clerk in the same whisky exporting firm as herself, carried the plate for the offerings. Their mother and one of the sisters stayed at home to cook the Sunday lunch, after which the family slept until tea-time when two gawky young men came to visit her sisters, and the married brothers called with their wives and children. They were a united family. There was a tremendous noise.

Amelia's first breach in this unity was scorning Presbyterianism to go to the Episcopal Church. It seemed to her to be more exclusive. Here she attracted a young man articled to a firm of solicitors. She seldom brought him home. She gave him only a restrained encouragement. His assets in her eyes were not his good looks and pleasant manners, nor his better social position. He had been educated at Oxford and might one day succeed to his uncle's law firm. His real attraction for Amelia was his accent. She wanted to get rid of her own. More and more their speech at home jarred her. Her parents were an admirable devoted couple but the Glasgow accent lay heavily upon them as on her brothers and sisters. She felt she must get away from them. Marriage might be a way of escape, but not marriage in Glasgow. She was aware of other worlds, revealed by the cinema and the pages of *Vogue*. She was now twenty-three and getting restless. The prospect of life in Glasgow as the wife of a lawyer would be alluring to many girls of her class. It would be a promotion, but not enough of a promotion for Amelia with her looks and ambition. She believed in the great god Chance, twin-brother of Luck. She must get out of Glasgow.

One day early in 1933, she had met at a friend's house a young Spaniard who represented a Jerez sherry firm. He was dark, suave, elegant. He had beautiful hands, her first experience of Latin hands. They fascinated her in contrast with the meaty, knobbly hands of the local swains.

"But he's an R.C.! You can't go round with a Roman Catholic, and a foreigner!" protested her sister Mabel.

"He might just as well object to your being a Presbyterian! And with a longer historical reason," retorted Amelia.

She had no intention of marrying the young Spaniard but, like the Oxford boy, she had a use for him. He was delighted when she said she wanted to learn Spanish.

She proved a quick pupil. She was also a baffling one. Within six months she was reading one of Blasco Ibanez's novels with him, but he was no nearer to getting into bed with her. Her red hair, green eyes and beautiful legs made him frantic. She tortured him with inducements and repulses. She grew more fluent as he grew more desperate.

A day came when Amelia spoke to the manager of her firm. It had a branch in Buenos Aires. She felt she would like a wider experience. She spoke Spanish. Would there be an opportunity for her to go to the Buenos Aires office?

The manager was delighted. That was exactly what they were seeking, a competent typist with a knowledge of Spanish and experience in the business. His cooperation was increased by the fact that he, a respectable middle-aged married man, suffered a considerable provocation when she came into his office to take the letters. She crossed her legs to cushion the shorthand notebook. They were exquisite legs. Better to banish temptation.

When a month later she told her father what had been arranged his mouth opened in silent astonishment. Her mother was equally dumbfounded. At last he became articulate. He was sitting in the kitchen, in his shirt sleeves, with his shoes off and his feet on the steel fender. For years Amelia had tried to reform him of this plebeian habit. She knew now she would never succeed.

"Well, you're a marvel!" he said at last, knocking out his pipe on the hob grate.

"Aren't you afraid—going to them foreign parts?" asked her mother, holding a dish-cloth after taking a rice pudding out of the oven.

"Afraid? I'm much more afraid of being stuck here!"

"I hope they're paying you well," said her father.

She told him her salary. It was three times his after twenty-five years of clerking. Also she would have her return passage and three months holiday every three years.

II

She had a royal send-off. The day before she left Glasgow to go to Southampton the family held a farewell tea-party. Her brothers, their two wives and their six children, her sisters, a brother-in-law and three children, two aunts, an uncle, five friends from the office, the curate from the Episcopal Church, the young articled pupil with the Oxford voice, and the suave dark Spaniard of the frustrated hopes, came to the drab house in the long squalid street where Amelia had been born. The parlour, the dining-room and the large back kitchen were crammed.

For the first time in her life Amelia was moved by the emotional atmosphere. She felt a little like a film star. She had a new trousseau. If only there had been photographers with flash bulbs! She wore a greenish grey tailor-made skirt and coat, and she was slightly made-up, with a restraint and a distinction that evoked general admiration. "My, you smell good," said her brother Alec, kissing her roughly when he came in with his onion-shaped wife. It was not the kind of remark she liked but she accepted his gauche compliment. She had never economised on scent. She bought Chanel. She had few clothes but they were of first-class quality.

"She's a fair knock-out!" said her brother Jack. "I wonder what she's really up to!"

"I wouldn't like to say," said his wife. "You don't go all the way to Buenos Aires to type!"

He let the remark go. Amelia made all the women mad.

The party was a great success. No one drank too much. Never had Amelia looked more lovely, been more gracious to family and friends. She had the feeling of getting out of prison after a life-sentence but she hid her exultation. Poor things, they were to be pitied. They had no sense of a larger world.

On the morning when her father and mother went to the station to see her off to Southampton she was a little afraid of herself, a little appalled by her own adventurousness. She was aware that, deep down, she was fond of her parents. With a great effort she controlled her tears, hugged her weeping mother and kissed the cheek of her watery-eyed father. To the last she astonished them.

"No, no! Not there! First class," she said to the porter who had not observed the ship's labels. From now on, free of Glasgow, she was going to travel through life first class. No more twinges from her father's accent and his stockinged feet on the fender. No more suppressed protests when her mother took dripping out of a jam-jar with the meat knife. No more wet sheets standing by the wringer in the scullery with the old brown stone sink, waiting for her father to give a hand, or for her to pull and fold before ironing. It was remarkable how she had endured that frowsty commonplace life in a Victorian villa with a closet at the bottom of the garden, in whose sooty sodden soil a few chrysanthemums succeeded in lifting their dowdy petals.

The whistle blew, the train began to pull out. Despite herself she could not see her parents at all clearly for a mist in her eyes. She leaned out of the window and watched them move away down the platform, her father's arm around the stumpy all-black figure of her mother. She did not hear her father's remark as they turned to leave.

"Amelia's a marvel," he murmured with a note of pride. "That girl'll come out all right. You'll see!"

CHAPTER TWO

I

LIFE on board the liner in which she sailed from England had been a revelation. She had entered a world unbelievably beautiful. The cabin was most comfortable. She was a good sailor. Her looks commanded immediate attention. At the Captain's cocktail party she made some pleasant acquaintances. She was always in demand at the ship's dances.

On the deck an opera *diva* occupied the chair on her left. She had come on board at Lisbon. The *diva* spent a considerable time hidden behind dark glasses, and holding up her hand to be kissed by a train of admirers. She was Argentine. Amelia was soon on cordial terms with her. They chatted in Spanish. Towards eleven o'clock, when the soup trolley came round, the chair on her right was occupied by a well-groomed, picturesque old gentleman. He was brought there by a valet. He had a grey Van Dyck beard, shapely gloved hands and small feet. Despite his years, he was a dandy. A Spanish *hidalgo*, obviously. For three days, always immersed in a book, he never addressed a word to anyone, though it was obvious he knew English, for among the books the valet brought out were some with English titles. He spoke Spanish with the valet. When the luncheon gong sounded the valet came to escort him to the dining-room. The Don was as tall as he was elegant. He wore a wide-brimmed black felt hat. He had a strange habit of always wearing light tan kid gloves. In the dining-room, where he sat alone by one of the port-holes, she observed that he had a finely shaped head with well-groomed wavy grey hair, white over the temples. It was a beautiful head.

14

One day, her curiosity now intense, Amelia called the Head Steward to her. The Don seemed to know most of the ship's stewards, who treated him with great deference.

"Can you, please, tell me the name of that distinguished Spanish gentleman sitting against the port-hole?" asked Amelia, indicating the subject of her enquiry.

"Yes, madam. He's not Spanish, he's English. Sir Anthony Slowdon. He's known all over South America as the greatest authority on horses. He's been travelling on this line for many years. He's very popular in the Argentine."

"He lives there?"

"He has an *estancia* there."

"He travels alone?"

"Yes, madam. I believe he's a bachelor—but a great lady-killer," he added with a smile.

"I don't wonder!" exclaimed Amelia, laughing.

From this time on she observed Sir Anthony closely, fascinated by his distinguished appearance, his aloofness, the strict regularity and precision of all his movements. Exactly at eleven o'clock he appeared, impeccably dressed, attended by his valet bearing a steamer rug, for they were still in the North Atlantic and the mornings had a chill in the air. He wore bluish sun-glasses. His shoes, long and narrow, were highly polished. Tight-fitting gloves covered his hands. There was an elaborate monogram worked on the white silk scarf that he sometimes wore. At twelve, when the ship's siren went, he pulled out of his waistcoat pocket a thin gold hunter watch, which he checked carefully with the noonday signal.

He had not been present at the Captain's cocktail party on Tuesday evening, but there was another cocktail party on Wednesday, and possibly he had been grouped in the second of these. The passenger list gave Amelia a fragment of information, filling in the Head Steward's identification of her deck chair neighbour. He was entered as Sir Anthony Slowdon,

Bart. So he was a baronet. This seemed to bear out her assumption that he was a man of breeding and not one of those innumerable commercial knights that the City produced with such fecundity.

The passenger list gave her another piece of information. He occupied a suite on the promenade deck. It bore out an estimate of considerable means, if not of wealth. A singular fact regarding this handsome old gentleman was that he never spoke to anyone. He sat alone, he ate alone, he walked the deck alone. Something in his aristocratic bearing seemed proof against the general affability that prevailed on board ship. Half-a-dozen acquaintances asked her what she knew about the distinguished old Don who was her neighbour. She could tell them nothing. On one occasion when she was invited to the bar for an aperitif before dinner she saw him sitting alone, drinking a sherry. He was dressed in a superbly cut dinner jacket, a glossy white shirt with a single pearl stud, and a very high stiff collar. What surprised her was that he wore white kid gloves this time. Were his hands deformed? He smoked a cigarette in a long gold-mounted holder.

The next day she particularly observed his gloved hands as he held the Spanish book he was reading, *Obras Completas de Góngora*—a book of poems. No, they appeared well-shaped and flexible as he turned the pages. The glove-wearing was an eccentricity probably.

One bright sunny morning as he appeared with his valet, who followed, rug and books in hand, she looked up when he halted by his chair. Their eyes met. He gently and ceremoniously bowed to her, and sat down, while the valet wrapped his legs in the rug. She waited expecting he might at last speak to her, for she had acknowledged his bow with a friendly smile, but he uttered no word, opened his book and began reading. When the deck steward arrived with the cups of bouillon, he had a short and affable conversation with him. He had a beautiful speaking voice, an accent befitting a man of culture. It was a little high in pitch. Amelia liked that, it carried a note of command. It belonged to a man who was assured that his wishes would be fulfilled. Yet it was not an arrogant voice. She admired the ease with which he spoke to the steward, affable without condescension, the patrician visible in his bearing. She much wanted to talk to him but the Grandee in him restrained her.

The *diva* on her left was tiresomely loquacious. She held court on deck, with a continuous gabble of high-pitched voices around her. She had a musical laugh and exercised it freely. There was a commotion when she appeared, wind-blown violet tulle about her neck, gold bangles loaded with trinkets jangling on her wrists, heels so high and ankles so thin that one marvelled that they safely carried the immense superstructure of bosom and abundant coils of glossy black hair. She was a large handsome woman of about fifty, a wide face above a double chin, every line creamed out, the eyebrows plucked and marked by black pencilled lines. She gesticulated freely, enjoying the commotion she created. A little French maid, like a tug attending a liner, fussed and manipulated her into the deck chair, bearing cushions and books, and a Pekinese dog with watery eyes and an immense blue bow. Two stewards rushed to assist at this berthing. The *diva* chaffed them all in Spanish, French and English, lavishly affable. Every morning she wore a fresh creation. On the fourth morning she appeared in scarlet trousers, and a gold-laced brass-buttoned blue jacket that made her look like an Algerian *poilu* at the end of a long term of service.

The most assiduous member of her entourage was a dapper little youngish man with a blue-black chin and soft white hands, whom she called Kiki. He shot his words out with the barking flow of a Gatling gun, accompanied by monkeyish pantomime. He was a dandy, effeminate, and taut as a violin string.

It was astonishing how he put out of face his competitors offering incense. He might be thirty or forty. He dusted his face with a bluish powder, had pale fingers that looked like parsnips, and smelt of sandalwood bath salts. There seemed to be no legs to fill the razor-edge trousers. His narrow feet were encased in yellow suede shoes. He had the air of a puppet animated by his irrepressible nervous energy. Amelia learned later that he was a Portuguese *marqués* with vast estates in Brazil. He was a renowned aviator, and had volunteered in the French Air Force, during the World War, gaining the Légion d'Honneur, the Croix de Guerre and three citations. Most surprising of all, married to a Braganza, he was the father of five daughters. "And a poppet!" exclaimed the *diva*, after giving Amelia the history of her *marqués*.

"Puppet?" repeated Amelia, a little surprised.

The *diva* opened her heavily mascaraed eyes wider and stared at Amelia.

"No—no! Poppet, not puppet! Don't you know—it's an American word for the most adorable creature!"

Every time Amelia looked at the Portuguese poppet she was more and more astonished by those five daughters. Poor little poppet. Would he try again?

There was a morning when the Grandee, as Amelia mentally termed Sir Anthony, made no appearance. His deck chair remained unoccupied. She asked the steward if her neighbour was ill.

"No, ma'am. Sir Anthony's moved to a chair by the verandah café," he replied.

She thought she knew why. Twice yesterday morning he had betrayed annoyance at the conversational racket around the *diva*. He had gone to a quieter spot. Amelia regretted the move. The possibility of any conversation with her Grandee seemed remoter than ever. She admired him tremendously. If only he were her father, or grandfather, how proud she would be to be seen with him! She thought of her father, sitting in his shirt sleeves with his stockinged feet on the kitchen fender. How strange, and unpredictable Fate was!

II

The days slipped by, smooth as the flowing sea. They had left Teneriffe behind. They were nearing the South Atlantic now. The wind was slight, the sun hot, the weather halcyon. Gay frocks, and white trousers began to appear. There was a crowd around the swimming pool. South American children, Spanish-speaking, with Spanish blood in their veins, screeched and flitted like tropical birds. The sunsets faded like dying fires, crimson above the darkening violet flood. A full moon silvered the sea. They played games on the deck, drank cocktails in the bar, swam in the pool, danced or played Bingo after dinner.

Within a week Amelia found herself in constant demand. Two ship's officers, a trio of Argentines, a young Polish pianist, a manager of a Brazilian coffee plantation, bound for San Paolo, an apple-cheeked Englishman representing the Rolls-Royce company, even the blue-chinned Kiki, the Marqués Alonso Varregas-Medina, took time off from the *diva* to pay her court. She was popular with the women too. They admired her figure, her abundant red hair and roseleaf complexion.

She could not compete in the matter of clothes, but she was elegant in her few frocks. The gaiety of youth, the excitement of a new wonderful world, the circumambient prosperity, brought a glow to her beautiful green eyes, a heightened flush to her cheeks. Sometimes she wondered whether she had ever lived in Abernethy Villas, caught a morning bus to the gloomy office where she typed letters in a glass cage, mostly under an electric bulb, hot on one side from a sizzling steam radiator, chilled on the other by the damp air of the fog-laden winter days.

Perhaps the greatest of wonders in this new fairy-tale life was a bathroom to herself. "We're doing you well, Miss Macreary—but we're able to get good terms from the Line because they handle a lot of our shipping." Yes, they were doing her well, she reflected, as she lay deliciously idle in her own bath. The nickel taps gleamed, the walls shone with white enamel paint, the thick towels came warm off the towel rail. To crown this new excitement she bought a jar of verbena bathsalts in the hairdresser's shop. At home, Friday was her bathnight. She followed one of her sisters, and often the water was not hot enough, and always she had to pick some loose hairs out of the imperfectly cleaned bath. She found the task revolting, and in repeated quarrels with her sister she was called a pernickety fuss-pot. "Anybody would think you were a duchess, the way you go on," snarled Annie. "I am a duchess," retorted Amelia, "when I compare your habits with mine!"

Now every morning she had a hot bath in a spotless bathroom in deliciously scented water. No duchess did better. Annie's insult had been turned into a prophecy.

She had a motherly, attentive stewardess. She received a shock when the little woman first spoke to her with a strong Glasgow accent.

"Are you from Yorkshire?" asked Amelia, knowing quite well she was not, but on no account would she let her stewardess know she also came from Glasgow.

"No, m'leddy. I'm from Glasgow. We're all in the shippin'. My father worked on Clydeside. My brother is chief engineer on the *Clan MacDonald*. My husband went down in H.M.S. *Renown*. Sea's in our blood, m'leddy."

My lady. She could have embraced the little woman for such a mistake.

That evening, seated in front of the long mirror, brushing

her abundant tresses before retiring, she addressed herself, a habit since childhood.

"Amelia Macreary, you're a snob! M'leddy indeed! And why not, I ask you. You've got out of Glasgow, you've a private bathroom of your own, you're sailing down the South Atlantic, tonight you've been uncomfortably hugged on the dance floor by a real marquis. And, truth said, you're only a swollen-headed little typist from Glasgow, going to be a typist in Buenos Aires. Face the facts, my girl."

She stopped brushing her hair, and looked at herself in the mirror, very pleased with what she saw. She gave a tug at the white silk négligé, half exposing her breasts until she looked like one of those ambitious women the French kings got mixed up with. She laughed at herself, brush in hand, and then began to sing as she resumed the brushing.

> My heart's in the Highlands, my heart is not here,
> My heart's in the Highlands, a-chasing the deer,
> Chasing the wild deer, and following the roe,
> My heart's in the Highlands wherever I go.

She sang the lines softly, and then stopped. "There never was a bigger lie, my lass. Your heart's neither in the Highlands nor in Glasgow," said Amelia to her pretty face framed in its red hair. "But there may be something true about following the roe, particularly if he's a dear."

With that bad pun she finished her toilet and got into bed. "Good-night, m'leddy," she said, switching off the light.

CHAPTER THREE

I

THEY had crossed the Equator and sighted Salvador. The vast South American continent lay on the western horizon. The passengers watched the officer who kept the chart of the ship's course move the tiny flag along the plotted line down the ocean, the line curving into Rio de Janeiro, looping out again to Santos, and then marking the final twelve-hundred-mile run to Buenos Aires.

Amelia began to regret the lessening distance to her goal. A year of this life of ease and pleasure would not have worried her. She was very popular in this friendly varied community, and had addresses of residents in Buenos Aires who wanted to entertain her. She had been somewhat secretive about her mission. Would they show themselves as hospitable if they knew she was only a typist going out to the Argentine office of her firm? Obviously some of these Argentines were very wealthy. The jewels worn by the women would have ransomed a king. Millionaires seemed as common as dominoes. Some of them were reserved and modest in their attire and deportment, an air of breeding emanating from them. Others had a flashy vulgarity. She was soon aware of the subtle social currents flowing about her. There was a young attaché of the French Embassy at Buenos Aires, going out for the first time, after two years in Rome. He was an excellent dancer and she soon became his preferred partner. He taught her the tango. He talked excellent English having spent a year at Cambridge. He was gay, exquisitely mannered, and adventurous. Soon he was enticing her from the dance floor to the boat deck, the purpose being very obvious. There was a moment, taking cover from the wind, in the lee of an officer's cabin, when he confidently took her in his arms and kissed her. She made a token resistance and then amply rewarded him. The French words he used lent intoxication to his boyish ardour. Very soon he was her slave. She was merciless, being at once reserved and enticing. She extracted his history. He was twenty-six, his father a retired colonel who lived with his mother on a small property near Avignon in Provence. He had two older brothers, a sister his junior, and an uncle who was an Ambassador. They belonged to the *petite noblesse*. Amelia teased him about being flirtatious, and unfaithful to his fiancée. He stoutly denied the existence of any such person.

"But every French boy has an *amie*," declared Amelia.

His blue-grey eyes opened wide.

"*Une amie*—perhaps, but that's not a fiancée!" Etienne de Lérin protested, a little embarrassed. "Where did you learn that?"

"Learn what?"

"*Amie*."

"It's French for friend, isn't it?"

"Not exactly, not always. It's a word of different meanings," he said, somewhat confused.

In her ignorance she blundered on.

"Can't I be your *amie*?" she asked.

She saw him turn red in the face, but his eyes danced as he looked at her.

"Alas, no," he said, with a mock sorrowful air.

"Etienne, have I said something awful?"

"Yes—but delicious because you don't realise what *amie* can mean."

She knew then, and they laughed together to cover their embarrassment. They looked out across the moonlit sea. The bright stars swung over the great funnel as the ship rolled.

Then his lips sought hers and they trembled a little in a wordless young ecstasy.

"Etienne, will you do something for me?" she asked, after a long silence.

"Anything, *chèrie*."

"I want to learn French. I am really serious about it. Will you teach me?"

"Nothing would have more pleasure for me!"

"Thank you, but that's not good English."

"No?" he asked.

"Nothing would give me more pleasure."

"Nothing would give me more pleasure," he repeated.

"I would like an hour in the morning, and one hour in the afternoon."

"And also two hours in the evening!" he added merrily.

That was another opportunity taken. She had not been long in making the discovery that French was an asset. There were French books in the ship's library, there were French films at the ship's cinema. Most of the passengers had an easy flow of French. The *diva* and the *marqués* went from Spanish into French with the ease of a gear-change in a sports car. They switched, without any apparent reason. It was beautiful to hear them. The pleasure apart, it was an asset one must have if one aspired to a certain social standing. It had intimate associations also, evading an awkward vulgarity. The sleek young crooner, Italian as it happened, in the ship's orchestra, sang an enchanting French song, his voice husky with amorous tenderness. *Parlez-moi d'amour*. It always brought loud applause.

"I'm just crazy about that song," cried an American dowager, flushed under a paper hat.

"*C'est ravissant!*" said a Frenchwoman.

"*Che bello!*" said an Italian.

"*Como hermoso!*" said a Spaniard.

Had the young crooner in the tight blue hussar jacket sung "Speak to me of love" it would not have been *ravissant, bella, hermoso,* or made anyone crazy. It would have been just silly. French was the language of seduction, just as Italian was the language of opera, and English the language of sport. In French a woman could be naked down to a perilous verge and they said she was *en grand décolleté*. In English there was not a word for it. She was just brazen.

Amelia made a discovery. She had learned Spanish quickly. She now astonished Etienne by her swift acquisition of French. By luck she found a French grammar in the ship's library. She learned the verbs *avoir* and *être* thoroughly. She made her tutor write lists of words, and learned twenty every day. Her natural gift was encouraged by her charming young teacher. The evening lesson on the boat deck often lasted until midnight. She read with him a novel by Colette that would have been considered improper in Glasgow but evoked young love in Paris with deceptive simplicity, if not innocence. Also her tutor produced a book, *Toi et Moi*, a series of reminiscent love-poems narrating the history of an *affaire* between an ecstatic young man and his *amie*. She learned that a *garçonnière* was not a waitress but a young bachelor's rooms—and might be a *nid d'amour*, a love-nest. Again, how expressive and delicate!

By the time the boat reached Rio, Amelia was tackling irregular verbs. She was firmly dealing with Etienne's irregular suggestions.

"You have a beautiful ear," he said. He made her repeat a phrase.

"That's not good English. You mean I have a good ear!" corrected Amelia.

"I mean both," he said, with an alluring smile. "You have an ear that is *belle* and *bonne*." He leaned forward and bit the lobe of her ear.

"*Vous êtes un méchant garçon!*"

"*Tu es!*" he cried with mock severity. "We are intimates."

"*Tu es—*" she began, solemnly.

"*Toi et moi!* You *tutoyer* when intimate."

His eyes played over her face, serious, ardent.

"Not too intimate!" she admonished him.

There were moments when she felt he was seventeen, just out of school. She did not want to hurt him, but she would not allow him to become a nuisance. And most probably this ardour of his was as evanescent as a rainbow-hued soap bubble. Meanwhile, he taught her French, he danced superbly, he fetched and carried, and was like a ripple of water through a springtime meadow. *Parlez-moi d'amour*. Like the Greeks, the French had a word for it.

I I

The vanishing of the Grandee, as she called him, disconcerted her a little. She saw him only at meal times, or when they passed in a corridor, or in the foyer. In the latter places he never failed to give her a courteous bow. She had found where he sat in the mornings, in a solitary chair in a recess between the verandah café and the swimming pool. Once, when he was absent from his chair, she saw a book lying on top of his steamer rug. With a boldness that surprised her she stopped, picked up the book and read the title. *Nostromo* by Joseph Conrad. She put it down very quickly and hurried on.

How very singular! There was an arty young man in the Glasgow office who always had his nose buried in a book. He was shy and gangly and once, as she encountered him coming out of a bookshop in Sauchiehall Street, he asked her nervously if she would have a coffee with him. It was probably a gesture of thanks because she had several times typed out some poems which he had written. They were modern, *vers libres*, and had no rhymes and, it seemed to her, very little sense, but she was not competent to judge such things. In the café he confessed that he longed to be a writer. He was working on a novel. She asked him what it was called. It was as if she had touched a button that operated a machine. He instantly sprang into life and was changed from something commonplace, encased in a shapeless suit and a cheap shirt, into a flame that burned incandescently, throwing a vivid light on human passions and problems. The suburban face took on a glow, the voice a warmth. Here was a 'Transformation' in Sauchiehall Street. She looked and listened. How little one knew of one's neighbours! Could it be possible that here, in Glasgow's raw clime, he might plant an acorn of immortality, strongly flourishing from the dust they were all bound for? Some such white-faced youth had once upon a time walked out of a factory, its name forgotten but his name alive after a century: Charles Dickens.

Amelia was a good audience. He opened to her like a marigold that had found the sun. There was a lot of drab dirt but also a blaze of passion in his story. He had created a local Casanova who functioned between the sour sheets, the bar-parlours and the workshops of the Clyde. The lunch hour over, they went back together to the office. On her last day there he made her a farewell gift of a book. It was one of many little acts of her colleagues which had touched her, freshly conscious of the warmth of these good people in the great city that had seen her birth. Ever rebellious to her home place, a pang of contrition smote her despite the firmness with which she took the way of escape.

When she opened the book of the office poet she saw it was a novel, by a writer unknown to her, called *Nostromo*. It looked heavy, and long, but she packed it for her journey. When she began to read it she thought she would not be able to finish it but she persevered. There was something that held her in the cave-like immensity of the author's theme, the slow

27

compelling rhythm of his prose. Presently she found herself hypnotised by some magic he exerted. She had read it greedily to the last page. And now here again, she found this book, of whose existence she had been ignorant a short time ago, lying on the Grandee's chair! If only she knew him well enough to compare notes of their reading.

One morning, from some cause unknown, she was wide-awake at six o'clock. The sky was already light, the sea opalescent. She got out of bed, had her bath and slowly dressed. It was still only seven o'clock. She looked out of the port-hole. The morning was radiant. Vast snowy clouds towered up over the horizon. She decided to take a walk on deck before ringing for breakfast.

Already there were a few promenaders. The deck stewards were distributing rugs on the empty chairs. It was possible to make a complete circuit of the ship. A strong breeze assailed her as she rounded the promenade below the bridge. Then came a heavy glass door closing the long sweep of the starboard deck. Just in front of her someone was opening the door. It was the Grandee. She was surprised to see him about so early. She hesitated, waiting for him to pass through, but seeing her he held open the door and smiled as she came up. He was without his sun-glasses, and she observed how keen and bright were his eyes.

"Good morning," he said, smiling, as she passed.

"Good morning, thank you," she replied. She paused while the door swung back under its vacuum pressure. He walked by her side.

"I deserted you a few days ago," he said. "The noise of the lady at your side was too much. And what nonsense they talked! If Madame Ramorra would only open her great mouth to sing!"

He made the criticism playfully.

"I have never heard her, nor of her," said Amelia.

He paused a moment and looked at her. He noticed her fresh loveliness in the breeze of morning.

"Ah, but you are so young. Miss——?" he queried.

"Macreary. Amelia Macreary."

"Thank you." He stopped, took off his black and white check cap. "Permit me to introduce myself. I'm Sir Anthony Slowdon. I must have heard Madame Ramorra sing these last thirty years—in Buenos Aires, Paris, Munich, New York, Barcelona. She was—no, that is not just, she is, a very great artiste. I heard her only last March in Paris, in *Elektra*. She has no equal in that rôle, even now."

"You are fond of opera?"

"To be truthful, no! But I hear a great deal of opera—by devotion rather than taste. My wife loved opera—and the jewels that went with it!" he added quietly.

They walked on. Amelia reflected that the Head Steward had misinformed her. He was not a bachelor. A widower?

"What days those were!" said Sir Anthony. "I remember hearing Madame Ramorra's first great triumph at the Scala in *Norma*—thirty years ago. That must indeed seem a very long time ago to you, my dear young lady!"

There was a ship on the horizon, sailing north. He halted, to watch it, resting his gloved hands on the taffrail. Then he turned, and, seeing an entrance to the cabins, said, somewhat abruptly. "I've had my exercise. I will breakfast now. Thank you for your company."

He raised his cap, and before she could make any reply, he had gone.

Fascinated by her Grandee, she rose every morning early and joined him on the promenade deck. It was astonishing how reticent he was but obviously he took pleasure in her company. One morning he invited her for an aperitif before lunch. She rarely saw him in the evenings after dinner, he retired early.

29

He was going to his *estancia* on arrival at Buenos Aires. He had not lived in England for many years and rarely visited it. He had sold his estate in Leicestershire. Twice she asked a question about his dead wife and his answers were evasive. She realised he did not intend to satisfy her curiosity.

A few days later it became their custom to take coffee together in the lounge after lunch while the orchestra played. Always, at the same time, he rose and excused himself. "My siesta," he said, with his gentle smile. She had solved the mystery of the gloves. Having somewhat impertinently said to him, jokingly, "You must be a good patron of the glove-makers," he showed no resentment. "I find nothing so unpleasant as the veins on the back of an old man's hands. It's better to hide them," he answered.

So he was vain. That had been obvious from the first moment she saw him. Sometimes she had detected him taking a small comb out of its case and combing his grey-white locks and trim Van Dyck beard.

Little by little he began to talk more freely to her. Etienne, who had observed each tête-à-tête, chaffed her about her old *hidalgo*. "He's very rich, very experienced. Perhaps one day he'll give you a string of pearls. You'll see dozens like him in Buenos Aires."

"What a monstrous thing to say!" she exclaimed.

"*Chère* Amelia—I'm only joking."

"I don't like that kind of a joke!"

"I am sorry."

She was very cool with him all that day. He was thoroughly contrite.

From what she learned of episodes in Sir Anthony's life Amelia computed that he was turned seventy. He had lived at different periods in Paris, Madrid, Buenos Aires, Lisbon and Rome. In the first World War he had spent most of his time in the Argentine buying horses for the British Government. He had been a great polo player, a friend of King Alfonso, and the Duke of Alba, having lived much in Spain as well as the Argentine. He had reminiscences of the Empress Eugénie, whose history was but dimly known to Amelia. "She was always very kind to me when I was a boy. My mother, who was Spanish, was a kinswoman, and one of her ladies-in-waiting before she married my father. I belong, my dear young lady, to a world that is dead, or at best, dying rapidly."

As they became more familiar she was aware of a compelling reticence into which he suddenly retreated. He was quickly evasive and changed the subject the moment it looked like running into a personal channel. It was very odd how solitary he was. He always sat alone, ate alone, and seldom engaged in conversation with other passengers. Amelia, fascinated by this handsome mysterious Englishman, who looked like a Spaniard, wisely refrained from any cross-questioning though her curiosity grew increasingly. Where had he been all these years? What other women had there been in his life? A man so attractive in appearance, manner and background, must have had some kind of history, unusual possibly, varied certainly. She was surprised when he told her that he had not lived in England for more than thirty years.

"You don't like England, you prefer Argentina?" she asked.

He was a long time replying as if he had to make a difficult decision. After a while he spread out his gloved hands in a gesture that was slightly foreign.

"I will not say I do not like England—after all I was born there. But my mother was Spanish, and I have lived much abroad, in Spain and in the Argentine. I am Leicestershire bred, and it was there as a boy I had my first love affair—with a horse!" he added, with a smile. "This early passion was confirmed when, at seventeen, I went to stay at my grandmother's villa in Seville. On that first visit I rode at the *Fiera*. You have never seen the *Fiera* at Seville?"

"No."

"Ah, then you have never seen the most perfect conjunction of lovely women and superb horses, in one of the oldest and most romantic cities in Europe. You rode all day, you danced all night to guitars and castanets, and you fell in love beneath orange blossom and the stars. I was seventeen, of course, and a pair of dark eyes plunged the first dagger in my heart."

He laughed awkwardly, then abruptly rose from his deck chair, picked up his book and cap, and bowed.

"I will go in now. Thank you for your company," he said, suddenly formal again.

III

"And how are you getting on with your old Grandee—still an enigma?" asked Etienne, one morning, having observed them in a long session on the promenade deck.

"He's not so much of an enigma as we thought. He's rather shy, really," answered Amelia.

"Shy? That's the last thing I'd say of that old Don Juan—he's wire and whipcord."

"I like him more and more."

"And me less and less?" he bantered.

"Don't be silly! With him the attraction is intellectual."

"*Mon Dieu!* What will the girl say next!" said Etienne, his eyes dancing. "What do you talk about—metaphysics, or are you investigating the autonomous psyche?"

Amelia opened her eyes wide, and he met her gaze tauntingly.

"I haven't the slightest idea what you are talking about!" she exclaimed.

"Have you ever heard of Freud?"

"No."

"Of Jung?"

"No," said Amelia firmly.

"A psychiatrist named Jung has spent years investigating what he calls the *collective unconscious*. He thinks the mind as well as the body has a long hidden ancestry. He attempts on the psychic plane what Darwin investigated on the natural plane. Darwin found irrefutable physical traces of our mammalian descent. Jung believes the mind has its antecedents also. He——"

"Will you please stop! Are you treating me to a slice of a lecture you heard at the Sorbonne or at Cambridge?"

"A little from both, *ma chère*!"

"Well, I'm greatly impressed by your command of English. It should lead you a long way into trouble. Let me say that I regard all psychiatrists as charlatans. Anyhow, what has this got to do with my talks with Sir Anthony?" demanded Amelia.

"Only that I feel you are investigating his *libido*!"

"Again, I don't know what you mean. Let's go and play shuffleboard, you want a little healthy exercise, my very clever young man. And we will talk French, please."

"*Chère, chère* Amelia! I'm not nearly as clever as you are—hypnotising that old cobra with your flute. Very well. *Allons au* shuffleboard!"

"I have a little news for you," said Amelia as they climbed to the upper deck. "Sir Anthony's very kindly offered to take me ashore for a short excursion when the ship reaches Rio."

"Disturbed normal processes, as Jung insists, are not entities in themselves," observed Etienne, teasingly.

"Are you being rude?"

"No, *chère* Amelia. I am only inferring what I have noticed from the beginning, with deepening admiration, that you are a considerable entity in yourself."

She looked at her attractive escort, and then repressed a comment. More and more she was beginning to feel he was right. She was an entity in herself. It was that which had taken her out of Abernethy Villas into this wonderful illimitable new world.

IV

Early one morning they turned in towards shining Rio de Janeiro, leaving the swell of the Atlantic behind. They sailed through the narrow entrance to the magnificent bay between two bold headlands, one of them the steep conical mass of the Sugarloaf. The city in its grand sweep round this bay, some ten miles of buildings fronting the beach, glittered in the early sun. Behind lay the irregular hills with green valleys between them, and, beyond, rose the great ranges covered with tropical vegetation. Prominent to the south-west, was the spectacular precipitous cone of Corcovado, familiar from posters and pictures of Rio. At the taffrail Amelia, her heart beating with excitement, watched the great city gliding smoothly towards them, a new land, a new civilisation, a new life awaiting her.

An hour passed before they could go ashore. Sir Anthony, with Carlos in attendance, came up from his cabin.

"And what do you think of it?" he asked Amelia, who was standing with Etienne on the promenade deck. She turned to him with shining eyes.

"I—I have—oh, I have no words for it—I never knew there was anything so beautiful in the world!" she said, her voice trembling with excitement.

Sir Anthony turned from her to Etienne. It was not envy but a heavy sense of the years that briefly smote him as he looked at the young man beside the slim eager girl, so flower-like and fresh in her blue and white striped print frock.

"There is a car waiting for us on the quay," he said, then, turning to the young Frenchman, "We are making an excursion, to Corvocado of course, for the panorama, and then along Copacabana for lunch. But you know the place of course?"

"No, sir—I am *en poste* in Buenos Aires, this is my first trip to South America—out of Europe, in fact," replied Etienne de Lérin.

"Then you should see Rio. Will you not join us, there is plenty of room in the car?" said Sir Anthony.

The young man looked at him, dumb with surprise. Did the old boy really mean it?

"I think, sir, that you—that I——" He was about to say "should be in the way" but checked himself in time. "It's most kind of you, sir, but——"

"Of course you are coming! Oh, what fun, Sir Anthony!" exclaimed Amelia, clapping her hands and making a little ecstatic jump.

V

Looking back across the years to that sunlit morning when they stepped on to a new continent, the vision was ever fresh, miraculous with surprise and delight. Sir Anthony was a quiet cicerone, known to all where he called, exchanging greetings, and received with a deference touched with homage. He seemed as fluent in Portuguese as in Spanish or French. The head waiter at the flower-laden restaurant under the shade of vast green awnings that protected them from the glare of the bay, greeted Sir Anthony and his party with an ebullient courtesy. They were escorted through a sea of thronged tables to the terrace, where a fountain rained its diamonds into a pool of flowering hybiscus and white-belled datura plants. A reserved table awaited them. The strains of a Mexican orchestra rose from the lower terrace and its dance plaza.

"Thirty years ago, when he was a very thin young man, Céleste, who is Italian, was my cook-valet in Paris. So I am *en famille* here," said Sir Anthony, when the head waiter had departed following an earnest conference over the menu.

It was the same everywhere they went. Even an old dock hand, half-negro, doffed his straw sombrero hat, and ran up to Sir Anthony as they re-embarked, his old face wrinkled in warm delight.

Day by day, as the ship bore southwards down the Atlantic, skirting the mysterious interminable continent with its immense withdrawn mountains, its vast rivers, its impenetrable jungle forests and illimitable plains, Sir Anthony evoked his own magic in the eyes of Amelia. They had long conversations, during the pre-breakfast promenades, at the tea-hour when he reappeared in the café verandah after his siesta. He talked of his ranch, four hours' journey from Buenos Aires, referring to it as just outside the capital. She noticed however how impersonal he kept his reminiscences. He spoke of the different countries and the cities in which he had lived, and a little of his work when he had been a British agent buying horses for the Government. It was singular how seldom he spoke of his own country, of England where he had passed his youth, though he told of his childhood in Leicestershire, his school in Switzerland, his three years at Trinity College, Cambridge, followed by a brief spell in diplomacy, with posts as a junior attaché at Teheran and Athens. He had no brothers or sisters, being an only child. His widowed mother had retired to Seville, which, from frequent visits had been like a second home. It was there, and not in Buenos Aires, as Amelia had first surmised, that he met his wife making a brief visit to relations.

Twice Amelia sought a little information about his married life. Obviously he did not wish to speak of it. Sir Anthony seemed singularly alone in the world and he left in her mind a feeling that he deliberately followed the life of a recluse. She had to dismiss from her mind, as his appearance had first suggested, that he had been a gallant, a roué of untiring promiscuity. How had a man who moved through the capitals of Europe, of good family, ample fortune, handsome and attractive to women, been able to confine his passion to horses, and a life on a distant and lonely ranch? Despite her delicate questions the portrait of this *hidalgo* remained obscure.

"You'll probably get a surprise in Buenos Aires," said Etienne. "A man like that must have quite a history."

Buenos Aires, surprisingly, knew little about Sir Anthony Slowdon. Later when she encountered her countrymen, of the Embassy and Consulate, they could tell her nothing. None of them had been there for long. Sir Anthony was merely a name on their books. They had rarely seen him. He played no part in the public life of the capital.

In those last days on the boat she had come to know him better as a person, and every day her admiration of this withdrawn picturesque *grand seigneur* had deepened. He treated her with a grave courtesy. Yet his shrewd glance had missed little. One day his eyes being tired, she offered to read from *Nostromo*. He accepted her offer gratefully.

"You read very well—your articulation is very clear. But there's an accent——"

"I'm Scots," said Amelia.

"Of course—your colouring, your sturdy *sangfroid,* if I may term your self-possession thus—yes, very Scottish. But what part of Scotland? Not the Highlands. My guess is the Lowlands."

"Your guess is a good one—I was born in Glasgow."

"You've studied phonetics?"

Her eyes opened in surprise. He smiled at her gravely. "I find much to admire in you," he added, quietly.

She did not speak for a few moments, but something in his solid qualities of breeding and good manners gave her a feeling of confidence that led to confession. She could not dissemble in the face of his tranquil and uninquisitive assessment of her.

37

"You've seen Shaw's play *Pygmalion?*" she asked.

"No—I'm almost a stranger to the English theatre."

"It's the story of a Cockney flower girl who is taken in hand by a professor of phonetics. He finds the girl and undertakes to turn her into a lady. The first thing he has to do is to get rid of her Cockney accent. He succeeds—almost—there's a moment in a West End society drawing-room when a young man asks the beautiful Eliza if she is walking across the Park. In a moment of denial she forgets her rôle and replies 'Not bloody likely!' "

Sir Anthony snapped his gloved fingers together.

"How very extraordinary! Of course, I've heard of the play! It was a great success, I remember, but I didn't see it."

"Well, I'm Eliza!"

"Eliza—what do you mean? You're acting the part in the play. You're on the stage?"

"I'm acting the part, but I'm not an actress and I've never been on the stage. I'm acting the part in life."

He looked at her keenly and noticed how intense was her young face, a face visibly struggling to control a wave of emotion.

"I suppose the Glasgow accent pops out—in some sort of not-bloody-likely moment," said Amelia.

"My dear young lady—is there anything reprehensible in a Glasgow accent?"

"Well, even good Scots make fun of 'tha mon fra Glesca'—Sir Harry Lauder pokes fun at us in the music-halls."

"So that's why, like Eliza, you've studied phonetics! I must congratulate you on your diction. It is sometimes so good, so refreshingly good in this careless age—particularly while you've been reading to me—that it seemed slightly unnatural, if you'll excuse me for saying so! You must have a very good ear—your Spanish is excellent, too."

"Thank you, Sir Anthony. What I really want to tell you is

that my people are working-class. They're very sound good people. But I'm ambitious, and their surroundings jar me, they always have jarred me, and I'm rather ashamed of myself for feeling like that sometimes. But there it is, and I was determined to get away from it. So I kept my ears open. I learnt my English from a young man, English, who'd been at Oxford, and my Spanish from a young man in a local sherry firm, who spoke Andalusian Spanish—he came from Jerez de la Frontera. I'm a typist-secretary in a Glasgow firm of whisky exporters. They have a branch office in Buenos Aires, and, as I know Spanish, they're sending me there. That's how I come to be on this boat!"

She finished her confession rather breathlessly. Having indulged in some subterfuge with Etienne and other passengers, she was surprised at the surrender of her secret to this grave and aristocratic old gentleman. He had treated her with such courtesy, with no element of curiosity, that she felt she could not in any way deceive him, instinctively certain that there would be no lessening of his regard.

His words bore out her surmise. He put forth a gloved hand and lightly and briefly let it lie upon hers as she sat holding the copy of Nostromo.

"Thank you. That little confession could not be easy for you. I am touched by your confidence and admire a worthy ambition. You are the fortunate possessor of a rare combination, Miss Macreary."

She regarded him questioningly, the flush from this confession still enhancing the colour of her cheeks.

"I think I may say it without flattery or the danger of dispelling your modesty—you combine beauty with brains, and a sensibility that disciplines you. Now, where had we got to in our Nostromo?"

She turned to the marker, and opened the novel.

Part Third. The Lighthouse. Chapter One. Directly the cargo

boat had slipped away from the wharf and got lost in the darkness of the harbour . . . .

Her voice wavered a little and she could hardly see the words
for the tears of relief in her eyes; but presently she recovered,
and read quietly on, as the ship, rolling slightly, ploughed on
southwards down the blue Atlantic.

CHAPTER FOUR

I

FOLLOWING her arrival at Buenos Aires, a wholly new life opened before her. The manager of her firm, Señor Anstruther, had been waiting for her on the dock. He took her back to his own home where his Argentine wife gave her a warm welcome. Her new chief was a Scot also, who had been settled in Buenos Aires for almost thirty years. Surrounded by his wife, mother-in-law, two sisters-in-law, and seven children ranging from ten to twenty, the house was like a bird cage hanging in a semi-tropical garden. They all talked, sang, screeched, gabbled, banged the doors, clattered over hard floors, slammed windows, kept the radio and gramophone going from dawn to sunset so that only exhaustion and sleep brought a few hours of quiet. It had become a completely South American home, with four servants, from off-white through coffee-brown to downright negro-black, who served the house in a genial haphazard manner. Señor Anstruther seemed to be utterly divorced from his native Aberdeen, and as if overwhelmed by numbers, and a desire to sink his identity in the home he had created, he had forgotten his sturdy Aberdonian Presbyterianism and embraced Roman Catholicism. He was so amiable, so unresistant, that Amelia believed he would have embraced cannibalism with the same adaptability. "It makes my wife and mother-in-law happy, so why not?"

Amelia was surprised to discover that, notwithstanding his lack of principle, or his sense of tolerance, as he termed it, he was a business man of razor-edged acuteness. He was a martinet in the office with a mania for punctuality and pre-

41

cision that seemed sadistic to the easy-going Argentine staff. Nevertheless, there was gaiety throughout the office, bright behind the sun-blinds that dimmed the glare of the immense radiant sky. The zest of youthful life flowed in the streets and through the great blocks of offices along the splendid wide avenues.

After a month she found for herself a small apartment off the Avenida de Mayo, looking into a garden of palms, oleanders and exotic cacti. She made a few friends and joined a tennis club, but she fought against the common tendency of the English, German and American colonies to segregate themselves, with the attendant stomach fetiches of bacon, eggs and tea, or pork, sauerkraut and lager, or waffles, hot dogs and coffee, that carried their nostalgic smells to the nostrils of the exiles. Amelia cultivated her Argentine friendships, made more widespread by the all-embracing conviviality of the vociferous Anstruthers. Only on Sundays was her racial bias in evidence. She went to the English Church, to which the chaplain's name of McGillivray brought a native air.

The acquaintances she had made on board ship faded away, as do those quick, ephemeral contacts. Etienne de Lérin took her out to dinner. They went to a country club to dance, to a French film, but his world was not hers. He seemed well-to-do, fashionable, bought a large sports car, a couple of polo ponies, and moved in the international set. There were abundant pretty señoritas of his own social standing; their brief ship-friendship appeared to have faded.

Two months had passed when, one morning, a letter awaited her at the office. It was from Sir Anthony Slowdon, written from his *estancia* at Tabara. He would be in Buenos Aires the next week. On Thursday Doña Ramorra was singing at the Opera House in Strauss's *Elektra*, one of her famous rôles. Would she give him the pleasure of dining with him and going to the performance?

The silence of two months duration had caused her to believe that he too had vanished into his different social world, that she would never see him again, unless by accident. She had made a few enquiries, as had Señor Anstruther. He ascertained from the Commercial Attaché at the British Embassy that Don Antonio, as he seemed to be called, was a famous but somewhat exclusive figure, rarely seen in British circles, though well-known among the Argentines as one of the greatest judges of horses on the South American continent. He had during these latter years become more and more of a hermit, making only sporadic appearances at the horse shows and the races. Don Antonio. She liked that name for him. She responded at once to the invitation. Happily she had just bought a new evening frock.

The intervening days dragged their feet. On the evening previous to the dinner Señora Anstruther called her on the telephone and asked if she could come to see her. In some curiosity she awaited the amiable, exuberant lady.

"Enrico tells me you are going to the Opera tomorrow evening. With the great Don Antonio! What a beautiful man! I have seen him often, at the balls and the races when I was young. I've brought you something I seldom wear. I want to lend it for your evening," she said breathlessly.

She opened her large handbag and took out a small box covered in green leather.

"Look, dear Amelia—Enrico gave it to me when our Carlos was born."

She lifted the lid and extracted from it a necklace of sparkling diamonds. It flashed fire as it swung on her fingers.

"I sent Enrico to the bank for it today. You must wear it for the opera."

"But Juanita dear, I should be terrified! What if I lost it, or it was stolen. It's a fortune!"

Señora Anstruther laughed, and hung the collar on Amelia's neck.

"Nonsense—and it's insured. It's so long since the poor necklace had an outing! And a beautiful throat like yours shows it off."

Excitedly Amelia turned in front of the mirror. Then she flung herself in Señora Anstruther's arms.

I I

That evening at the opera remained vividly in her memory throughout the following year. The great auditorium, the beautifully gowned women with their escorts, the tiers of boxes, the stalls, the buzz of conversation, the glitter of jewels, the hush when the lights fell and the vast curtain rose on the opening scene of *Elektra*. The grim Greek drama spread its hypnotic spell. Amelia could not find in the passionate, intense woman, sister of Orestes, motivated by revenge, the gay, gossiping *diva* who had occupied the deck chair next to her. Some power seemed to have descended on her, a daughter of Agamemnon, as she moved to her fell purpose. The timbre of her voice, the intensity of her acting, held the vast audience in a trance. It was Doña Ramorra's most famous rôle, and this was her last appearance in the theatre where she had won homage for a generation, if any announcement by a *diva* could be believed concerning final appearances. For thirty years she had dominated the great opera house.

The final curtain fell. For a few moments there was a deep hush throughout the dark auditorium, followed by an acclamation that reached hysteria. It was Amelia's first opera. It ever remained her most memorable one. As they sat in the automobile, a Mercedes driven by the faithful and taciturn Carlos, Sir Anthony paid her a compliment:

"I've been admiring your necklace," he said.

44

"Yes? Of course you know it isn't mine! It's been lent to me by my chief's wife, Señora Anstruther," replied Amelia with her characteristic candour.

Sir Anthony smiled at her. "I don't know Señora Anstruther —but she has never had her diamonds better displayed," he said.

Amelia thanked him for a wonderful evening as he escorted her into the hall of her apartment. She rang for the lift.

"I leave for Tabara tomorrow. One day I hope you will pay me a visit there. You will discover what a hermit I really am. I will take you riding over my domain."

"But I can't ride, Sir Anthony—the only thing I've ever ridden was a donkey at the seaside, and I came off that!"

They laughed together. The lift had descended. He held open the door for her.

"Then I must teach you. I know you have a good ear. We'll see if you have a good seat."

He waited until the lift carried her out of sight, then turned and went out to his car. The night was warm, starry. Even so late the avenues were full of automobiles, the cafés still open.

A month went by with no word from her Grandee. It was likely that he had forgotten his half-formulated invitation to visit Tabara. She would be deeply disappointed if she did not see him in his most characteristic setting, among the horses he loved so dearly. Meanwhile, until his invitation was fulfilled, if such was to be her good fortune, she had been amusing her-self. Not far from her apartment there was a delightful park, with a restaurant café, a small wooded lake with boats, and a riding ring that circled the park. Here, on the tan, she had watched the equestrians, young men, women and children, most of them in riding habits, taking daily exercise. At the beginning of the ring there was a corral for horses and a small club house. She saw a notice setting forth the tariff for the hire of the horses, and that riding lessons could be taken. She had learned Spanish, she had learned French, so why not learn how to ride? The exercise would be good, and if Don Antonio ever asked her to his place she would not appear a raw beginner—and make a fool of herself. It was part of her nature to learn anything that added to the pleasures of life. At the Anstruthers she had taken up bridge with enthusiasm in spite of her poor card sense. Years ago she had been amused in the Glasgow office by someone saying of her, "That girl's got plenty of horse-sense." She would find out now whether the adjective was applicable in its correct meaning.

The price of a dozen lessons was not excessive. When she learned that if they were taken before breakfast there was a reduction, she was delighted. The riding ring opened at seven. She would go five times a week.

That same day she went to a store and bought a pair of light brown jodhpurs. Never had she imagined that she would ever wear such garments, which she had seen only on the films. When she tried them on she was delighted with the result. She looked like a slim young boy. They displayed and enhanced her neat figure. She put on a white silk blouse, and tied her hair up in a bun. The long mirror revealed someone who looked like a Governor's daughter. She could see herself running down the steps at Government House as the syce held her horse.

"You little fool!" she said to herself, turning in self-admiration. "You'll come a cropper in all senses of the word!"

But that was just what she did not believe. She was eager to take all the hurdles that an adventurous life offered.

She made a mental note that one day she would be photographed in her riding kit, crop in hand, standing by her mount. Such a juxtaposition of fashionable frailty and horseflesh was always impressive. A copy would go to the family in Abernethy Villas. She could see it standing on the kitchen mantlepiece, and her father, as he shifted his stockinged feet on the fender, would exclaim, "Just look at our Amelia!" Yes, it would shake them.

The eagerly awaited invitation came one morning. A friend, Doña Lucia de los Rivos, would be travelling to Tabara. It was four hours by rail and then one hour by car to the *estancia*. The train left at 8.30 a.m. and they would arrive for lunch. The visit was from Saturday to Monday. Amelia had no difficulty in obtaining leave for Monday morning. They were very satisfied with her at the office. She was alert, her typing was flawless, her Spanish astonished them all. She could now ride fairly well, had a good seat and hands. Perhaps one day she would have a horse of her own, when her salary had been increased again.

The day prior to her visit to Tabara, to her great surprise, she was invited to a cocktail party at the French Embassy. It was an invitation from the Ambassador but she knew who was behind this invitation. She went and had a veritable triumph. Etienne de Lérin presented her to the French Ambassador and his wife. There were more than a hundred guests who spread themselves over the lawns of the Embassy. The women were gowned in the height of fashion but Amelia, in powder-blue, with a small hydrangea-petal hat to match, felt in no way outclassed. Etienne's eyes shone with admiration. He had had some misgivings but they were dispelled the moment he saw her. She moved like a princess, assured and cool in manner. She scored over a number of English women present, with her French and Spanish. When it was all over he drove her away to dine at an alfresco restaurant in the park, where an orchestra played and there was a dancing floor.

"I am very proud of my protegée," he said. The head waiter placed them at a corner table overlooking a patio in which canaries sang, and a thin silver fountain played into a lilied pool full of goldfish.

She let his possessive claim go by.

"I knew you were a born linguist—but I never met anyone who made such progress. You must have worked very hard, my dear Amelia."

"I have had a good tutor." She changed the sex of her teacher, saying '*maître*', knowing it would arouse his curiosity. The only masculine thing about Madame Dupont who gave her three lessons a week, was the incipient dark moustache on her upper lip which she vainly tried to bury under powder. "My poor Alphonse made me shave—everywhere. Ah, dear Miss Macreary, it was a grave mistake, but Alphonse was a persistent man," confided the little widow.

"*Tiens!*" exclaimed Etienne, as he raised his apéritif glass to her. "So that explains your fluency! I am jealous!"

"It's your own fault, if you will do a vanishing trick," said Amelia, smiling over her glass.

"*Touché!*" cried Etienne. "It is my fault, yes, but I have much excuse with too many things to do."

"Much excuse doesn't ring right either as English or as an explanation. You wish to tell me that you have a good excuse, having too much to do—or too many to see?"

"*Chère* Amelia, you have an enchanting frankness—it was the first thing I noticed about you after your face——"

"And my ankles!"

"Oh, oh—so you think——"

"I've learned the difference between an Italian and a Frenchman."

"So? What is it?" asked Etienne.

"A Frenchman looks at a girl's face and then at her ankles. An Italian looks at her ankles and then at her face," answered Amelia.

"And an Englishman—how does he look?"

"I can only speak for a Scot. He doesn't look. He asks you for your golf handicap!"

"*Formidable! C'est drôle*—but how dull!"

"The overture may seem indifferent, but the performance is the same," replied Amelia.

He leaned towards her over the table, his eyes engaging hers with a mocking seriousness.

"My dear insouciant girl—how should I know? I've never got beyond the overture!"

She laughed quietly and let him cover her hand beside the flower bowl. He pressed it gently. The head waiter came with the menu. It was like one of those ship's menus, a gastronomic voyage through all the continents. He consulted her, ordered the dinner with great seriousness. Then, the order given, he said, "Shall we dance?"

They moved on to the floor of the patio. The Argentine jazz band played a current air. The floor was not crowded. Again he was aware of his partner's perfect rhythm.

"How lovely you were at the Embassy! I saw my chief watching you. This is a beautiful frock—Argentine or English?"

"Neither. Believe it or not, out of Glasgow!"

"Beautiful—and the hat is adorable. It is all the better because it does not hide your hair, your ears, your eyes!"

"An anatomical triumph! Thank you, the compliment gives special pleasure—I made it myself."

"No!—you are a hatter, a milliner woman?"

"Etienne, sometimes your English is so exciting I could not wish it better—or worse! A hatter is a man who makes men's hats——"

"No women are hatters?"

"No."

"But men make women's hats—the best hats are made for women by men. They are famous."

"Yes—but if a man makes a man's hat, he is a hatter, and if he is crazy he's called 'a mad hatter'."

"He makes crazy hats?"

"No—it comes from a character in a famous book, the Mad Hatter in *Alice in Wonderland*. This conversation is getting a little mad hatterish——"

"Yes, *chérie*. The English, as one says, have a peculiar humour."

"To return to our English lesson. A man can be a hatter and make hats for men, but if he makes them for women he's a hat designer. A woman can't make hats for men. She can make hats for women, and then she's a milliner, not a milliner-woman."

"There are no men milliners?"

"Yes—but we don't call them that."

"Why not?"

"They're like ballet boys, a phenomenon. I made this hat with my own needle."

"Then you are a needlewoman?"

"No—yes, in a sense, but—Etienne, this conversation is making me dizzy!"

"I shall never understand the English language. If I make a hat for a man I am a hatter, but if I make a hat for a woman I am not a hatter but like a ballet boy. A woman who sews, she is a needlewoman and, like you, she can make a hat and not be a hatter or a milliner! Well, however you describe yourself, your hat is a triumph," said Etienne. "Everyone looked at you at the Embassy. Your hair and your Scottish freshness and flawless complexion, your green eyes, your—your——"

"Go on, you're doing beautifully, Etienne—and all in English!"

"Please do not laugh at me. I go on, then. I thought you

exquise, so fair, so Nordic among all the darker beauties, like Venus at the Court of the Ethiopians!"

The band stopped. They stood still a moment. Perhaps he was a little in love with her. They went to their table. He began to be curious about what she did, who were her new friends. Was she happy with her work? Did she like Buenos Aires? What did she do in her spare time?

"In the morning before breakfast, I ride. On Saturday and Sunday I play tennis."

"You ride?" he exclaimed, surprise in his voice. "What an enterprising girl you are! You learn Spanish, French, you play tennis, you ride. You cook?"

"No. I am not fond of the frying pan, the oven and the sink. But I type," she said, mischievously. "I work for my living!"

"*Et moi?*"

"*Toi?* Not very seriously, Etienne. You go to lunch parties and cocktail parties and dinner parties. You serve your country in a white tie and tails, you know the finer shades of protocol. If you behave yourself, and are attentive to the ladies and tactful with the politicians, and wear good clothes and drive expensive cars, and have the right parents, the right education, several languages, and refuse to be too clever, you cannot help going a long way. One day you will be an ambassador and recall with wonder how you once found the courage to invite a Scotch typist to a French Embassy cocktail party and got away with it."

He stared at her, easing his collar with a finger. Had she had too many cocktails?

"But my dear Amelia—I—I can assure you—I swear—I work! I——" he stammered.

She gave a laugh, a silvery laugh that harmonised with the tinkle of the fountain.

"Etienne—can't I tease you with a little bit of truth?" she asked, picking up a rose lying on the table, and playfully brushing his chin. "Our worlds are so very different, aren't they? It makes the situation piquant. As the Duc de Guermantes said——"

"*Mon Dieu!* Where on earth have you got hold of the Duc de Guermantes?" exclaimed Etienne, shaken by surprise.

"I'm at the second volume of *A la Recherche du Temps Perdu*——"

"Amelia, my dear! I refuse to be taken out of my depth! You have been unkind. You have suggested that I have patronised you."

"Of course you have—and I've enjoyed it immensely! This is the first Embassy I have ever been invited to, and a French one at that! You are the first Secretary, although a Third, I've ever danced with. But I am an ambitious girl and one day I hope to dance with an Ambassador——"

"You will dance with me when I am an Ambassador?" he exclaimed, catching her hand.

"Too long to wait, Etienne dear!"

"How cruel you are!"

"I couldn't enjoy dancing with you more—even if you had a blue ribbon and a star."

The waiter arrived with *mousse de poisson Newburg*. A *sauterne* like spring sunshine filled their slender glasses.

"A toi!" said Etienne softly, raising his glass.

"A toi!" repeated Amelia.

This was sheer romance. The band, under enormous straw hats, throbbed a rumba. Festoons of lights under the trees in the glade were switched on. They looked like little moons, a lunar fruit pendant in the foliage.

"To return to your many accomplishments, *chèrie*. You ride. I too ride. Can we ride together?" asked Etienne.

"If you get up early enough."

"I am the early worm. Do you ride tomorrow—where?" he asked.

"Tomorrow I'm not riding. I am going away for the weekend." She paused to give full effect to her little surprise. "I am going to Don Antonio's, at Tabara."

Their eyes met. He noticed more than ever before what lovely teeth she had as she laughed at him.

"*Tcha!* So the old Don's still pursuing! An excursion in Rio, a night at the Opera, a weekend at the *estancia*. I approve of the nicely graded approach. And now you will ride together!"

"I hope so. I've been having riding lessons in case I was invited," she said, quickly.

He drank, put down his glass, and looked at her steadily.

"Perhaps the most attractive quality among many is your destructive candour," said Etienne.

"I think the word used is 'devastating'. I'm not destructive."

"Devastating, of course. You are an astonishing creature— a little reckless too!"

"How do you think I escaped that cage in my home-town, dear Etienne? A typewriter is a very odd flying machine—but it's brought me here!"

"Your courage, your beauty have brought you here!" declared Etienne.

"A whisky firm in Glasgow is not moved by feminine beauty, *cher ami*."

"No. I am quite wrong! It is something else—your—your —Amelia, how lovely you are tonight!"

"My native Scottish wits have brought me here," she said, ignoring his compliment. "But you would be surprised how I tremble sometimes. There are moments when I feel I'm getting out of my depth."

"Out of your depth—what does that mean?"

"That's our difficult English again—it really means quite the reverse—into the depth where you can't touch bottom, as in swimming."

"Do you swim?" asked Etienne.

"Of course!"

"You speak English, Spanish, French?"

"Yes, but my French is not very good, is it?"

"It is most amusingly terrible—like my English," said Etienne, candidly. "Your typing?"

"Very good."

"You have shorthand?"

"I'm considered a first-class secretary-typist, or I shouldn't be here!"

"Can you drive a car?"

"Yes, I've a driving licence. I took lessons in Glasgow."

"What's your car?"

"An O.P."

"O.P.? What make is that? I've heard of an M.G. I had one at Cambridge. It's very good. What's an O.P.?"

"Well, it can vary. You see, dear Etienne, I've never owned a car—I drove Other People's! A young man from Oxford taught me to drive. He also proposed to me."

"Oh! You didn't like him?"

"I liked him very much—but not that much. I chose him as a tutor, not as a lover. He taught me good English as well as to drive."

"You used the poor lad?"

"Yes," said Amelia, frankly.

"There are some moments, Amelia, when I think you are the most objectionable girl I've ever met. And at other moments quite the most astonishing, quick-witted, adorable creature."

"I plead guilty to all those charges. You've not said one thing about me which is also true—I'm an *arriviste*."

"I think you are a *petite gamine*. I love you!"

"You have said that before," retorted Amelia.

The band began a Blues. "That's one of my favourites, shall we dance?" she asked.

54

"Very well," he replied and signalled to the waiter to take away the plates. "But only until the next dish comes—you shall not get hot or breathless. Lucullus is a god. You must attend him in a right spirit."

They took the floor. She slipped into his arms.

"You're very fond of food?" asked Amelia, as they threaded the crowded floor.

"Fond is not the proper word, my green-eyed child. Unlike the Americans, I reverence food. I am an acolyte at the altar of Brillat-Savarin."

"Where is that?"

"It's not a place, it's the name of a person. Brillat-Savarin is the high priest of the gourmets. He wrote a masterpiece *La Physiologie du Goût*—the physiology of taste. He lived two hundred years ago. He became a mayor and they put up a statue to him in Belley, where he was born."

"How appropriate for him to be born there!"

"There—why? I don't understand."

"In Stomach!"

"Stomach?"

"In Belly!" said Amelia, with a little wriggle.

He stopped dancing and tried to look severe.

"Yes, you are *une vraie gamine*! That is a most atrocious pun. You have no reverence. You do not deserve the next course—which I see is coming. We'll go to our table."

They seated themselves. A waiter in a crimson monkey-jacket wheeled up a trolley and lifted the silver salver cover. There was a golden feather protruding from the rump of a brown trussed bird. Amelia clapped her hands together in delight.

"Etienne—what is it?"

"*Le Faisan doré aux truffes*. Golden pheasant with truffles. I much teach you to reverence food—and Brillat-Savarin, *chère* Amelia."

"I'm most contrite—your humble scholar."

"For this we are opening a bottle of Dom Perignon, 1920. I must inform you, *chère petite arriviste*, there are many ways of reaching immortality, and the invention of a superb dish is perhaps the most sure. Who remembers the Ministers of Louis XVI? Where would Chateaubriand be without his steak? Béarn has disappeared with the Department des Basses Pyrenées but its Sauce has survived. The name remains, though sometimes the birthplace is no more. When I was in England I motored to Stilton, in Huntingdonshire, to see the home of your famous cheese, to learn that it was made in Cheshire. I went to Melton Mowbray, in Leicestershire, home of your excellent pork pies, to find they were made in Wellingborough, Northamptonshire. It is refreshing to learn you can still find Gruyère cheese in Gruyère, but there are no Madeira cakes in Madeira—these names live on, immortal on the palate. Do you like this?"

"It's delicious!"

"The chef is a Frenchman—I followed him here from Edmond de Rothschild's in Paris. You're having *Coupe aux Marrons Chantilly* to follow," said Etienne.

"Why did you say the Americans have no reverence for food? They crowd the best restaurants," asked Amelia.

"They crowd the most expensive restaurants. You have never been in the United States?"

"No."

"I was there for two months. What an incredible adventure! America is the land of extremes. Their automobiles are too long, their pedigrees too short. They have contaminated music with negro rhythms. They have too much energy and too much money. They do strange and cruel things to their food. They put it in a 'deep freeze'. They implant a white blob of processed cheese on a yellow ring of tinned pineapple, which is given an air of 'gracious living' by resting on a leaf of de-iced lettuce—that is a salad! They ruin their palates with cocktails, and they smoke while they eat. There is more sex and less love, more food and less flavour, more luxury and less comfort, more wealth and less satisfaction, more speeches and less sense, more creeds and less religion than anywhere else in the world."

"Didn't they throw you out of America?" asked Amelia, interrupting his flow of denigration.

"No—on the contrary, they gave me the place. They're the most generous people on the earth. You can squeeze money out of them like toothpaste out of a tube for any worthy cause. Don't forget they invented the words 'boob' and 'sucker', as well as Rotarianism. Every sensible European has at least one favourite American to keep fresh his hope for the human race. But don't take me too seriously—I'm just Pommarding!"

"Pommarding?"

"Whenever I drink Pommard I get reckless like this. I'm not drunk. I'm uninhibitedly happy. *Chère, chère* Amelia, I want to make you open your lovely green eyes wider and wider. I want to give you a thousand kisses, and to go to sleep with my head on your bosom, lulled like a sea-mew on the undulant wave."

"I really think it's time we had a dance," said Amelia. "There's going to be no sea-mewing here."

"Not until we've had the *Marrons Chantilly* and a *Fine Josephine*. Darling Amelia, *charmante arriviste aux yeux verts,* I love you!" he said, reaching out his slim brown hand, that Latin hand again, towards her.

"Nonsense, Etienne. You're in love with yourself loving me!" said Amelia.

"That is too difficult for me. What a girl! You reject my devotion and you go to spend the weekend among the cows and the horses of your be-gloved Don Antonio. Can you play bridge?"

"Badly."

"Ah, thank God, there is something you will fail in when he puts you through your paces."

"You talk as if I were a filly."

"*Mais oui! Filet Mignon!* Who was Mignon, who was Helen, who was Cleopatra?" exclaimed Etienne, waving a fork, his boy's eyes glinting.

"You are a little drunk, and delightfully absurd. Come along, we're going to dance!"

But at that moment the *Marrons Chantilly* arrived.

I V

They went home at two o'clock. Etienne took her in his car. There had been a little battle of wills. He wanted to show her his small apartment. It had everything, a balcony, a view, an American kitchen, and two paintings that travelled with him everywhere, a water-colour of Rome by Corot, and a street scene of Paris by Raoul Dufy.

"They represent the past and the present—you must see them. You love pictures?" asked Etienne.

"I love pictures, but not at 2 a.m. in a young man's bachelor apartment," responded Amelia.

"I do not understand you! You are young, pretty. Why are you so afraid—is it your Scotch blood? I want to love you. It would be such a beautiful thing. Am I repulsive?" he demanded.

"On the contrary—you are very attractive!"

"It could be so beautiful!"

"Do you want to sleep with every pretty girl you meet?"

"Yes—why not? It is a beautiful thing, to lie in one another's arms, to make love, to sleep, to wake! We are young, it's what youth is for. When we are old we shall have no fire in our hearts," said Etienne, turning up the palm of Amelia's hand and kissing it, as they sat in his car before leaving.

"I'm not denying anything you say, but dear Etienne, I'm not going to be made a recurring decimal."

"What do you mean?"

"I mean that I'm not willing to be a repetitive number in your sum of love," she said.

"That is very clever. You will be so very clever that you will have no fun if you go on like that."

"Etienne, you've given me a lovely evening—don't spoil it."

"Spoil it? *Mon Dieu*, I want to crown it!"

"It's going to remain uncrowned, dear Etienne."

"You insist . . . You really mean No?"

"Yes."

"Yes—No?—Yes? I'll go crazy!"

"Oh no, you won't. You'll find a victim tomorrow!"

"I hate you!" cried Etienne, slapping his hands on the dashboard.

"Love, they say, is next to hate—so I am not too surprised," retorted Amelia, smiling at his clouded face.

He started the motor, and let in the clutch.

"My apartment is on the way," he said.

"If mine is too far, I'll walk! I shall never forget the *Faisan doré*, the *Coupe aux Marrons Chantilly*, and the lecture on Brillat-Savarin," said Amelia mischievously.

He threw her a look. "Heartless minx!" he said, as the car moved forward. "When you are old, with a scraggy neck, you'll be sorry for this!"

He softly recited some French verses as the car glided down the lamplit boulevard.

> *Le jour où la pluie viendra*
> *Je t'emmènerai, j'en suis sûr,*
> *Dans mon lit,*
> *Petite tête de gamine mouillée de pluie.*
> *Ce sera, ce jour là,*

Te serrant dans mes bras,
Je t'embrasserai sur la poitrine,
Là, où est ton coeur,
En y laissant une petite goutte,
Limpide, nacrée, de pluie—ma vie.

"I don't get it all—perhaps it's better not!" laughed Amelia.

"It's a poem by Nguyen Dang," he said. He repeated it softly in English, to the accompaniment of the tyres on the tarmac.

> The day when the rain comes
> I shall take you, I am sure,
> In my bed, little head
> Of a gamin moist with rain.
> That evening, on that day
> You are clasped in my arms,
> I shall kiss you on your bosom,
> And there, where your heart is,
> Leave a little spot of rain,
> Limpid and pearly—my life.

She said nothing when he had finished quoting, and they drove on into the silent street where her apartment stood. He got out and accompanied her to the door. As she took out her key he said—

"You will not ask me in?"

"No."

"How inhospitable! How cruel!"

He embraced her, and kissed her warmly. She disengaged herself, thanked him and added—"Alas, *cher* Etienne, it's not a day when the rain comes!"

He raised his hands with a shrug of despair and waited until the door closed.

CHAPTER FIVE

I

SHE had very little sleep. It was foolish to have stayed so late with Etienne. The alarm clock woke her at seven. She dressed and at eight prompt the bell rang. It was Señora de los Rivos. When Amelia went down into the hall an elderly woman stood waiting for her, with a taxi outside. She was about sixty-five with white hair and black eyebrows. She was smartly but plainly dressed in a dark blue coat and skirt, and a simple straw hat. She wore dark sunglasses. She came up to Amelia as she left the elevator.

"You're Miss Macreary—I'm Lucia de los Rivos. I've a taxi waiting. We've plenty of time. You are prompt—a good Scotch habit!"

She laughed very gently. Her voice was soft and musical.

"You've not been to Don Antonio's *estancia*?"

"No—I've never been out of Buenos Aires," replied Amelia, as the taxi started for the station.

"You've not seen the Pampa?"

"No."

"Then you don't yet know what space is! It goes on and on and on—flat, flat, flat, scarcely a tree, not a stream, nothing but grass and cows and horses and gauchos," said Señora de los Rivos. "It either hypnotises you or drives you mad."

"What has it done to Sir Anthony?" asked Amelia.

"Both, I think!"

"Have you known him long?"

"So long it would give me away if I told you!"

"What very good English you speak."

"But I am English!" cried the Señora. "I came out here when I was a girl. My father was a railway engineer. He brought us all out from England with him. I married a young Argentine banker. Now I'm an elderly widow, with five sons and four daughters and eighteen grandchildren!"

"Are you ever homesick?" asked Amelia.

"Never—if you mean England, and Bedford in particular. This is my home. I wouldn't live anywhere else. Now, tell me something about yourself. You see, I'm playing chaperon. Don Antonio's very old-fashioned, and a stickler for the conventions. He wouldn't invite you until he knew I would come. You met on the boat?"

"Yes—he was very aloof, for a long time—I was fascinated," answered Amelia.

"Every woman who sets eyes on him falls in love with him. But it's quite useless. He has dismissed women from his world. We're going to a place where you won't see one except *peons*, for a hundred miles."

"But I was told Sir Anthony was a great lady-killer!"

"It was the lady who killed him."

"The lady—what lady?" asked Amelia.

Señora de los Rivos looked at the pretty young woman beside her.

"I see you know nothing," she said quietly.

"What is there to know?"

"There was a great tragedy. He was madly in love with his wife. She ran away with a gentleman-gaucho working on his *estancia*. Poor Antonio took it very badly. It would have happened later anyhow. She was man-mad. The gaucho was a hot-headed young Austrian. He came of some broken-down family, an aristocrat. He'd got something that turned all women into wax—sinewy, flame-lit, a grey-eyed devil if ever there was one."

"You knew him?"

62

"Knew him! I was one of a dozen women who made idiots of themselves over him. He had, my dear, what Hollywood calls 'It'—but he was a no-good. Everyone saw what was happening. But Antonio was blind. He thought Kurt Weninger one of the earth's wonder-boys because he was a great *domador*."

"*Domador*? What's that?" asked Amelia.

"Horse-breaker. We believe he had Hungarian blood, something out of the Puszta where horses are more important than women. He was tall, slim, long-thighed, with cool grey eyes in his dark face. He was a wizard in the corral. He could drop a lasso on the neck of a horse with the delicacy of a girl stringing pearls. He handled a troop of *potros*—broncos—three-year-olds, wild as cats, as no other fellow on the pampa. Antonio was good but Kurt was a masterhand. What a man!"

"Were you in love with him?"

"Yes, we all were!" said Señora de los Rivos. "We were at an age when those things get out of hand. When the blow fell, when he vanished with Carmen—Antonio's wife—we were stunned, but not really surprised. It might have been any one of us he could have lassoed."

"So that's Sir Anthony's tragedy?"

"Part of it. To have gone off with her lover—women do things like that every day, even when they've got a Don Antonio for a husband—but to have taken the boy, that was unforgivable!"

"There was a boy—Don Antonio's son?" asked Amelia.

"Yes, a boy of eight. That really broke up dear Antonio. Carmen—he might have got over, but taking the boy was a deadly blow. Don Antonio began to get odd ideas. He came to believe that—— My dear, we're at the station! I've told you too much, perhaps, but you must know where you are. No, no, I'll take care of this," said Señora de los Rivos, opening her purse as they got out of the taxi.

The train journey was fascinating. They were bound for Rosario, one hundred and eighty miles from the capital. They left behind the sprawling sophistication of Buenos Aires, its warehouses, outbuildings, and entered the flat plain. There was soon nothing visible except great stretches of wheat and corn crops, and herds of grazing cattle. The skyline was broken only by the iron scaffolding of windmills, with scattered *estancia* huts, crudely built for the most part, set in a treeless waste divided by wire fences. The roads had degenerated into dirt tracks that were straight brown trails across the plain, leading to the lonely ranches. There were carts pulled by horses or oxen, and very few automobiles on the dead-straight roads. The Argentine Republic covered one and a quarter million square miles and had a population of twelve millions. Three of these lived in Buenos Aires.

The train continued to run through a flat silent green landscape. They stopped at little wind-swept stations, some with English names, all with cattle docks. A lame boy, a *mestizo*, of mixed blood from his colouring and Indian black hair, came along with a tray. Señora de los Rivos bought from him two *matés*. They were pear-shaped gourds with narrow ends that contained 'yerba', a Paraguayan tea, infused with hot water. This national drink was sucked up through a metal tube. Amelia was familiar with it. It was refreshing.

Amelia restrained her curiosity about Don Antonio's tragedy. She wanted to hear the whole story but her companion seemed reluctant to tell her any more. Twice she turned aside a reference Amelia made. How long ago had all this happened? Was the fugitive wife still living? And the boy? He must be a grown man now. Doña Lucia seemed not to know the answers.

After three hours they arrived at their first destination,

Rosario, a considerable town of over half a million inhabitants. In the station yard was a large Mercedes car, driven by a lean brown-skinned young man. He was an odd kind of chauffeur. He wore a coloured silk scarf round his neck, and carried a *facón*, a long knife in a broad leather belt studded with silver coins. A thin green shirt tautly covered his lean torso and sinewy muscular back. He wore half Wellingtons, with brown leather cuffs and highish heels. He seemed more equipped for the corral than the car. Black curls thickly clustered on his head and the nape of his neck. The Doña knew him and addressed him as Juan. He had a slow musical speech and a lazy smile. What might have seemed a cool arrogance of manner was dispelled by a singular air of breeding. He might have been an *hildago*, disguised in blue jeans. He could not have been more than twenty-five. His candid dark eyes leisurely appraised Amelia. When she spoke to him in Spanish there was a flicker of surprise. His strong white teeth flashed a smile. He placed the portmanteaux in the boot. It was an open car. They threaded their way down a thronged *avenida*. The place had an air of prosperity. It was a port, derricks lined the river docks, and there was a forest of grain-elevators.

"We have sixty miles to go. I hope you won't be afraid," said the Doña.

"Afraid?"

"Juan treats an automobile like a bronco that must be broken in. We'll be off the earth half the time."

The resolute slim brown hands on the wheel, the young taut body, gave Amelia confidence. From time to time this was rudely shaken. The car seemed to stand up on its hind legs and whinny at pot-holes in the dirt track. The speed never relaxed. Sometimes Juan sang a tune, sometimes he dismayed Amelia by lighting a cheroot, one hand on the wheel while he struck a match on his lean muscular thigh. From time to time he glanced back, with an ivory grin, to see if his passengers were still aboard. He made observations at intervals; on the state of the road, on two bearded beggars he blotted out in a cloud of dust. He greeted people by name as he roared through a village, startling a group by the local *almacen*, the store that sold everything. They passed thriving truck and dairy farms, and cows, cows by the dozen, hundreds, in herds. The pampa, which covered one fifth of Argentina was a vast agricultural factory that fed a hungry world with meat and cereals. Amelia reflected that from the haunches of one of these innumerable animals would come the piece of bloody beef that her mother bought at the butcher's in Fitzroy Street. It was the pillar of the midday Sunday lunch, sizzling with gravy and fringed with potatoes as it came out of the iron grate by which her father, reading the *News of the World*, twiddled his toes. As if conscious of her thoughts, Juan turned his young head. If beef went to Scotland, it also came from there.

"Don Antonio," he announced, "last year imported two Scotch bulls to improve the herd. Olé. How they are doing it!"

They went on and on. The road lay like a ruler over the rich prairie, with its clover, green lucerne, giant sunflowers, the windmills, the wire fences running for mile on mile, and a few *ombu* trees, the national tree that gave a deep shade; and everywhere, following the curve of the earth, to its wide horizon, the illimitable pampa.

The long straight railway line was punctuated by small stations, all receiving-depôts for a ceaseless traffic of 'packets of meat', as a modern poet put it, that went on to the ports, with their refrigerator ships, and to their final destination, the butchers' shops of the United Kingdom of Great Britain and Ireland.

In busy Rosario, a freshwater port on the Rio de la Plata, once ambitious to become the Federal capital, the national prosperity, based on beef and grain, had been very visible, in the wide avenues, the good hotels, and the mixture of nine-teenth-century and ultra-modern architecture.

"The grass of the pampa has made all this," commented Doña Lucia.

At every stopping place there was a grain and cattle depôt Amelia was seeing an Argentina unsuspected in Buenos Aires. The pampa was the soul of the country, Buenos Aires was only the decorative head, the show place of the wealth flowing in from the *estancias*. The pampa, the vast patchwork rug, hill-less, treeless, stoneless, a flat prairieland that ran from the Atlantic and the bank of the Rio de la Plata monotonously on to the western foothills of the Andes, embraced everything. Its silence, its vast sky, its unreachable horizon, were a revela-tion to Amelia.

At last Juan raised a hand and said simply—"Tabara!" They deviated from the straight track. On the skyline there was a low cluster of buildings standing in an oasis of giant eucalyptus trees and Lombardy poplars. They drew nearer, encompassed by wire fencing, and, passing under a dense arch of trees, entered through a gateway into a patio. They had scarcely halted when out of the door of the house came Don Antonio, hatless, dressed in a light brown suit, perfectly tailored, with highly polished shoes, and gloved as ever, still the dandy in the green prairieland.

He greeted his guests with a courtly air.

"Beautifully timed—lunch will be in ten minutes," he said, as he shook hands with Doña Lucia and Amelia. "Well, what do you think of my little retreat?" he asked.

Amelia did not answer for a few moments, surveying the eucalyptus trees shading the patio, and the long low house.

"I feel as if I had just landed on another planet. The space, the light, the air!" exclaimed Amelia.

"You have thirty thousand acres to breath in, so I do not think you will feel cramped!" said Sir Anthony.

Two women, dark, portly, all smiles, appeared with Carlos the valet, and took their bags. Their host conducted them into a large *salon*. A vast window commanded a surprising view of formal gardens with clipped hedges, a flagged terrace, lead garden statues, a Mercury fountain, a tiled loggia, and a beautiful wrought-iron gate leading from the patio to a grassy walk bordered with flowers. It was surprising after the primitive plain to find this highly cultivated garden made in the English tradition on the grassy prairie.

"This is not a characteristic feature of the pampa, it's an English eccentricity," explained Sir Anthony. "There are moments in this illimitable waste when one craves a cloistered retreat. I've attempted it here."

Another maid appeared and led Doña Lucia and Amelia to their rooms, which were adjoining. Again Amelia stared in amazement. Her bedroom might have been in an English manor house, with its Tudor bed, its thick pile carpets, kidney dressing-table, chaise-longue, deep armchairs, Chelsea china ornaments, and bright cretonnes, in a house where she would not have been surprised to find boarded floors and a truckle bed. Even the walls had a Chinese flower paper.

Doña Lucia was amused at Amelia's childish delight.

"But how is it possible—all these thousands of miles away from Europe?" asked Amelia.

"It's explained largely by having a Harrods in Buenos Aires, and an imported race of interior decorators, English, French and Italian, who will create for you a Blenheim, a Versailles or a Caserta, if you have the wish, and the money," exclaimed Doña Lucia. "I can take you to the foot of the Andes, where you'll be surrounded by bare-footed *peons*, and sleep in a boudoir that Madame de Pompadour would have envied. Here, if you have the whim and the money, anything is possible. This country is founded on the cow. It is reverenced as much as in India, but here we don't worship it, we cut it up."

They drank an apéritif on the flagged terrace, seated under a large yellow umbrella that shaded them from the fierce sun. Lunch was served in a long cool room. Juan appeared again, this time as a waiter, in a short white gold-braided jacket, wearing cotton gloves. He served silently but observed them from under his long lashes with a blend of humour and gravity. He had changed from his riding jeans into black trousers, his slim waist encompassed by a green cummerbund. He trod panther-like on slippered feet. Amelia, watching him, recalled Doña Lucia's comment: "Sometimes he's so coolly insolent I want to horsewhip him. He flaunts his sex and you couldn't count the children he's fathered round here. Unfortunately he has Don Antonio in the hollow of his hand. He's menacingly efficient at everything."

"But he's a mere boy!" exclaimed Amelia.

"He's not as young as that—though he behaves like an adolescent sometimes. He dominates Pepe."

"Pepe?"

"The old butler. Juan can do no wrong in Don Antonio's

eyes because he's the finest *domador* within a hundred miles. I've seen bulls go weak in his hands. As for the girls . . . ."

Whatever his faults Juan treated his master with a grave deference. He was swift, ubiquitous, silent in Sir Anthony's presence.

The lunch was excellent. They took coffee on the terrace under the awning. The heat had grown.

"We take a siesta until five o'clock. I propose then that we go round the stables. Perhaps you are not interested in horses? We *aficionados* can become great bores," said Sir Anthony.

"I love horses !" exclaimed Amelia. "I should ride every day if I could."

"You can ride? I thought you said——" began Sir Anthony, trying not to betray surprise.

"I've had some lessons," said Amelia.

"Miss Macreary asked me if she should bring riding kit. I said 'Yes'," interjected Doña Lucia, removing a long cigarette-holder from her mouth.

"Splendid ! Then when we have chosen your mount we will take a ride. Tomorrow morning I am putting on a little show for you—a *domada*, a horse-breaking. The gauchos are bringing a troop of *potros*, three- and four-year olds. You'll see something !" said Sir Anthony, with a slow smile.

They went to their siesta, a deep silence enfolded the house. Not a leaf stirred. Only very faintly, there was the wavering monotone of the fountain playing on the terrace below Amelia's window. She put on a négligé gown and lay on the chaise-longue in the beautiful room with its Chinese flower-and-bird wallpaper. There were some books on the small Chippendale lamp table at her side. She glanced over the titles, Spanish, French, English. A volume of Pierre Loti, a book of short stories by Colette, *Madame Bovary*, Stendhal's *La Chartreuse de Parme*, and an Italian novel *Il fuoeo* by D'Annunzio. She must learn Italian next. There was a large Italian colony in Buenos Aires, and two of the girls in the office were Italian.

Amelia picked up a volume by Hugh Walpole, *Fortitude*. He had once lectured at the Celebrity Series in Glasgow. He was plump, rosy, urbane, she recalled.

Glasgow. How far away, what aeons in time, what miles, what dissimilarity in its civilisation! Here, on a Saturday afternoon, on a chaise-longue in the bedroom of an *estancia* on the immense pampa, on the South American continent, she, Amelia Macreary, was the guest of an English baronet! Now, on a winter's afternoon, grey, drizzling, in cap and mackintosh, with three thousand other men similarly clad, her father would be shouting himself hoarse at a football match, and her brother Alec would be digging, as usual, on his grimy small-holding, excited about a row of snail-eaten cabbages! She reflected on the vagaries of life. It was all largely what one made it. Lady Slowdon for instance, who might have been living here, had chosen to go off with a herdsman, a baronet's wife ruining herself for a mere male!

A mere male. Could the Austrian have been anything like this Juan, with his blade-like body, long lashes and smoky smile? How old had Lady Slowdon been? Where was she? Dead? Alive, full of regrets? She must ask Doña Lucia. And what was Doña Lucia's own story? An English girl become an Argentine. There were so many questions to be asked in this entrancing new world.

She opened *Fortitude* and read but presently it slipped from her hands. The warm afternoon overcame her.

III

There were twenty horses in the stables grouped around a large yard. Don Antonio was a slim elegant figure in his riding kit. He wore a soft black sombrero, a blue blouse with an orange kerchief, and cream whipcord trousers tucked into

71

highly polished neat half-boots. He threw an appraising glance at the slim figure of his young guest in her brown twill jodhpurs. She wore a white panama hat that set off her red curls. Doña Lucia had remained in her room.

There was a couple of native boys in the stables. Juan was in attendance, cool, slim, watchful. They visited the stalls. Amelia knew nothing about horses, but that they were thoroughbreds was quickly visible. Crown Prince, Don Antonio's favourite, was already saddled.

"Now, a nice quiet mount. Here we are, an Argentine *Criollo*. Bring him out and saddle him," he said to a boy. The horse's colour was a cross between a dun and a bay, with sturdy legs and a shortish thick neck. "This is Moko, he's a sixteen-year-old, quiet," said Sir Anthony. He stroked the horse's neck while it was being saddled. "He's a native—as far as any Argentine horse is a native. He's descended of a breed brought over from Spain by the man who founded Buenos Aires four hundred years ago. He's out of the finest Spanish stock with Barbary and Arab blood. They all came overseas. There were no horses in America until the Spaniards came here. When they were massacred by the Indians—they wiped out the first Buenos Aires—these horses ran wild over the pampa. Only the toughest survived the enemies that attacked them, animals and hunting Indians. We've brought them back and civilized them. There's nothing on earth to match them for toughness and spirit."

Amelia stroked the velvet nose of Moko as the boy saddled him. Then she mounted. The saddle was comfortable. Moko was not high or hardmouthed. Don Antonio's mount was a hand higher. He seemed restive. Behind them, on a thoroughbred that made a spirited display coming out of the yard, rode Juan, poised, smiling, keeping a distance of twenty feet behind.

They took a dirt track that led from the eucalyptus avenue

out to the grassy plain. The sun was westering, a blue haze lay over the vast expanse of alfalfa grass. They rode quietly, Sir Anthony slightly abreast of Amelia.

"I suppose you know that this is the *Sábado Inglés*, the English Saturday, that we brought to the Argentine?" asked Sir Anthony. "They shut all the shops at noon following our tradition. We've brought them football, golf and tennis. We've built the railways—and the water works. We've done much more than any other race, more than the natives, to develop this country. When I came out here as a youth we were the most influential, I'd almost say, the ruling race here. The *estancias* learned from us how to improve their breeds of cattle and sheep. But now young Englishmen are ceasing to come and we are slipping in power and prestige. Much of the banking is still in our hands and you'll find British managers directing big businesses here—as your own, for instance. But we are vanishing, we are no longer the Argentine's largest customer. Germans, Italians, Slavs are coming and infiltrating—and the Russians too."

They passed a great herd of cattle and traversed a settlement of huts. They rode for an hour and yet they seemed to have made no progress; the plain went on and on over an immeasurable wilderness of grass, to the level horizon, under the unclouded dome of the blue sky. Slowly the fascination of this empty land, with its rich black soil, its grain and grass, its cattle and horses, began to hypnotise the senses of the young woman riding with her elderly host. She came to understand the reason of his repose, his seclusion here away from the great cities he had known. The mystery that cloaked his personality on the boat had not been dispersed. He was still an aloof proud figure, not given to confidences. But she began to comprehend a little of the forces that had set him apart from other Englishmen. Now from Doña Lucia she had learned of the tragedy in the background of his life. It explained part of the singularity

73

she had felt on that first day when, attended by Carlos, he had come to his deck chair, the *hidalgo*, aloof, and always the great gentleman.

The immense ball of the crimson sun had touched the western horizon. They turned homewards, encompassed by a golden light. In the cooler air they galloped towards the homestead set amid the eucalyptus trees. The golden glow had quickly gone. There was now a sharp violet light, level over the landscape, that seemed to magnify details. Glancing back Amelia saw that Juan followed, a slim black silhouette against the crimson sky. Man and horse moved as of one piece.

I V

Before retiring that evening Doña Lucia said to Amelia. "Are you Catholic or Protestant?"

"Protestant—Episcopal Church of Scotland," replied Amelia.

"I ask because there's mass at eight o'clock in the morning. A priest rides over from Webster, and the family and tenants go to it."

"Is Sir Anthony Catholic?"

"No—but he is sympathetic. He was married both by the British Consul and by the Church. The Church is all powerful in Argentina. Nearly every *estancia* is connected with and supports a local church with its priest. It is all part of the paternalism that the *estancias* exercise over the district. We are still feudal, despite the politicians! Don Antonio has always been a generous supporter of the Church. He has built a small chapel, which has been consecrated."

"Where is it?"

"Here, in a wing of the house."

"Does he attend the services?"

"Yes, and he insists on all his employees attending—of course guests please themselves."

"I should like to come," said Amelia.

"You'll have an interesting view of the people on the *estancia*."

"How many come?"

"About sixty," said Doña Lucia. "The men all in black, the women in high-necked dresses of serge. Some of the young *cabelleros* are dandies—they let themselves go, with their boleros and braided trousers."

"Was Sir Anthony's wife Catholic?"

"Yes, but his son, like himself, was not. He was much criticised for this. He agreed that any daughters should be Catholic but that the boys should be Protestant."

"The boy—what was he called?"

"Roderick," replied Doña Lucia.

"How old is he now—where is he?" asked Amelia.

"He must be over forty now. We don't know where he is."

"Don't know. But surely Sir Anthony——"

"He took a strange attitude towards the boy. He regards him as illegitimate."

"Illegitimate?"

"Yes," said Doña Lucia. "He believes he's Karl Weninger's son. We think it is utter nonsense, but he has an *idée fixe* on the subject. He will never discuss it. That is one of the things you must never allude to. I've known Don Antonio all my life, but it is the one thing I've never dared to discuss with him. No one dares."

"Did you know his wife?" asked Amelia.

"Very well—both before and after their marriage."

"What was she like?"

"Carmen was a great beauty. She came of one of the first families. Her mother was English, a Beaumont of the Beaumont family. They met at a *Fiera* in Seville. She was deeply in

75

love with Don Antonio. No one wondered at that. He was the handsomest young man that ever drove up to the Jockey Club. She turned down all the other *estancieros* for him."

"And the marriage went wrong?"

"Not at first. They seemed the happiest couple on the earth. He worshipped her—but she was very temperamental. Within two years, Roderick was born. There was one flaw in it all. Carmen hated life here on the pampa. She wanted the races, the opera, the theatres. She wanted always to be on show, to have adulation, a court of young men, and to be the best-dressed woman in Buenos Aires—which she was. She made him buy a town house there. She had no sense of the value of money. A time came when he had to make a protest, he was getting into difficulties. To remedy this he wanted her to go to England, to the place he had there, a family place, very old and lovely. But she hated it. She hated England. After six years the strain began to show. Anthony was often employed by the British government, buying horses. It entailed a lot of travel, here in Argentine and in England. She refused to accompany him. He wanted to send young Roderick to school in England when the time came—you have to write down a boy's name at Eton a long time ahead, I'm told. They had a scene over that, and she brought the whole phalanx of her Spanish relations into the battle and he had to give way. Then something began to happen. In Anthony's long absences the management of Tabara gradually fell more and more into the hands of Kurt Weninger, the Austrian gentleman-*domador*, who had been here since Anthony's marriage. It was useless to warn Anthony, he had such confidence in Weninger, also, let me say. Anthony is in some ways terribly lazy. *Mañana*, the vice here, took possession of him. So Weninger soon had everything in his hands. It went on like that for five years or so. Then nasty rumours began to spread. Carmen used to come here more and more during Anthony's absence on business. It was odd because she hated *estancia* life. One day my husband and I rode over from Webster, where we were staying. Carmen was in her room so I went up to her. She was in her bathroom. I saw at once from the pillows side by side that two persons had occupied the bed. There was a smell of tobacco in the room, strong tobacco. The folly of it, with the servants around! I said nothing but it bore out a rumour I had heard and disbelieved. They were often out riding together. They seemed quite reckless. A friend saw them dancing in a night club in Buenos Aires. Later, we heard the Austrian had a garçonnière in the Barrio Norte district. As you know, you don't keep a garçonnière there for nothing. I was miserable about it, about Anthony's utter blindness, about her folly. One day I found the courage to tackle Carmen. She only laughed in my face. There must have come a time when Anthony learned the facts, for one day a bombshell fell. We heard that Carmen had gone. She had sailed for Europe, taking the boy with her."

"And the man?"

"Kurt Weninger had disappeared too—but he wasn't on the boat. Later they joined up in Vienna. There was a terrific scandal."

"Sir Anthony—what did he do?"

"Nothing," said Doña Lucia. "He shut himself up here, and if anyone tried to discuss the matter they met a stony barrier. I never saw a man change so. He had been very gay, very *simpatico* to everybody, a wonderful host. He became a morose recluse here. He saw no one, he went nowhere, except on his British government commissions."

"Did he divorce her?"

"There's no divorce in the Catholic Church. I don't think he'd have done so had he thought it possible."

"Surely he wanted the boy—he must have been fond of him?"

"He loved him very much, a good father. The strangest part of all was that he never, so far as we all know, attempted to get the boy. He had got it into his head that Roderick was illegitimate! That's something we've never been able to understand. My husband was his closest friend, up to the day of his death. He told me that he once spoke to Anthony on the matter. 'If you want to continue our friendship, Alvarez, that's a subject we can never discuss,' he said to him. All this was in 1900. From that time on we saw very little of him. Then the War broke out—he was sent all over the place. He came back here in 1919, more aloof and enclosed than ever. We heard that Carmen had died. She had been living with Weninger in Vienna. Her brother in Spain had seen her and Roderick there in 1912. She called herself Frau Weninger, and seemed quite happy. She died very suddenly in 1914, soon after the Great War broke out. Weninger, we heard, had been killed fighting on the Russian front."

"And Roderick—does he never write to his father?"

"So far as we know, never. We don't even know where he is —we surmise he's still in Austria. If Anthony ever received any letters from Carmen or her son, we don't know. He's never spoken of them. In some ways he's a man of granite behind his polished exterior. You will never quite know our Don Antonio. He's very lonely, very proud, very reticent. It all began by letting his affairs get into the wrong hands—Kurt Weninger's. I suppose, au fond, it's laziness. Anthony will not bother about anything."

Doña Lucia looked at her wrist watch. "Eleven o'clock! How I've talked! Please, don't let Don Antonio know I've been talking about him. He detests any gossiping, particularly concerning his affairs. I've known him intimately—as intimately as is ever possible with him, for over forty years. My husband admired him tremendously but said he never really knew him."

Doña Lucia rose. They had been sitting in the library. Their host had excused himself. He had rigid hours. He retired at ten and rose at six.

Doña Lucia and Amelia left the library and mounted the wide wooden stairs to the long landing.

"Good-night," said Doña Lucia at her door.

"Good-night—and thank you for all you've told me. It explains a great deal that has puzzled me. Poor Sir Anthony!" said Amelia. "What a tragedy!"

"Yes, we are all sorry for him, but we daren't show it. He hates any sign of sympathy. Good-night!"

CHAPTER SIX

I

THERE must have been forty persons attending mass in the little chapel the next morning. It seemed a singular mixture of races. Sir Anthony was undisguisedly English, aloof, handsome. The little fat priest seemed almost a peasant, buried in his vestments. There were Indian faces, half-breeds, *peons*, *mestizos* of mixed white and Indian blood, cattleboys or herdsmen, the gauchos of Spanish-Argentine stock, some high-cheeked women of Russian origin, blond Germans, Italians, half-a-dozen negroes, and black-eyed, black-haired children; it was an interesting polyracial community. Their clothes were for the most part sombre, but singular in design. They all comported themselves with the *dignidad* on which Argentines set such store.

After church they waited until Don Antonio, with a word of greeting to them, had left the chapel, and then the young *cabelleros*, in their Sunday clothes, began to chaff the girls. The little fat priest followed Don Antonio into the house where he was given a glass of wine and a cake before he rode on to the next chapel. He treated Sir Anthony with great deference. "He gives generously to the Church and is in very good standing," explained Doña Lucia.

When Father Martinez had gone they all changed into riding kit and, after breakfast, set off for the next event of the day. In honour of Amelia there was to be a *domada*, a horse-breaking. They rode off in a considerable company to the corral three miles away. The morning was still cool and cloudless. The green prairie shone wide and flat. It being Sunday morning the men were in gala attire and took some of their womenfolk along. The men's black felt hats with soft brims and chin straps, had all been newly ironed, the younger men sported black caps with coloured tassels. They all wore bright silk kerchiefs around their necks, with loose blouses, and wide baggy trousers, *bombachas,* tucked into their soft leather riding boots. They had silver rowel spurs. At their waists they wore heavy leather belts studded with silver coins, into which they had tucked large murderous-looking knives. The girls, vivacious and vivid with their glossy black hair and flashing dark eyes, sat sideways behind their swains. They wore ornaments of native workmanship and beautiful neat shoes.

A company of about twenty followed Sir Anthony and his guests. He was dressed in a tight-fitting light grey bolero jacket with a black sombrero, and high glossy leather boots; his hands in gauntleted gloves with wide embroidered cuffs. With his grey hair, pointed beard, fine hawk-like face and trim body, he made a commanding figure. No one could doubt who was the *hidalgo* present in that group. He sat his mettlesome stallion superbly.

At the corral they found a larger company. The gauchos, mostly springy lean-thighed young men, had come in from all over the *estancia.* The word had gone round that a young blonde beauty with a marvellous complexion and red hair was a guest of the old Don, and the *domada* was in her honour. There was a great sweep of hats in courteous greeting when the company rode up. In one corral were seventy or eighty horses; a second corral, lowly-fenced, with a centre post, was empty. Half-a-dozen young horses were let into the corral. Four agile young men followed, lassoes in hand, shouting and waving their ropes. The animals started to gallop wildly round. A horse had to be selected. The intended victim quickly divined the lassoer's intention and, in order to evade the rope, turned and twisted and took shelter between its companions. A moment came when the *criollo* was detached. With unerring aim the lasso slid over its proud neck. The assistants left their colleague to play the wildly careering horse. Suddenly the rope went round the post in the centre of the corral. Before it knew what had happened, the *criollo's* legs were roped. Madly bucking and kicking, it was brought down with a crash. At once the assistants rushed in. It was deftly blindfolded and the *bocado*, a bit made of a piece of raw hide with reins attached, was slipped into the animal's mouth and bound tightly about the lower jaw. With hind legs unroped they let the horse rise, one foreleg slung up, the head fastened close to the post. The saddling of the helpless *criollo* began, despite his snorting and quivering. This completed, the rope was loosened at the post and the horse, one foreleg still slung, was permitted to move. He still kicked wildly as he moved on his three legs, and the lads were very wary. Out of the smaller corral he came, tossing defiantly his bridled head, the resented saddle on his back, the two gauchos firmly tugging at the reins. They led him into the open arena. The great moment had come.

A tall, thin, belted young man in half-boots and tight jeans, hatless, cool-eyed, approached. He was the *domador*, the breaker of this wild creature. He leapt into the saddle. The assistants loosed the blindfolding bandage and the binding ropes. The wild game for mastery between man and animal began. The bronco reared, plunged, kicked and twisted madly. At every buck down came the raw-hide lash. A wild rush down the field followed, but in vain, for the bronco found itself herded by other horsemen away from the fence on which it had hoped to brush off its rider. Hounded by other horses, wildly kicking and turning, alternately reined in and loosened to induce exhausting rushes, the mad play went on, the rider still in the saddle. There came a moment when the lathered horse conceded victory. It stood still for a time, puzzled, humiliated. The rider lightly slipped down from the saddle, gave a half-sympathetic cuff on the muzzle of the animal, handed the reins to a boy, who then slowly walked it out of the arena. The first lesson had been learned.

Three times a horse was selected from its fellows and broken in this fashion. The wildest had been kept for the last. It entered with the troop.

The two assistants went into the corral. With them went a third. Amelia knew him at once. It was the *peon*, Juan. Tall, slim, sinewy, he was a magnificent figure of young manhood. Lean flanked but muscular, with straight back and wide shoulders above the thin waist bound with its heavily studded belt, he commanded attention. He lassoed his choice coolly, brought it neatly to the *palenque*, where its head was tethered, and waited while the seething bronco was blindfolded and bridled. He watched the assistants saddle the horse, firmly keeping the reins. A foreleg slung, the horse was led, still vicious and rebellious, kicking madly with one of its three free legs, out of the corral into the wide arena. With a spring Juan was in the saddle, the men let go the ropes, the foreleg was freed, the bandage came off its eyes. In a frenzy of rage the bronco leapt in the air and bucked. Down came the raw-hide whip. Twisting, bucking, rushing, with sudden checks, it was incredible that anyone could keep mounted under that tornado of furious movement. Vainly the enraged creature sought to throw its rider. It foamed at the mouth, it pulled the bridle reins until it seemed they would snap, or the strong wrists fail to hold them. Again and again the maddened bronco rushed for the rails with a cunning intent to sweep the rider off, but the other riders skilfully headed him away. For twenty minutes the battle raged. Then came a moment when the bronco stood still. Was it a pause before another tornado of bucking and rushing? The spectators breathlessly waited. Nothing happened. The horse lowered its head, admitting defeat. Juan turned it, and slowly rode his mount to the exit. There he slipped down from the saddle, patted the horse's neck and gave the reins over to a boy. Calmly he took out a packet of cigarettes from a hip pocket and lit one. He pushed back a damp black lock, rubbed the nape of his neck with a brown hand, and under his sweeping dark lashes gave Don Antonio and the ladies a cool confident smile.

"Bravo, Juan," said Don Antonio, proudly.

The young man came over to them. There was a touch of arrogance in the slight roll of his hips, the set of his torso. The sweat stood in beads on his dark brow. Here was a male animal as superb as the horse he had broken, with the difference that he was the *domador*, the breaker. Could anything tame him? Soft hands hold him, loose tresses bind him, dark eyes enslave him, tender mouth prove its mastery? Perhaps. There were other powers than muscle and courage.

As he talked easily with them, Amelia understood how one like this had worked a tragedy on this very *estancia*. A lonely woman, youth fading, had been overwhelmed by sheer physical potency. It was singular how the proudest fell, how rank was swept aside, how even thrones toppled and the current of history was diverted by those who possessed what this virile young man flaunted before them.

The young *domador*, cigarette on lip, smilingly acknowledged their congratulations, then withdrew from Don Antonio's party. He slowly walked across to a young girl, raven-haired, with sparkling dark eyes, and a head superbly poised on her slim throat. She laughed at him as he came over to her, took from her bosom a rose, and stuck it over his ear. She stood with a court of señoritas, noisy with laughter and chatter. Not one of them seemed to be more than seventeen. Juan glowed with an assumed indifference to their hero-worship.

The company began to remount their horses. The sun, climbing to its zenith, burned with increasing force, and a slight haze of heat palpitated above the level plain.

"I hope you enjoyed it?" asked Sir Anthony when they had come to the stable yard.

"I shall never forget it! It was quite amazing. Don't those gauchos sometimes get badly hurt?"

"Very seldom. They get thrown, of course, but they know how to fall. They're all rubber and whipcord."

"And a lot of steel!" laughed Doña Lucia.

"I had one gaucho thrown and kicked by a violent *potro*. The poor fellow died in hospital. But that was many years ago—and the only fatality I've known. It's dangerous, of course, but not quite so dangerous as bull-fighting—and I think more sporting!"

11

Doña Lucia and Amelia left early on Monday morning. Another young man drove them to the station at eight o'clock. He was Alonzo, a sleek lad who surprised Amelia by addressing her as 'Miss'.

"You speak English?" she asked.

"Leetle—I two months wait me for make new boat at Clyde-side."

"Clyde-side! You know Glasgow?"

"Si. I have nice girl, Glasgow. Scotch, *muchos* fresh skin. *Hermoso!* I like would marry that girl—one day perhaps. She write often. I write often. She teach me dance reel. Scottish Reel. I bring home kilt, wear, do reel. *Muchos* sensation. *Olé! Olé!* they cry when I do cross-dagger dance. Yes, Miss, Bonnie Scotland good, whisky good, people good!"

"Were you there in summer or winter?"

"Winter, Miss. December. Cold, the fog nice. You get girl closer!" He laughed, raised a hand from the wheel. "Annie

—that her name. Her people nice. We have parlour alone. Big coal fire. Christmas, we eat. All family drink, dance. Scotland very nice. Three cheers Bonnie Scotland!" said Alonzo.

"Well, you couldn't have a better report than that!" laughed Doña Lucia.

Amelia made no reply. She could not. For some silly reason she was almost near to tears.

In the train they talked of Sir Anthony.

"He is really a shy man. His pride is only a façade," said Doña Lucia. "He's a very lonely man, and now he's getting old he feels it more and more. But he won't leave his beloved *estancia*."

"Has he no relations?"

"We never see or hear of any."

"I suppose that Mr. Carson really runs the *estancia*?" asked Amelia.

"Yes, I don't know what Don Antonio would do without him. But Mr. Carson is getting old and he tells me he would like to retire. The staff is good and loyal."

"Sir Anthony seems quite attached to Juan, the *domador* in charge of his stables. He seems to go everywhere with him."

"The Don Juan of the *estancia*!" exclaimed Doña Lucia, laughing. "Yes—he's rather a spoilt lad. He's very attentive to Anthony, and he seems to get his way in everything. My brother, who visits here occasionally, says he's a sly young rascal. I won't say I'll go as far as that. He's quite a remarkable fellow. As for his morals—well, we'd better not go into those! So you've noticed him?"

Amelia did not answer for a few moments. Then she said—"I find him a little mysterious. He looks at you so—so——" She hesitated for a word.

"Do you wonder that he plays havoc with the girls on the *estancia*? I'm very glad that I'm not young and impressionable, I wouldn't dare to go into his corral! He'd rope one up as easily as that poor bronco yesterday morning!" said Doña Lucia. "That was poor Carmen's end with her handsome *domador* Kurt."

They turned to other things. The train reached Buenos Aires. They took a taxi and Doña Lucia put down Amelia at her apartment. There was a warmth in the elder woman.

"I'll give you a call soon," said Doña Lucia. "You must come and dine. And you shall meet some young men. You deserve it after being so kind to the old folks!"

She waved her hand, and the taxi went on.

CHAPTER SEVEN

I

ANOTHER month passed swiftly by. Amelia was kept busy at
the office. Etienne de Lérin was now her frequent companion
in the early morning rides. At the Anstruthers, which became
a second home, the good-hearted noisy Anglo-Argentine family
seemed to have adopted her. She made shopping excursions
with Señora Anstruther, she went to a Catholic convent school
where the twin daughters performed in a play. They played
bridge, they took her on river excursions.

Doña Lucia de los Rivos had not forgotten her. The Doña
moved in a different world, a wholly Argentine one of an exclusive set of *estancia* owners. Amelia discovered that this was
a kind of landed aristocracy. They intermarried, they passed on
their *estancias* within a small circle, firmly aloof from the cock-
pit of Argentine politics, and were patrons of the Church,
though in no way subservient. It was a male oligarchy. The
father ruled his family strictly, he submitted to no other
authority except the old mother who was enthroned like a
deity and dictated the destinies of the family clan. Though the
girls were not given in marriage without some exercise of their
preferences, they were expected to conform to their parents'
wishes. The sons of the house followed a similar patriarchal
direction.

The great *estanciero* families were a cattle aristocracy, auto-
cratic. They kept their town houses, but lived in them only
seasonally, going to the opera and to the exclusive Jockey Club.
They travelled in lavish style, taking houses in Paris, at Deau-
ville and Pau. The younger sons had an international renown

as polo players. They ordered their suits in Sackville Street. The women bought their gowns in Paris. They were jewelled by Cartier, they kept exquisite their hair and complexions at Elizabeth Arden's. They were finished at French schools and given a season in London, Paris or Madrid.

Behind all this refinement and luxury stood the virile primitive life of the *estancias*, the silence of the vast level pampa, the tough gauchos, kerchiefed, black-hatted, in espadrilles or booted and spurred, displaying their maleness with a half-provocative arrogance. The estate women, like clusters of hens, cackled around their strutting cocks, the drivers of herds, the tamers of broncos. One saw them at dawn, a race of centaurs, herding the cattle to the railroad docks, with an almost theatrical vanity imposed on their phallic consciousness, black locks clustered and curled over their brown necks. They wore rings on their strong hands, a fine gold chain with crucifix on their tawny chests, and soft riding boots with silver spurs. They were not without guile, the glance of their clear eyes under the dark lashes sometimes had a conscious allure. Ruthless, possibly cruel, certainly not to be thwarted, with the knife in the belt and the raw-hide lash in hand, they bridged a primitive and a sophisticated civilisation. With the strap of their black hats under their firm chins they had an air, sometimes, of state police. It was not wholly tactful to call them gauchos, indicative of European and American Indian blood. Some of them were pure white, adventurers, lost younger sons who sought oblivion. They had graces, their supple bodies could not only tame wild horses. They could dance a saraband. A guitar was often slung on their lean bodies. They had a repertoire of melancholy songs, sung to a guitar in the shade of the dense *ombu*, or on still moonlit nights by the walls of their huts. None of them lacked his girl for dalliance. Promiscuous, careless breeders, they laughed at the church, went to confession, and sinned vigorously; stallions that could tame stallions and remain untamed.

From these *estancias* came also the delicate señoritas, with their European graces. They shone, jewelled, at the operas and the balls, displayed an exquisite delicacy and elegance at the races, or driving in the still favoured open *calêches* as they circled the park, reminiscent of the Empress Eugénie at St. Cloud, or the *Feria* at Seville. And then in turn they appeared on the wind-swept emerald pampa, superbly mounted, Dianas of the radiant day.

Every hour in this new world was intoxicating to Amelia. She blossomed, bright-eyed, rosy-lipped, vivacious. Gradually the inherited inhibitions fell away. Only the occasional letter from home recalled the dour soil that had produced her. Her Spanish was fluent, her French good. Etienne was very proud of his pupil. He no longer playfully called her *ma petite gamine*, although the rain never came for him and he patiently attended her through an unrewarding drought—*je t'emmènerai, j'en suis sûr, dans mon lit.*

He was no longer sure, rain or no rain, but he was still assiduous, attentive, playful. His admiration of her grew daily. She continued always to be exquisitely dressed, although he knew her budget must be slender. She had a natural chic, *une vraie duchesse*. It was a gift more than an achievement. He invited her out, in his own set. The women were a little cool, with a few exceptions. The men were eagerly attentive. There was a sad little scene at a dance one evening. A rose-leaf lad of seventeen, son of the First Secretary at the French Embassy, had fallen into a state of dumb adoration. He filled her room with flowers. He suffered agonies on the morning ride when he came with Etienne, for he had no seat and was often thrown. Somehow he had failed to get a dance with her one evening, and when, after midnight, he sought her and she had said she was too tired and was going home, his eyes suffused with tears, and he rushed out on to the terrace. Contrite, Amelia followed, and found him seated in the cover of a giant hydrangea, crying. It was embarrassing. What could one do with this shaken boy? She smoothed his sleek head, made him look up, and with her handkerchief proceeded to wipe his tears away.

"I love you! I love you, Miss Macreary!" he cried, his mouth trembling.

"Yes—yes. But now you're going to behave yourself, Emile. We'll have one dance together, and then I must go. You know, I'm a working girl and must get up in the morning!"

"Oh, yes, oh thank you!" he cried.

She put his white tie straight, adjusted his gardenia, and patted his cheek. He smiled desperately. They went indoors and danced.

With all her social success she kept away from the British Embassy set. Some of the younger women were nice, some frigid. She wasn't going to be patronised. She went to the annual garden party on the King's birthday, shook hands with the Ambassador and his nice wife. And that was all.

With Doña Lucia she had a rewarding friendship. She was a good musician. She was delighted when Amelia played duets with her at the piano. It was through Doña Lucia that she saw more of Sir Anthony, who stayed with her when he came to Buenos Aires, having given up his town house. He was always grave and courteous, but there was a point beyond which one did not advance to an informality or intimacy of manner. A strange solitary figure.

With Doña Lucia Amelia paid several week-end visits to Tabara. Sometimes there were other guests, usually Argentines. They rode. In the evening a couple of boys on the *estancia* came in and played rumbas or tangos to which they danced. Always in the background, supervising, watchful, a mysterious smile on his handsome dark face, was Juan. He occupied a curious place. He was not only a *domador*, a magnificent equestrian, he was something compounded of an estate superintendent, chauffeur and factotum. He never presumed despite a condescension masked by the manners of an *hidalgo*.

"Has he Indian blood?" asked Amelia.

"Yes—he's a *peon*. He came here as a small boy, an orphan. He had from the beginning a hypnotic touch with horses. Anthony took a great liking to the boy. He had him educated by a priest. You find him interesting? Everyone does, and is a little afraid of him!" laughed Doña Lucia.

"How old is he?"

"About twenty-five or so, I should say."

"And single!" exclaimed Amelia, for all these Argentines married young.

"Oh no, he's married and has two small boys—and a good many others elsewhere, I'm told!"

"His wife's here?"

"No, one never sees her. He keeps her in his quarters, two miles away. Once he took me to see her, a pretty dark little thing—a Sicilian, I believe. He married her when she was fifteen."

11

Amelia had not been a year in Buenos Aires when she was faced with a difficult decision. From the time of her arrival she had been pestered by young men, and older ones. They were shameless and persistent in their advances. Etienne, for all his suggestions, was of another order. These sleek dark young men could not understand why she would not sleep with them at the first overture. They all seemed to have large cars and small *garçonniéres*. She dealt very peremptorily with them. Perhaps it was the climate as much as a tradition. Everything mated. Very odd, for the male put tremendous emphasis on the chastity and virginity of the fiancées they courted, as behoved a Catholic society, but unrestrictedly flouted these virtues themselves, before and after marriage.

One evening, very late, at a restaurant where they went to eat and dance, Etienne said, without any preliminary approach, "*Chèrie*, will you marry me?"

She laughed and said, "Don't be silly—I might accept you at once, *cher* Etienne."

"I want you to accept me at once. I'm not being silly, or frivolous. I'm very serious. I love you. I want to marry you."

She looked across the table at him. He was serious. He could not be drunk, they had only had one bottle of *Château Cheval Blanc*. And now, after midnight, they were drinking a Dom Peregrine champagne—the bottle in its ice pail still half full.

"I think we should dance this number," said Amelia, smiling at him.

"No, that is an evasion. I've asked you, *chère* Amelia, if you will marry me," he said quietly, his hand crossing the table to cover hers.

She made no reply, and looked down at the table. After a silence she spoke, her eyes meeting his so intently observing her.

"You must know you've greatly surprised me and overwhelmed me. I suppose it's something every girl wishes will happen to her, but usually, I surmise, she's not wholly as surprised as I am. If I answered you at once, I'd say I couldn't, Etienne. Will you let me think it over? I'm moved, and proud of the compliment."

She smiled and answered the pressure of his hand. She couldn't see him quite clearly, and divining her emotion, he said, "Yes, think it over but don't keep me too long in suspense, *ma chèrie*. Shall we dance?"

They rose and went on to the floor. But there was a constraint on them, and when she suggested leaving, he agreed at once. He drove her home in the new sports car he had just purchased. He went into the hall and waited until the lift came down. Then he kissed her, holding her for a few moments and gazing in her eyes. "I've told you nothing about myself— you'll have to take so much on trust. You must forgive me over *Le jour où la pluie viendra*—I'm a very young man after all, and I haven't grown up in a monastery."

She made no reply, but her lips touched his cheek and her hands rested on his shoulders.

"Good-night, *cher* Etienne, I'll call you," she said, entering the lift.

"Soon, Amelia?"

"Soon," she replied, as the lift ascended.

Amelia slept badly that night, her mind in a turmoil. All the next day at the office she could not concentrate. In the evening, instead of eating in a restaurant she bought some food and took it back with her. It was the evening of her French lesson with Madame Dupont. She called her and put it off. It was a very warm evening. She changed into her light rose négligé gown, and carried a tray from the kitchen, setting it down by the open window of the balcony. She looked out on to the leafy trees in the *avenida*. While she was eating, someone in another apartment, the window open, had turned on a radio or a gramophone. One of the songs was *Parlez-moi d'amour*. She recalled she had first heard it on the boat. They had made a dance tune of it and Etienne, her partner, repeated the words softly to her, and from him she had learned them. "*Redites-moi des choses tendres.*" Tell me tender things. It had all been so newly exciting, and it was not a year ago. What had happened was beyond the most ambitious of her dreams. Here was a young Frenchman, good-looking, elegant, well-born, and of an entrancing gaiety, in a career that would lead him to high positions in the Diplomatic Service, probably an Ambassadorship, who offered her marriage.

Was it an intoxication of the flesh, the headiness of youth, a rashness in his nature that had brought him to this point of declaration? Supposing the day of the rains had come, and she had gone to his apartment, as he had urged, would this proposal have been made? Most surrenders were fatal to any continuity of passion. All young women knew that. Each *embarquement pour Cythère* grew a little less exciting. That an ardent, passionate young man, bred in the continental tradition, had not had his *embarquements* was past belief. She remembered a remark he had made when they looked in an art dealer's window one day. There was a painting, a reproduction by Jordaens, called *La Fecondité*. It showed the ample back and flanks of a nude female.

"How revolting! I've not got the callypigian mania. Could you imagine dallying with that!"

"Callypigian?" asked Amelia.

"Venus with fat buttocks—they made statues of them in the Roman era. And old Rubens too, how he loved *les fesses énormes*! I want the slender amphora"—his expressive quick hands made a slim curved pattern in the air—"not the Flanders mare!"

Twenty-six, travelled, French, he was surely not inexperienced. He had strained at the leash. The relief of passion encountered few obstacles in Buenos Aires. But this, she believed, was something different.

Solemnly considered, he offered much in comparison with her own assets. She was beautiful, clever and had much spirit —"*beaucoup de courage, petite gamine*," he would say playfully. He complimented her on a dozen things, her taste in dress, her deportment, her vast appetite for life and radiant enjoyment of all that came her way, or she attracted to her— but these things set against all he offered? What were they? He had breeding, an innate birthright. She had none. Every embellishment of manner had been patiently acquired by a steady rejection of all that her background involved. Even her voice and accent had been assumed. She had natural good manners, something unconsciously possessed and conveyed by her mother. Behind Etienne, unsought, stood the tradition of a landed aristocracy—she had seen photographs of his parents, his sisters, the old château set behind its ornamental gates, statuary and parterres, deep in its Provençal meadow. What would they say, his mustachioed colonel-father, his fine-featured mother, née Colbert, and all the de Lérin clan? And in the Service, an exclusive diplomatic set that recruited itself from the scions of the aristocracy, or holders of the *cordon bleu* of scholarship, how would she, the ex-typist, the Glasgow *gamine*, be received by the women of the profession? Her beauty, her wit, her courage, how would they wear against the steady attrition of rivals assured in their position and the banyan-rooted strength of family? And, lastly, a foreigner within the gates. Had Etienne considered all this? And if he had was he not challenging an impregnable fortress of prejudice and tradition?

Individually she could take on all the women. She had as much beauty, possibly more brains, greater resolution, and the strength engendered by an incessant attack on adverse conditions. There was Scots blood in her. It had planted its flag in many a hostile domain. She had the driving force of necessity and ambition.

Did these assets justify so great an adventure as was now offered to her? She would not have weighed the pros and cons so carefully but for one fact. Much as she would like to think it, she was not in love with Etienne. Why she was not, eluded her. The alchemy of love could not be explained. Physically, he was attractive. His body was shapely. Voice, hair, skin combined in a compelling masculinity that excited and pleased her. She knew enough to have no doubt of his ardency in love, his masculine allure. The play of his mind delighted her. They seemed matched in their mental quickness though his experience, education and social status were far beyond hers. He also offered a complete fulfilment of her material ambition. But, perversely, she did not love this attractive young man. What more was required to do so she could not define, but the compelling force was absent, the potent force that had driven Lady Slowdon into the arms of an Austrian adventurer.

It was frightening to see what power love had and how everything else lost all value in comparison. If she rejected Etienne no man might again make such an offer. Certainly no man so personable, with so much to further the fulfilment of her ambition.

All that evening her mind went round and round. The magnitude of what lay within her reach seemed to crown the fairy-tale that started in Glasgow. The wife of a First Secretary in Athens or Sofia, the wife of an Ambassador in Brussels, Teheran, Peking, Vienna, Rome—or even London! The pageant of progress fired the imagination. Madame l'Ambassadrice. The State dinners, the Presidential receptions, the gala performances, the palladian Embassies with their wide ceremonial staircases, herself standing, gowned and tiara-ed, at the side of her starred and ribboned husband, under the portrait of the President of the Republique Française. Her vivid mind saw it all. To reject all this for something that might never come into her life or come with a drab setting of commonplace surroundings, of struggle perhaps? What folly to gamble all this on the unpredictable chance of meeting a man she loved.

Over and over she debated the question. It was nearly midnight when she retired, the matter unsettled. From sheer mental exhaustion she slept until six. She awoke with the same roundabout of indecision goading her. When she breakfasted at eight o'clock she thought of Etienne fresh, well-groomed, hopeful, awaiting a call. Twice she picked up the instrument, then replaced it. He must wait another day. To-morrow she would see him.

While eating she picked up a copy of *El Hogar*, the lavish magazine devoted to the Home Beautiful. She looked at the coloured illustrations of houses, apartments, patios, boudoirs, *salons* and American kitchens. She could have a home finer than any of these. She could live in regal splendour, for ambassadors were the last royalties surviving this age of democracy and crushing taxation. The State's art gallery lent its master-pieces of tapestry and painting for the Embassy walls. The Rolls-Royce, C.D'd, waited at the door. She saw herself in white satin, decolleté, going to dine at the Quirinale, the Hofburg ... 'Madame de Lérin, the wife of the French Ambassador, had the honour of dining with Their Majesties at Buckingham Palace last evening' . . . a long way for Amelia Macreary of Abernethy Villas, Glasgow, to have travelled. But history had many such fairy tales of Cinderella's progress.

It seemed too much to reject for so iridescent and fragile a bubble as love. And why couldn't she love him, or come to love him, a charming, gifted handsome man who offered her so much?

He had suggested they should dine and go to the cinema to-morrow night. Until tomorrow night she would think it over.

She went to the office, distraught with concentration. Etienne got into the typewriter's keys, the filing cabinet, even into instructions from her chief.

"Have you a headache, Amelia?" asked Señor Anstruther kindly, as he received the wrong dossier. Yes, she had a head-ache but not of the kind he suspected.

Of course Etienne might not make the grade. He might never be more than a First Secretary or a Minister. Her rôle would then not be so difficult. But she would have given herself to someone who had not achieved the height. What a horrible mercenary thought! Did it matter where the man you loved got to, whether he failed entirely? If you loved, you loved. Wasn't that the test, the real triumph?

"It's the 26th, not the 25th," said Señor Anstruther, quietly, correcting the date on her typed letter.

The 26th. And tomorrow, the 27th, she must make her decision.

She dined at home again that evening in a high state of nerves. She wasn't really in love with Etienne, and all he stood for was outside her own world, even if she had loved him. She foresaw the tremendous opposition of his family, his colleagues in the service. It might damage his career. She had no background. She had no 'dot', a fatal thing in French families. They would treat her as an adventuress, or she would be patronised. She had never allowed anyone to patronise her. She never would.

After a second sleepless night she decided to end this indecision. She rang Etienne early. He greeted her warmly.

"Etienne, dear, it's No. I'm sorry!" she said.

There was a silence.

"Etienne—are you there? Did you hear?"

"Yes."

"Don't be angry with me."

"I'm not angry. I'm deeply disappointed. Are you quite certain, chèrie? Would you like to wait a little?" he asked in a quiet voice.

"Quite certain, darling. Will you forgive me?"

"There's nothing to forgive."

"We're still good friends—we can see each other?" asked Amelia, her voice wavering despite her effort of control.

"Still very good friends, chère petite gamine, but I'll be a bit lame and out of song, chèrie."

"Darling Etienne, how very sweet of you. Do you mind if we do not dine tonight—I am very tired."

"Very well. Can we meet Saturday? Let's go to Mar del Plata and bathe, I've friends with a villa there."

"That would be lovely."

"I'll pick you up at nine o'clock. And Amelia!"

"Yes?"

"*Il pleut dans mon coeur.*"

"Darling Etienne! Thank you and bless you. I'm crying a little also."

She put down the receiver. She had done it. She got up and went over to the cheval mirror and looked steadily at herself.

"Why couldn't you? Why? Why? You'll live to regret it all your life," she said to herself.

She arrived at the office mentally exhausted, and quite unprepared for what awaited her. Señor Anstruther had died of a coronary thrombosis early that morning. He was her best English friend, kind, paternal, wise. She felt terribly alone. She was conscious for the first time of the great distance between Scotland and the Argentine. She contemplated calling off the excursion to Mar del Plata. But if she stayed home her nerves would break. She decided to go.

III

Whatever Etienne may have felt he was his young debonair self when he arrived on Saturday morning in his long, low sports car. He had flowers for her. He kissed her tenderly and all the way to Mar del Plata he talked easily. The road was magnificent, he drove confidently at eighty miles an hour. They stopped only once for an aperitif and covered the two hundred and fifty miles in four hours, arriving at his friends' *casa de weekend* in time for lunch. All Buenos Aires seemed to be in Mar del Plata, massed in luxurious hotels, pensions and villas, that catered at the height of the season for half a million *nouveaux riches* families, ebullient business men, clerks and shopgirls, at this Brighton of the South Atlantic.

After lunch and a siesta they went water-skiing, towed by a rampant motor launch. Their host was 'in oil', a tycoon born in Mauritius who, in twenty years, had built up a vast fortune, which he spent freely. To her surprise and pleasure Amelia found the *diva*, Doña Ramorra, in the house-party. Etienne told her she was the tycoon's *amie*. He financed opera seasons, *futbol* teams, and the ballet. Four Narcissian youths displayed their sleek oiled bodies and gyrated on the edge of the beach with six young girls with legs of polished steel. They were from a company dancing in Mar del Plata. That evening thirty sat down to dinner. The native servants were directed by the Hawaiian butler, a grinning mountain of flesh, his great brown belly naked above a vivid *lava-lava*. He was the person of the house, called Taku by everybody. He played the ukelele superbly and had taught a languorous young *peon*, with scarlet hybiscus blooms tucked behind each ear, to sing Hawaiian love dirges to the undulation of his slim torso and the rolling of his large doe-like eyes. They ate a lot, drank a lot, danced a lot, amid a deafening babel of languages and the strumming of guitars.

At eleven o'clock Etienne drove back to Buenos Aires. It was a still moonlit night. Amelia slept some of the way. Then she woke, leaned her head on Etienne's shoulder and to his amazement began to cry quietly. He put an arm around her shoulders, caressed her hair, and drove with one hand on the wheel without any reduction of speed. Later, as they neared the city she sat up, brushed back her fallen hair, and smiling wanly, said, "I can't think what's the matter with me."

"I can," replied Etienne, "you're the girl who doesn't know what she wants. And you're tired, you want putting to bed."

He said it playfully. After a silence he heard her say, very softly, her head seeking his shoulder. *"Le jour où la pluie viendra."*

"Je t'emmènerai," he quoted, his low voice joining hers, *"je suis sûr, dans mon lit."*

He bent over and kissed her mouth while the car kept its speed.

She smiled at him.

"The rain has come," she said, almost inaudibly.

"Tu es sûre?" he asked.

She made no answer, her head still on his shoulder, warm and firm.

At the fork of the *avenida* leading to her apartment he turned left in the direction of his own. They drove on, wordless, until the car slowed up at his *garçonnière*.

IV

He mixed a drink in the dimly lit sitting-room. Then, kissing her, he left her and went into the bedroom. He came out shortly, pyjamas and slippers in hand.

"You'll find everything," he said quietly.

She rose and went into the bedroom. There was a shielded bedside light, a dressing-gown on a *fauteuil*. The bed was turned down.

He closed the door softly on her. He undressed, changing into his pyjamas. Then he nervously lit a cigarette and looked at himself in the mirror. He was astonished by this sudden surrender. It was three by the clock on the mantelpiece. He finished the cigarette, switched off the lights so that only a faint light came in between the slats of the Venetian blind. He went to the bedroom door and tapped gently. There was no response. He tapped again, called "Amelia!" and, receiving no answer, he slowly opened the door. She was not in bed. She had removed her shoes and stockings and her blue silk blouse, revealing a thin low-cut bodice of white lawn, with lace insertion and shoulder straps. She was sitting immobile in the *fauteuil* holding her head in her hands. She was crying, almost inaudibly.

He went down on his knees so that his face was level with hers and took her hands from her face.

"*Chère, chère* Amelia—what is the matter? Why do you cry?" he asked gently.

With a sudden gesture her arms went round his neck and she clung to him swept by a paroxysm of tears. She pressed a tear-stained face against his, like a frightened child.

"Amelia, don't cry. Please don't cry! You wanted to come?" he asked, his mouth finding her bare shoulder. The tears were running down her face, her body quivering as he pressed her to him.

"Oh Etienne, I'm sae worrit, I'm sae daft," she cried, lapsing into the dialect of her youth. "Ye mon forgive me. I'm that daft!"

"You're a wonderful person, Amelia, I love you!"

"Nae, I'm only a puir fool that kens nae be'er waur she's going."

He took a handkerchief from his pyjamas and gently wiped her wet cheeks.

"Ye'll tak me hame, Etienne. Ye'll tak me hame?"

"Yes, yes, there's nothing to fear, nothing, *chère enfant*," he said, stroking her hair and smiling into her tear-suffused eyes. He took her hands and kissed them slowly, tenderly, "Darling Amelia, you mustn't tremble, you mustn't be afraid!"

She gazed at him, and her hands reached to his hair and played in it lightly. A wan smile came to her face. "Oh, Etienne, what must you think of me!" she cried.

"I think you're adorable, *petite tête de gamine mouillée*," he said softly. He rose from his knees. "Sit there, I'm going to get you a whisky and soda to warm you. You are cold and trembling."

He left the room and came back with a tumbler.

"Drink that," he commanded, going down on his knees before her, folding her hand over the glass.

She drank slowly and he watched her until the glass was empty.

"Better?" he asked cheerfully.

"Yes, much better. Forgive me, Etienne. You are a dear boy."

"There's nothing to forgive. Now you must dress." He picked up her stockings. While she pulled them on, he sat back still kneeling, holding a shoe in either hand. He kissed her foot as he put each one on. They stood up. They looked at one another, not speaking. He gave a little nervous laugh, to which she responded. She picked up her blouse, slipped it over her head. He waited while she tucked it into the waistband. He smoothed the back of the collar, his soft hand warm against the nape of her neck.

"Have you a brush?" she asked.

He opened a drawer and took out a silver-backed brush with a handle.

"*Comme tu es méchant!*" she said as she took the brush, a woman's brush, from him.

"I am a good host, *vraiment?*" he answered wryly.

He watched her brush her hair. Then he led her into the sitting room. His discarded clothes lay on the settee. "*Oh, la, la!*" he cried, gathering them up. "Only a minute, *chèrie,*" he cried, and disappeared into the bedroom.

When he returned she had switched on a light. It was a quarter-to-four. He lit a cigarette for her and mixed himself a drink.

"Ready, *chèrie?*" he said, putting down his glass.

"Are you furious with me?" she asked.

"No. Do I look furious?"

"No—but you are a diplomat!"

He made no reply, took her face between his hands and kissed her mouth lightly. Then he opened the door into the little hall. When they emerged into the avenue the moon had set and the ghost of dawn was over the silent city. Only the noise of birds stirring in the trees could be heard. They got into the long grey Ferrari. Except for a watercart whirring around a plaza there was no traffic. The avenue of her apartment house was wide and empty. He followed her through the door into the hall and waited until the lift descended.

"Darling Etienne, thank you!"

"Sleep well," he said softly, kissing her brow.

He waved as she went up in the lift. He got into his car.

"*Tiens! Gentilhomme! Idiot!*" he said under his breath as he changed gear. "*Aucune pluie ne viendra pour moi!*"

V

Amelia went to the Anstruther funeral. She had lost a good friend. Her position at the office among the Argentine employees had been made most agreeable by the paternal interest he had shown in her. She was always welcomed in the Anstruther home, and became very friendly with Señora Anstruther, vivid, busy, loquacious, a good mother, and a most hospitable hostess in a home brimming over with an old mother, two spinster sisters and seven children. The house was like a birdcage of twittering parakeets. Now, in a moment, that colourful scene was transformed by the doleful mourning garments in which all Catholic races seemed to exult, making a panoply of their grief.

Amelia felt as if a storm had swept down upon her out of a halcyon sky. Her life, since the escape from Glasgow, had been one of progressive excitement and success. The boat journey, the exhilaration of a new continent, with its sun-intoxicated gaiety, the kindness of her business chief, Sir Anthony's hospitality, Doña de la Rivos's friendship, her language lessons, her riding, the excitement of having her own little apartment after a rabbit-hutch environment at Abernethy Villas, all these things had built up a new world of colour, beauty and enchantment.

And with all these there had come into her life a well-born, well-placed, ardent young Frenchman, at once her tutor and her critic, playful, cynical, assured. What had begun as a light flirtation, pursued by an amorous young man accustomed to easy conquests, had developed into something more serious. Etienne had swept down on her, with his sheer physical and mental allure, and she had been almost carried away. The day at Mar del Plata, amid that boisterous and somewhat raffish gathering of cosmopolitans, the swimming, the water-skiing, the food and the wine and flashing repartee, had followed the mental exhaustion from his proposal, and from her employer's death. A contingency of naked bodies in sunshine, the awareness of Etienne's svelte figure in his seal-like play, excited her as they swam. His firm hands on her cool flesh, his wet mouth swiftly over her breasts, as seeking her, elusive, submerged, they gambolled, half-playful, half-purposeful in the pellucid water, all this had made it a day out of paradise after her mental ordeal.

And then, exhausted, lazily happy, had come the long drive through the moonlight, his confident hands on the wheel, his body so near, warm, assuring. A deep tenderness, a need of him in her frailty, had suddenly seized her. She wanted to know the relief of complete surrender, a release from all her inhibitions. In that impulsive mood she had fed the flame of his desire. And she had failed him. What had possessed her? When she had gone to her room in the half-dawn she flung herself on the bed, dressed, and lay there. For the first time in her life she knew fear in a shape more frightening because it was a fear of herself. Her high confidence had deserted her.

She had kept to her room all the day. Thank God, it was Sunday. There was no office. She made herself a meal in the kitchenette. She tried to read, to write letters, to sew. A terrible loneliness encompassed her. If Etienne had come, compelling, she would have surrendered to him. But he did not come. He must be very angry with her, despite his smooth-mannered reaction to her feminine capriciousness.

On Monday the office was closed for the funeral of Señor Anstruther. Amelia was about to leave her apartment to go to the service when the door-bell rang. A boy from the florist's stood there with an immense bouquet of flowers. She tipped him and took them in. She knew by its extravagance from whom it came. In the attached envelope she found Etienne's visiting card. There was nothing written on it.

VI

The heat of the summer waned, the autumn passed. The heavy rains began. Amelia was restless and unhappy. Her twenty-fourth birthday had gone unheralded. She still saw Etienne. They ate at restaurants, they danced together. He took her to various social entertainments. He remained playfully amorous but she knew it was superficial. He made no overtures. Something perverse in her nature, vanity surely, hoped that he would. Then one day she learned with a shock that she had lost him. He was being moved to Cairo. There was a last evening when they danced and dined together. She was on the verge of tears when he took her home. Had he repeated his offer of marriage she might have accepted him. But he said nothing. He kissed her goodbye in the hall, and said, gravely—

"Thank you, *chèrie*, for a lovely friendship."

Friendship. The word sounded coldly in her ears. If she had

become his wife there would have been no farewell. If she had become his mistress, the severance would have been more emotional. Or would it? Affairs, from all she read and heard, went stale in a satisfied passion.

From Cairo he sent her a long amusing letter describing his journey, his new apartment. He signed it playfully, *"Ton Etienne, sans pluie—au moment!"* How characteristic! She answered, with a cheerfulness she did not feel. And then no more.

Her spiritual malaise was increased by the successor to Señor Anstruther in the office. He was a fat little Argentine who had been waiting long for his chief's shoes. He wore them heavily. He rang his bell peremptorily. He was a clumsy dictator, duplicating and altering his words, but resentful of her ability to supply the right text. His manners were abrupt and he showed resentment of the social contacts she had, superior to his own, being a *petit bourgeois* with a heavy plain wife and two podgy children. She was never introduced to her or invited to their home.

Happily Doña Lucia de les Rivos became a warm friend. Her house was a second home. Two of her graceful birdlike grandchildren adored Amelia who took them riding and swimming. Their parents had been killed in a plane crash. Together with Doña Lucia she went repeatedly to Tabara for week-ends, and whenever Sir Anthony came to Buenos Aires he included her in his parties at the Jockey Club, at the opera and the theatre. He had a weakness for the cinema. "One can shut one's eyes and go to sleep in them, and no one knows!" He was a lavish entertainer. "Too lavish," said Doña Lucia.

"Isn't Sir Anthony very rich?" asked Amelia.

"No—he was. But there have been heavy losses on the *estancias* these last years. Three years ago there was a ruinous plague of foot-and-mouth disease. He lost fifty of his Shorthorn champions. Then there was a locust plague. Anthony was never a sharp business man and runs the *estancia* on the old paternal lines. He has too many lazy *peons* and too many sharp-handed gauchos. And the Government's breaking up the large *estancias* and heavily taxing them. It imposed income-tax for the first time two years ago."

Amelia in this period of depression, increased by the heavy rains as well as the new manager at the office, was not without her admirers. There was no one as debonair as Etienne, with his beautiful clothes and dashing car. She met a young English-man working in the Anglo-Argentine Bank who sought her company. He was a nice well-mannered lad of good education, Harrow and Trinity College, Cambridge, but there was no spark in him. He would sit dumbly looking at her. He danced badly and seemed never to read a book. When he had had a few drinks he came alive. He tried to paw her with sweaty hands, but two words would bring him to order. "Why do you everlastingly wear that school tie, haven't you got others?" she asked him one day, irritated. "Oh, yes," he replied, "Don't you like it?" "Not for six consecutive weeks," retorted Amelia. He changed it, and wore the substitute for a whole month. How different in mind and dress he was from Etienne! But he had a kind, dog-like nature. When she had a cocktail party he patiently took round the glasses and stayed behind to wash up. He was quick to pay for taxis and would never let her go 'dutch' in the restaurants. He did not mind being put off if she didn't want him. He responded immediately if she did. He bought her flowers and boxes of candies so lavishly that she was constantly reproving him, without result. She became rather ashamed of the way she used him, for she sent him shopping, let him carry parcels, and get theatre tickets. He was twenty-three, and when they went swimming astonished her. Stripped, he became an Apollo, magnificently but propor-tionately muscled, with a satiny skin. When she remarked on his physique, he said, casually, "Oh yes—but I don't get any practice now."

"Practice at what?"

"Boxing. I was in the Cambridge boxing team."

He provided another surprise. One day when he took some papers out of his pocket, always untidily crammed, in search of his car key, she saw an envelope with his name on it. It read 'Hon. James Fayne.' She made no comment. There was a Debrett's *Peerage and Baronetage* in the small library at Tabara. She had already sought out Sir Anthony Slowdon, second baronet, married 1890, to Carmen Juanita Beaumont y Cardenas: son and heir, Roderick, born 1891. She tracked down James Fayne. He was the eldest son of Lord Antley, V.C. fourth Baron, of Antley Manor, Nether Antley, Somerset. His mother was Lady Priscilla Carneley, second daughter of the seventh Duke of Aberforth. He was born in 1912.

The son of a baron, the grandson of a duke. No wonder he was so well received at the British Embassy. He had invitations to everything there. After her discovery he was never quite the same young man in her eyes. "You snob!" she said to herself.

"You never told me you were an Honourable?" she remarked.

"No? Well, I can't help it, can I?" he laughed.

"But it *is* something!"

"Um! But not that much if you haven't got a bean!"

"What made you go in for banking?"

"My uncle's a bank chairman. I was licking stamps in Lombard Street a year ago. I grumbled when they promoted me to here. You see, I didn't know what I was in for."

"And what are you in for, precisely?"

"You!" he said simply. His blue eyes on her face.

"Your luck's out, I'm afraid, Jimmy dear!"

"You're the prettiest woman in the whole British Colony. Everyone agrees about that."

"Not much competition there, to be catty!" retorted Amelia, laughing.

She reflected on the matter that evening. A red-haired typist out of Glasgow running around with a duke's grandson! Things like that only happened if you got out of England. She'd heard of a girl here who had been typist-secretary to a Scottish shipping magnate. He had been sent out here by the Government during the War. She married him here. When they got home he was made a peer. She was now famous for her tennis parties. Amelia had heard her 'open' a bazaar. You could cut her Aberdeen accent with a knife. Well, if she played her cards well with the Honourable Jimmie she might walk into the peerage. She could open bazaars very much better than the other girl, and without an accent.

"No, no!" said Amelia to the mirror, powdering her neck and beautiful bare shoulders. "A nice boy, but dumb and sweaty. He would run to fat."

She preferred them lean and dark, like Etienne, or like . . . She saw leaning by a wire fence a gaucho holding the reins of a horse, a dank curl on his brow, a thin gold chain and cross hanging from his tawny throat.

She stopped powdering herself, and sat still for a moment, critically admiring herself. Yes, she was beautiful. It was not always an asset. It would lead her into trouble. Beauty was power but power provoked men in various ways. It irritated Señor Anstruther's successor at the office. It had resulted in that scene after the return from Mar del Plata for which she still felt a guilty shame.

CHAPTER EIGHT

I

SIR ANTHONY had been in town and gone. For the first time Amelia noticed a frailty in him. He was seventy-one, she learned from the *Peerage and Baronetage*. He was not a young seventy-one. He still sat a horse well, but he was cautious in his movement. When his gloves were off she observed the thin dark veins of his emaciated hands. He had little intervals of sleep when company was talking. But he was very erect in his posture, his mind was keen. Two days after his departure from Doña Lucia's there was a telephone call from her. She had something very special to communicate. Amelia went to see her.

"It's about Sir Anthony," said Doña Lucia as they sat in the canary-haunted glassed annexe to the *salon*. "He's given me a commission. It concerns you."

"Me?" queried Amelia.

"Yes. You know how shy he can be about some things, especially anything that entails business? Well, I have long thought, and he has come to agree, that he should not live so much alone at Tabara. I would like him to be more in town, but he won't leave his beloved horses. For some years after the tragedy he wouldn't go near Tabara. Now, he doesn't want to leave it. There's a great deal of business connected with the *estancia*, and his manager, Mr. Carson, whom you've met, is getting old also and feeling the burden. I've talked it over with Anthony and I hope we've found what might be a solution. You're not very happy now at your office? You've spoken of looking for another place?"

"Yes. I don't feel *simpatico* towards Señor Diaz, and I think the antipathy's mutual! He's imported a niece who now takes some of my work."

"Would you consider going to Tabara?"

"To Sir Anthony's?" asked Amelia, astonished.

"Yes. We've discussed the idea. It would please him if you would go there to help."

"Help?" repeated Amelia.

"In the rôle of secretary-companion. The idea is that you should live in the house, and take general control under Mr. Carson. Anthony has great faith in your ability, as I have. He would pay you the same salary as you are receiving. What he fears is that after Buenos Aires you would find it very dull. There are no young people around. Of course he would be willing for you to come back here from time to time. I'll confess it's my idea, but he likes it. He refused to talk to you about it. He hates anything to do with financial arrangements. Anyhow, that's the proposition. What do you think of it?"

Amelia was silent for a time.

"There's something you haven't mentioned," she said quietly. "I'm to live in the house, part secretary, part companion?"

"Yes."

"Would there be gossip, or would the difference in our ages protect us?" asked Amelia.

"I don't think we need be apprehensive. If you were a guest there, frequently, alone, there might be talk. But you are there with a defined status and with a definite task."

"It wants very carefully thinking over," said Amelia. "You see, I've made friends here, you and others. I've a little apartment I'm very attached to. Sir Anthony wouldn't want me always running in to Buenos Aires, and I, too, would feel reluctant for his sake."

"Yes, I see all the drawbacks. Anthony realises very clearly what a change in your life it would make. He had a suggestion that might lessen your reluctance. He suggested that you retain your apartment here. Your salary would make provision for that. Also, if it didn't work out as we hope, you would have a place to come back to. You would have your own car, and horses. I suggested you should try it for six months or a year. He agrees to that."

"How soon must I make a decision?"

"There's no hurry. He wants to be quite assured that the post would be agreeable to you. If the isolation is not an insuperable drawback, I think you could be very happy. It would certainly give Anthony and myself great satisfaction and relief. Take a week to think about it, my dear."

"Very well, I will. Thank you for making the suggestion," she answered.

For three days she considered the proposition. It was one thing to be a man's guest, another to be his employee. They had not been continuously in each other's company, they were ignorant of each other's foibles. The luxury of the house, with its servants, horses, cars, might sap her independence. Above all, to be considered, there was the question of her isolation. Theatres, cinemas, restaurants, dances, and the continuous contacts with people of her own age, with agreeable young men that her youth craved, from all these she would be remote. She admired Sir Anthony immensely. She had seen enough of the pampa to know its curious fascination, but for all that she must relinquish were the gains sufficient compensation?

She consulted a few discreet friends. "You'd be crazy," said one. "I'd jump at it—the peace, the luxury!" said another. "Perhaps the old boy would leave you something. He can't last for ever. It wouldn't be the first time nursey-nursey's swallowed the lot!" observed a more candid and mercenary companion. "Could you ask friends down to stay? Jove, all those horses to ride!" exclaimed James Fayne. "But I'd hate you to leave."

Amelia carefully considered the proposition made by Doña Lucia. She loved Buenos Aires. She reviewed all its attractions. The magnificent avenues, the great Plaza del Mayor, the lovely Calle Florida, with its evening when all the traffic was stopped and the pavements were thronged with promenaders, the Paseo Colón, the Paseo de Julio with its succession of formal gardens, the great Teatrò Colón with its dazzling jewelled women on gala nights and its world-famous artistes, the gay Richmond Bar, the exclusive Jockey Club to which Sir Anthony took her, its racecourse with its vast grandstand and canopied tea-tables set out on the red gravel forecourt, the gay newspaper kiosks—she bought *La Prensa* daily, the oddly old-fashioned peanut vendors with their little carts along the *avenidas*, the liveliness of the streets, the splendid new buildings. No wonder the Argentines regarded Buenos Aires as the Paris of the American continent! She loved it all, for its vivid throning life, its cool mornings when she rode before breakfast, its torpid noons during which the city briefly slept, its warm sub-tropical nights full of stars, when the long *avenidas* blazed with lights and gay music came out of a hundred restaurants, cafés and bars. And how dearly she loved her modern little apartment in a side street off the Avenida de Mayo, quiet, with a balcony and a vista of tree-tops. It was her one extravagance. She was earning good money but saving nothing. Like the Argentines she had an easy faith in *mañana*.

The life of the pampa, at Tabara, was a wholly different thing, with the solitude of the vast prairie, the odd mixture of native and imported luxury at the great *estancia* houses, the primitive living conditions of the polyglot cattle boys and farmhands—Poles, Greeks, Hungarians, Germans, Italians and the dark gipsy-like band of swarthy *mestizos* of mixed Spanish, Moorish and Indian blood. Could she give up the thronging vivid life of Buenos Aires for this world of silence, of endless grass plains, wire fences, long level railway tracks and solitary stations, often carrying, oddly enough, English names, in tribute to the pioneer English *estancia* holders and builders of these railways that ran on and on across the vast plains to the foothills of the Andes, the only link with the civilisation of sprawling, prosperous Buenos Aires? Also she had to consider her own personal relationship with Sir Anthony. She would live in the atmosphere of *estancia* life, of these cattle barons who, in their luxurious living, might be compared with the rajahs and pundits of India. Many of them maintained houses in Paris. They travelled with teams of polo ponies, if that was their pastime. They kept suites at the Ritz in Paris, or the Hotel de Paris in Monte Carlo, they hired *palazzi* in Rome, they bought clothes and cars in London, gowns and shoes in Paris, often not visiting their *estancias* for two or three years, confident that these goldmines would be well managed by their overseers.

Into this strange world of extravagant contrasts, of herds and gauchos, *peons* and immigrants from Southern Europe, of proud millionaires with Spanish blood, of Englishmen who had settled here in a kind of squirarchal state, how would she blend her own life? Would she barter her independence? She knew nothing really of Sir Anthony, an aloof, silent, mysterious man. He was at once proud and reticent. He had turned his back on a fine English inheritance, the manor house and estate in Leicestershire. In himself he was half-Spanish through his mother's line, which, coming out of Andalucia, had established itself in the pampa of the Argentine. He was so very English in his reserved deportment, yet he was Spanish with his panache for display, with the clothes he wore denoting the *hidalgo*, and the horses he rode with the air of a conquistador.

There was his deeper, mysterious nature, betraying a fierceness under the polished graces of his suave demeanour. A dark tragedy had been played out on the *estancia* from which he had banished all signs of his betrayal. No article, no portrait held evidence of the lovely dark young mistress who had reigned here. Her name was never heard. Doña Lucia had told her that within a week of her flight he had changed every servant in the house, and every horse she had ridden had disappeared from the stables. The house of Kurt Weninger, a mile distant, had been pulled down. Sir Anthony's young son's room had been locked since the day of the flight. For five years Sir Anthony had never visited the *estancia*. Strangest of all, more unaccountable, was his surrender of little Roderick, the son and heir. He had made no move for possession of the boy to whom he had an undeniable right. Only once had Doña Lucia, a life-long friend and confidant, mentioned the young son. When the news of Lady Slowdon's death came, in 1914, out of an Austria in a death-grapple with her enemies of the World War, Doña Lucia had spoken of Roderick, who was then twenty-two.

"He's probably an Austrian soldier, fighting for his country," said Sir Anthony.

"But he's British!" protested Doña Lucia.

"I am not sure of that," said Sir Anthony quietly.

She had stared at him, incredulous of the suspicion that possessed him, revealed for the first time. Before she could say anything he had left the room.

"He thinks the boy isn't his?" asked Amelia when Doña Lucia narrated this. "It's Kurt Weninger's?"

"The idea is quite monstrous! The boy was like an English rose. A lovely little fellow."

"Sir Anthony was fond of him?"

"Yes. But he saw little of him, he was always travelling on missions for the British Government."

"And his mother? She loved the boy?"

Doña Lucia hesitated. "I did not consider Carmen a good mother. She treated him like a little toy and left him too much in the hands of his governess. She left the child for long periods at his grandmother's, at their *estancia* at Mendez. She loved life and was often in Buenos Aires or Paris."

"Not with Sir Anthony?"

"Sometimes—but I think he bored her. Anthony was always a serious person," said Doña Lucia. "In his reserved way he loved her deeply. I don't think she really loved him—it was one of those *estancia* marriages."

"What do you mean?" asked Amelia.

"The pampa is largely owned by dynasties of cattle barons. Here the men are overlords, the women their chattels. The daughters are disposed of with a thought to conserving the estates in the leading families. Anthony was a very handsome young man. Carmen was twenty-four when he married her."

"When was this Austrian on the scene?" asked Amelia.

"He was here when Anthony married. But I am positive there was nothing between them until years later—until there was a rift between Anthony and Carmen, and he left her and went off on his missions. She was a beautiful woman who wanted constant adulation. She got it. The men were crazy about her. Once in England there was a little trouble. Anthony gave her a London season. She had a wild success. She met a young Marquis of Morne—he's now the Duke of Aberforth —who lost his head over her. There was a rather wild launch party on the Thames that he gave one evening. They challenged one another to swim under the Waterloo Bridge and then back to the launch. They all jumped in dressed as they were—it was after dinner on a fading June evening. One of the boys got into difficulty, and a guest and a girl friend went to his rescue, but the current took two of them away. There was an inquest and a great scandal. Carmen was one of the swimmers. I was in England at the time, on my honeymoon. Anthony was furious when he learned Carmen had been on the launch. He cut the season short, gave up the house he had rented, and brought her back here. The trouble started,

I think, from that time. The affair with Kurt Weninger began to be talked about soon after. Poor Carmen, she was impulsive and loved a court of admirers. Unhappily she'd married an autocrat in Anthony."

It was from Doña Lucia that Amelia had learned all this about the Master of Tabara. The story behind the formal mask of old Sir Anthony was one of passion and wounded pride, hardening into suspicion. There was something a little frightening to Amelia in this history of a man who never forgot or forgave, and nourished a resentment to the exclusion of an innocent child's rights. It was an aspect of her prospective employer's nature that dismayed her and hampered her decision.

Then, while evaluating the risks of a new life at Tabara, an incident at the office provoked a decision. On a morning of a torrential downpour she had failed to get a taxi to the office. Taxis were the only cheap things in Buenos Aires. Late, she then tried to get a bus. But that morning, owing to the demand caused by the downpour, she failed to catch one. Two buses were full in succession. She had to walk a considerable distance before she succeeded in boarding a third. She arrived at the office, her feet wet, and twenty minutes late. "Señor Diaz's been ringing for you," said a clerk, on arrival. She picked up her shorthand pad and went to the manager's office.

He let her stand for some time while he slowly perused his papers. Amelia had never liked the way the black hair ran down two sides of his neck. She now had an opportunity of observing this unpleasant characteristic *ad nauseam*. At last he looked up from his papers and put a podgy hand on a desk clock.

"Good morning, Miss Macreary. This office opens at nine o'clock. It is now nine-twenty-five. You should not let a very active social life interfere with your business life, but you seem to take the opposite view. I cannot agree," he said slowly, "for it affects my life also. For twenty minutes I have been waiting to give you these letters. Will you take one to——"

"I'm loath to interfere with your life, Señor Diaz. It must be dreary enough. You shall have no further cause for worry. I'm leaving you, and ask you to take a month's notice," said Amelia, composedly.

She saw him pat his crescent belly, a habit when annoyed.

"Your directors in Glasgow should have notice of that. I don't know what are the conditions of your service here."

"It's in the file. I'll find it for you. The only condition was that after three years' service I was to have three months holiday and my return fare. I'll forego that. I'll give you my notice in writing, to forward to Glasgow."

She had burned her boats. She was not afraid. Already a friend in the Bovril Company had told her of a good job going. The atmosphere had completely changed since Señor Anstruther's death.

She now decided to accept Sir Anthony's offer for a year's trial. Doña Lucia was delighted. Within a few days Sir Anthony came to Buenos Aires. They had a long discussion after a dinner at the Palace Hotel. The salary proposed was generous. She would have her maintenance in a manner she could never have attained on her own. Sir Anthony also was responsible for the rent of her small apartment. "When I wish to come to town and there is business to transact you will then have your own quarters. You may find life at Tabara uneventfully dull. I am quite willing for you to leave if after three months you aren't happy."

It was another leap in her life. Her courage was rewarded. Within three months at Tabara she felt that she would never wish to lead another kind of life. Sir Anthony was always the grand seigneur in his dealings with her. There was plenty to do. She found the estate records in chaos and spent long hours trying to achieve some order. Mr. Carson, the manager, helped her, but he was ageing and had an imperfect grasp of figures. He was only interested in livestock and outside management. He cared nothing about market prices. Like Sir Anthony, he was reluctant to make changes in machinery and staff. They were still hauling the grain bags in the old waggons. This form of transport went back to the primitive times on the pampa. The waggons had wheels ten feet high, and were covered with leather hoods on hoops. They were pulled by three yokes of oxen and could carry ten tons. These prairie waggons lumbered along at a slow pace driven by sleepy *peons*. They were good enough, said Mr. Carson. Amelia thought they were not good enough.

One day she got Don Antonio, as they all called Sir Anthony on the *estancia*, to take her to Cordell. It was two hours up the railway line, the property of another Englishman, a young man who had inherited it and had a passion for modernisation. They saw camions running all over the estate. Some of the gauchos herded with Ford cars. "Horrible, an outrage!" was Don Antonio's private comment. But the journey bore fruit. He finally consented to an order for two camions. They engaged Italians from Calabria to drive them. Another little tussle came in which Don Antonio and Mr. Carson joined forces against her. Young Cordell came over for a couple of nights. He was a scientific *estanciero*. He had done away with all the old wells on his vast ranch. The water had been drawn by lowering a bucket over a crossbar and attaching the long rope to a horse, which then hauled up the bucket. He installed windmill pumps. Tabara had only ten windmill pumps, the others were all the rope-and-bucket model. "All right for my grandfather but not for me. The boys' wages are too high these days to waste time like that," said Cordell.

"Do I hear you've opened a school and make all your

gauchos' children go to it four hours a day, collecting 'em in a motor bus?" asked Sir Anthony.

"Yes, sir. It's quite a success."

"You're stirring up a lot of trouble for yourself. As soon as they can read they'll start reading about those strikes in *La Prensa*, and get ideas."

"They're getting ideas on the radio already. The gaucho as we've known him is dead. The boys all want to get to the town, for their own sakes and their children's. We are already deeply worried. We'll only keep the boys if we give them civilised living conditions. There's a labour shortage now. We'll have to go in for scientific farming if we're going to survive."

Sir Anthony made no reply. Cordell threw a glance at Amelia. A servant said the drinks were served. They went out to the patio and sat under the pergola.

Later he said to Amelia, "I didn't dare to tell the old boy that we have a cinema show for them all once a week in the granary. He thinks I'm a Bolshie already!"

Sir Anthony had another shock a few days later when Cordell came to dinner. He told him he was putting another ten thousand acres under the plough. He advised Sir Anthony to increase his acreage of wheat and corn and reduce his grassland.

"But we'll have no *estancias* if we go on like this."

"The *estancia* as my grandfather knew it has gone. The invention of wire killed it, dividing up the prairie land into grazing areas. It was the death-knell of the old wild herd-chasing gaucho. My grandfather told me they killed a cow to get one chop for a meal and left the carcass for the wild animals to eat. They used to burn horse-fat in the street lamps in Buenos Aires! We don't raise cattle any more just for the hides and the tallow. The railways have altered all that. We breed scientifically from pedigree stock, and so do you, Don Antonio. We fatten them on good grasses, we get them down

122

to the slaughterhouses and ports by train. That's progress, sir," said young Cordell, filling his pipe. "And now the farmers are breaking up the ranches, we can import all the labour we want only if we make the farms attractive enough. We can become the breadbasket as well as the meat market of the world. I bought thirty motor ploughs and four new harvesters at the show last month."

"You'll go bankrupt," said Sir Anthony grimly. "Where are the fellows coming from to work them?" he asked.

"I've sent twenty of my gauchos to be trained in the workshops."

"Good God! You'll be sending them to Eton next!"

They all laughed. When Cordell left he said to Amelia, "I'm afraid I irritated Don Antonio. He's a real old cattle baron who wants his gauchos to wear whiskers and carry ponchos. In twenty years round here you'll see all the boys riding motor bikes as well as they ride broncos. We give our bulls as much care as a Hollywood star, so why not the boys? There would be no *estancias* without them."

A car was waiting to take him to the station.

"Well, goodbye," he said, holding out a brown hand. "I hope dear old Don Antonio won't have a heart attack after I've gone! Do you go into Buenos Aires?"

"We're going in next week, for a month—operas, cinemas, dinners!"

"Oh, where can I find you?" he said, and added, with a twinkle in his clear eyes, "Alone!"

"I've a telephone in my apartment," said Amelia, and gave him the number.

He noted it down in a little pocket book.

"I'd like to take you out to dinner and dance the prettiest young woman in Buenos Aires," he said, frankly.

"Very prettily said, Señor Cordell. And what about me,

with the handsomest and most up-to-date young man?" she responded.

They laughed together merrily. Then he got into the car and left with a gay wave of the hand as it turned out at the gate.

I I

There was one thing that increasingly perturbed her at Tabara. It was the ever-growing consciousness of Juan, the gaucho. She ignored him but was always aware of him. She gave him sharp orders which he accepted with a quiet deference. As a foreman-*domador*, in command of the stables, he was very efficient. He had an hypnotic way with horses. At a word, a touch, a flick of his whip they fell into obedience. Sir Anthony relied on him for everything connected with the stables and the corrals. They rode much together visiting the distant stations. In a manner Juan seemed to hold more authority than Mr. Carson. He had the air of a thoroughbred, as mettlesome and proud as anything in the stables, yet he was a *peon*, with mixed blood in his veins. Always, vaulting into the saddle, grooming a horse, leaning silently against a post, carrying grain, his maleness communicated itself. It spoke in the line of his back, the proud carriage of his dark head on the strong neck, in the sinuous curve of his body. He discarded the gaucho's baggy trousers for blue denims that tightly moulded his thighs and the long legs encased in soft-leather boots. He had a habit of wearing his flat-brimmed Spanish hat hanging down behind his head by its leather strap. It emphasised the column of his throat, and the head with its tight cluster of black curls. He moved with the easy grace of a gymnast, unhurried yet quick and sure-footed. He was taciturn, but his eyes spoke. Ubiquitous, he seemed always near before being summoned. Svelte, agile, he was the panther out of the jungle. The animals

124

seemed aware of this. They were tense at his approach until a word or a touch relieved them.

If his class was that of the employed *peon*, he had no awareness. Every movement, the proud swing of his shoulders, the swagger of his buttocks beneath the broad belt encasing his waist had a male assertion. When he looked at Amelia, if she addressed him, his eyes rested directly upon her face. His voice, answering hers, was firm, controlled. He had the same assurance before Don Antonio. The difference was that his eyes left his employer, whereas they lingered on Amelia as if he awaited some further word. It was she who felt conscious, who seemed to feel her words to him unfinished. It was like being aware of someone who had entered a room and stood behind you silent, in suspended motion.

"How long has Juan been here?" she asked Mr. Carson.

"Since he was a small boy—an orphan."

"He is a *mestizo*?"

"Yes—why do you ask?"

"He seems to have tremendous self-assurance," said Amelia. "Sometimes he has the air of an *hidalgo*! Have you seen his wife—he's married, with children?"

"Two children officially. His wife is very young. He keeps her shut up. Juan is the Casanova of the *estancia*. He may one day have a knife in his back—that is not our risk. He is the most efficient gaucho we have, a first-class foreman. He regards himself as an aristocrat among them. They accept the distinction. He has the surest lasso and the lightest touch on a guitar of any man within a hundred miles. But he's damnably touchy. If you say anything he doesn't like he'll disappear for a month. He once disappeared for six months. He somehow got to France, to Chantilly, in some young Frenchman's stable. Sir Anthony brought him back. He was then only sixteen. Have you heard him speak French?"

"French—he speaks French?"

"Stable-boy French, I believe, very amusing. He brought back a repertoire of questionable French songs gathered from a little cocotte he linked up with. He's adroit, a diplomat in his way. He can wheedle anything he wants out of Don Antonio," said Mr. Carson. "In many ways he's a menace."

CHAPTER NINE

I

Two nights later, a thundery oppressive night when the bull-frogs were croaking around the fountain, just after she had retired and was reading in bed, Amelia heard through her window a guitar being played. The tune was very soft and lilting. Her room was in a wing overshadowed by an enormous silver-leaved eucalyptus tree. Turning out her light so as not to be seen, she got up and peered out of the window. She could see nothing, but the player seemed to be somewhere by the tree. She withdrew within her room. The guitar music continued, faint but lovely. The player was an artist. It must be Juan the gaucho, amusing himself.

Amelia did not go back to bed but sat in darkness in a chair by the window. In the quiet night the music was inexpressively beautiful. It continued for about five minutes, then it stopped. She waited but it did not begin again. Without turning on the light she got into bed. Just as she did this, the guitarist began again. This time the music seemed much nearer. Then after a few bars a very low soft voice began to sing. The words were a little indistinct but it seemed to be a Spanish lullaby, a cradle song, tender, melancholy. The voice had a velvety quality. The song ended. She waited in silence for the next song but the silence continued unbroken. The singer had departed.

Amelia turned on the bedside lamp and read a while but she found she could not concentrate on her book. She was curiously restless. The silence lay heavy over the house. It was a silence she half hoped would be broken by the singer with the guitar.

Was it Juan, whose touch Mr. Carson had praised? The voice had a haunting quality. It was a pity she had not understood all of the words. It seemed to be about a girl who had lost her lover. *Oh Pepe mío, han pasado ya muchos años.* "Oh Pepe, the long years have passed by." She had got that. And—*Oh, Pepe mío, querido amant a quien tanto hace que perdi . . .* "Oh Pepe, my beautiful long-lost lover," *entonces sentiré tus brazos a mi* —"I shall feel your arms around me," *esperando, esperando*— "waiting, waiting."

The song had a deep melancholy. It died out in the still night but left a tremor of sadness.

At half-past eleven Amelia turned out her light. She could not read. As she lay awake she became aware of a motion in the air. She heard the leaves of the trees stirring. Was a storm getting up? A shutter banged somewhere. A quick gust of wind struck the house, and then she heard another roaring in the windbreak of trees that surrounded the farm. She got up and went to the open window. The night had turned black, with no moonlight, no stars. Surprisingly the wind was cold. It rose violently and howled over the roofs. She fastened her window and went back to bed, but the tumult increased and there was a tremendous commotion in the upper air. A thunderstorm? There was no thunder, no lightning. Then, without warning, something happened that made her sit up in bed, her heart beating wildly. There was a tremendous bombardment of roofs, windows, patio, garden. The uproar was deafening, continuous, demoniac. She switched on the light but there was no electricity. The current had failed. It seemed as if a thousand hands were hammering at the roofs, doors, windows. She got up, crossed the room and looked out. She was aware of something like a white avalanche descending on them. It might have been snow but for the force and noise of its descent. It was hail, tremendous hail. She saw it bouncing off the walls and on the patio in a wild dance, devilish in fury.

The patio, the garden, were blotted out under a curiously luminous white flood. There was no abatement of the terrific storm.

She heard sounds of someone running in the house, along the corridors. Presently there was a tapping on her door. She opened it. Two maids stood there with hurricane lamps. They gave her one, and passed to the other rooms. A little later there was another tap on the door. It was Carlos, almost unrecognisable in odd garments, barefoot. Don Antonio and others were down in the sitting-room. He had sent word to her not to be afraid, asking her to join them if she cared.

Amelia put on a thick dressing-gown and slippers. When she reached the bottom of the stairs she saw an odd sight through the open doors of the long sitting-room. In the semi-light of the hurricane glasses, candles in deep glass funnels, she discerned a company, variously attired, that comprised Sir Anthony and the eight guests in the house. The former was a surprising sight. He was in a long green silk gown that was folded over his lean figure. It had short sleeves and no collar and at the bottom there was a vent on each side. The long gown was fastened about him with a yellow sash.

"What a wonderful dressing-gown!" exclaimed Amelia.

"It's not a dressing-gown, it's an Egyptian galabieh. I bought it at Luxor in Egypt many years ago—most comfortable. I hope you were not frightened?"

"A little," said Amelia. "But a hailstorm—I've never seen anything like this before! What hail!"

"It's our speciality," said Mr. Carson who had come from his wing. "It comes in from the Andes. The last one we had, two years ago, killed fifty cattle—hail as big as ping-pong balls —and crushed dozens of the *peons*' houses. Two million pounds worth of wheat and corn crops were lost. It knocked out our lighting plant—looks as if it's done it again! I didn't like the look of the sky last night—blue-black in the west. I'm afraid this is a bad storm."

"The worst is that all the roads will be deep in mud for weeks," said a guest.

"If it isn't mud, it's dust; if it isn't dust, it's hail; if it isn't hail, it's wind; if it isn't wind, it's drought; if it isn't drought, it's locusts; and if it isn't any of these pests, it's the worst of all, the politicians! Why, in God's name, do we live here!" growled a wrinkled, sun-tanned, elderly guest named Bishop. He was a large *estancia* owner, of an old Anglo-Argentine family.

"Now, come," said Sir Anthony. "If you were banished from the pampa you'd be like Dante languishing out of Florence! You know there is nothing on the whole earth that holds you like this corner of it! Did you ever know a fellow who, once he has it in his blood, can get away from it? No! Here we live! Here we die!"

"With intervals in New York, London, Paris, Madrid? Now admit it, Don Antonio, you are always away!" cried the *estanciero's* wife.

The servants came in bearing a tray of coffee and maté tea. The hail still beat on the house with an uproar that almost drowned their voices.

"It's a foot high—we'll be iced in!" observed Mr. Carson, looking out of a window.

"Well, it's an experience. I wouldn't have believed it," said de Lesseps, a Frenchman, who had come out to the Argentine for a tour with his polo team. He had a pretty young wife, formerly in the Comédie Française. They were Parisians, always perfectly dressed. Even now, by some magic native to the art of elegance, they were beautifully turned out in pyjamas, and kimono. "You said something about politicians —you don't mean to say you have that pest in the Pampa?"

"Don't get Freddie going on that, please! His doctor's

warned him of a coronary thrombosis," pleaded Mrs. Bishop.

Nevertheless, Freddie, maté gourd in hand, started, the torrent of protest broken only by recurrent draws through the *bombilla*, the metal tube mouthpiece of the gourd.

"Have we politicians? We have the most pestilent brood of scallywags on earth, sir! They're out to steal our railways, steal our ranches and start a bloody revolution among the *peons*! They are going to destroy the cattle industry, this country's goldmine——"

"And ours!" interjected Sir Anthony, quietly.

"Yes, but it isn't what it was, is it? They're out to cut up our estates. I don't know, since you're a visitor here, M'sieur de Lesseps, if you are aware what that entails. It's the custom for us to move our cattle over the *estancia*. This enables us, by changing about, to give them a grass feed, in summer to fatten them up on alfalfa, and in winter on grain. We have to rotate our herds. That means space. Those vote-catching politicians in Buenos Aires don't care a damn about that. Cut up the *estancias*, give the land to the *peons*, make them all small farmers scratching just enough to eat, sleep and copulate——"

"Freddie!" protested his wife.

"I'm sorry!—and bang goes all that meat and grain for export. It's on exports that Argentina lives. Do you know, sir, what these monkey boys in office are up to? Before the last election they ran like rats all over the *estancias* in Buenos Aires Province, with big-scale maps and blank entry books. They called on all the little farmers and the *peons*. "If you want more land vote for us and our policy to cut up the *estancias*." Naturally all the half-wit *colonos*—farmers, and the illiterate *peons*, voted for them. They haven't got their slices of land, not yet; but it's on the way. Look at me, sir! I'm the third generation of a family owning a large *estancia*. In less than a hundred years we've converted a wild prairie into one of the richest, most productive soils in the world. Down at Rosario you'll see vast docks and hundreds of ships, all taking, overseas, meat and grain. We've been feeding the world from the pampa. Our export sets the price of wheat on the Liverpool Exchange—the pulse of the grain world. Where does this colossal trade come from? It comes from our *estancias*, feudal if you like, but with happy people in them, even the *peons* and *mestizos* have full stomachs, clothes, things they never knew before. In this treeless, grassy, stoneless plain, in a three-hundred-mile radius from Buenos Aires—which is only a big belly-full of windy politicians who create nothing—we've made an earthly paradise—wind, rain, hail, drought, locusts notwithstanding. We British, Irish, Spaniards and others have had a long pull here. We came to a wilderness overgrown with thistles, we contended for every mile with treacherous native Indians. We fought them and tamed them. We brought here our money, our know-how. We cultivated grasses, clover, alfalfa, and banished the thistle. This pampa was empty in 1870, nothing but a waving sea of wild grass and skulking Indians. Cattle and horses apart, now two hundred and fifty thousand square miles of it produces wheat! The early Spaniards landing here, four hundred years ago, didn't do much. The only sea-trade they'd allow was through Porto Bello in the Panama, and it took nigh on two years to exchange goods between Cadiz in Spain and the sporadic Rio Plata settlements. Goods used to come down to them from Peru and Panama along the Andean mule tracks. There's thirty thousand miles of railways now—you've seen them, made by English capital, English engineers. They've brought more and more land under the plough, carried the meat to the docks with the refrigerator ships. And now those hustlers in Buenos Aires are out to embezzle the railways. They've a fresh restriction every month to squeeze us out!"

"I prophesy that twenty years from today we shan't own

a single yard of the thirty thousand miles we've laid with English capital," interjected Sir Anthony. "My father spent his life here, building railways. You've perhaps noticed that the stations along the line carry English names very often—little pockets of our people who settled there," he said, addressing de Lesseps. "What your country did in Louisiana we did here. We civilised it."

"We did more," asserted Bishop, after another swig at his maté. "The Pampa Indians tamed only three animals here— llama, alpaca, guanco—all of the same species. They'd never seen a horse until the Spaniards imported them. They hadn't got a word in their language for horse. They'd never seen cattle until 1552, when two Portuguese brought in seven cows and one bull. From their progeny, escaping control, came the wild herds. For two hundred years the gauchos went on hunting them, massacring them for the tallow and hides. Then we brought in fencing wire and had the herds under control. We erected windmills and conquered the drought that killed thousands of cattle."

"It's odd to think," said Carson, "that but for these wind-mills there'd have been no export of dried beef; but for dried beef there'd have been no slaves working the American and Jamaican tobacco and sugar plantations. They fed 'em on our jerky!"

"Jerky?" asked Amelia.

"Jerky's dried salt beef," explained Carson. He paused, the noise of the hail drowned his voice. When it subsided, he said, "I'll show you the drying sheds where we rack it."

"Is this cannonade going to stop?" asked de Lesseps.

"Yes, it'll be over in half an hour."

"And have cost us a million pounds with its destruction," added Bishop grimly.

They talked on. About two o'clock the hailstorm passed.

There was a strange silence. The hail lay piled up outside, a white world.

"It will take a day to melt it off," said Carson.

The company dispersed to resume their sleep.

11

Three days later when Amelia went into the stable, Juan was saddling a horse. The *domador* greeted her with his quiet smile.

"Was it you who sang on the patio the other night?" asked Amelia.

"*Si*. You heard me, *señorita*?"

She felt sure that he knew quite well she had heard him.

"I enjoyed it very much."

"*Muchos gracias, señorita*."

"Do you remember the songs you sang? I could only get a few words here and there. One was rather sad, the lament of a girl waiting for her lover—*esperando, esperando!*"

"Yes, she waited many years for him. She was faithful, so the song tells us—it was *La Canción del Husar perdido*."

"You don't think girls are faithful?" asked Amelia, amused, as he told her of *The Song of the Lost Hussar*.

He thumped his chest and laughed. "*Nada, señorita*—not the pretty ones!"

"But you men aren't faithful," replied Amelia, aware of his reputation.

He showed his strong white teeth in a wide smile, and with a brown hand stroked the horse's neck.

"Why should we be, *señorita*? What would the poor girls do if we were!" he said. "When I make love the girls are happy."

"And the other song?" asked Amelia, not pursuing the subject.

134

"It was an old song here, everyone knows it. *Adios, Pampa Mia.*"

"It was rather sad too."

"The pampa is sad."

"But you love it?"

"When I am here, I dream of going away. When I am away, I cry to be here."

"Señor Carson tells me you ran off to Paris as a boy. Did you like it?" asked Amelia.

"Yes—no. I did not run away. I never run away. I just go. Why not? A young Frenchman, he offered to take me. I groomed his horses. He was very rich, very strange man. He bought me beautiful clothes, but no money! He was afraid I would buy girls! He was afraid I love his wife. He was afraid I dope his horses!"

He laughed and stroked the neck of his horse again. "I was sixteen. Then I grew homesick for the pampa. Don Antonio arrived in Paris, he had a house there. One day I ring his bell and say 'Please take me home or I shall die here.' He was very angry with me. He brought me home."

Amelia went into the stall to get her horse. He followed her and saddled it. He led it out and watched her mount.

"You are very beautiful on a horse, *señorita*," he said quietly, looking up as he adjusted the bridle. Then, almost inaudibly but with his eyes slowly resting on her face above him, added, "You are very beautiful anywhere!"

She made no answer, but gave him a faint smile and rode off. Was he being insolent, forgetting his place? She could not be sure. His manner was correct, deferential, but his eyes had a disconcerting assurance. She was aware of him, of his lean body, his voice, his way with a horse, his lithe, confident bearing. He was too noticeable, too forward. She would talk to him less.

135

Little by little in her daily rides with Sir Anthony and Mr. Carson, or with the overseer, Amelia came to know the life of the pampa and its *estancias*. She saw it through the seasons. They made visits and stayed on other large *estancias*. There was an oligarchy of Anglo-Argentine families, an aristocracy of the pampa. The sons of the family were often educated at English public schools and universities; the girls at schools in France. Their speech was Spanish and English, with equal fluency, their traditions were largely British.

Every race in Europe seemed to have made its contribution to Argentina, which gave freedom and equal facilities to all. Much of the labour on the farms was Italian. The Irish had settled well. They came penniless, worked hard, acquired small farms, married Argentine girls, marriages facilitated by their both being Catholics, and prospered. The odd thing was that whereas the Irish who emigrated to North America were implacably hostile to Britain, down through generations that had never set foot in Ireland, the Irish who emigrated to Argentina proudly claimed membership of the British Empire and took part in all the communal activities of their fellow countrymen. They prospered, and in time became proprietors of large *estancias* because they laboured with their hands. The gaucho had lost his inheritance and was disappearing from the scene because of his insensate pride. Manual labour involved a loss of *dignidad*. They had been born hunters of the wild herds on the pampa. They could lasso cattle, brand and skin the animals, sell the hides and tallow. They decimated the herds with ruthless killing. They cared nothing about importing prize stock for breeding. They watched with scorn the Irish, Italian Polish and Slav immigrants earn large wages, ditching and fencing. Their *criollo* pride, the Spanish blood dominant over Indian, would not let them stoop to creative labour. They were as tameless as the horses they so proudly rode and corralled. They became a dying clan, *peons* deriving no permanence, no wealth from the fertile pampa.

Since the defeat of the Spanish Armada the Spanish influence, with its restraints and taboos, had steadily fallen, while the British prestige had steadily mounted until its influence was out of all proportion to that of the native Argentines. Politically this fact was denied. A steady aggression, fostered by the politicians exploiting the envy aroused by the prosperity of a small powerful oligarchy of English *estancieros* and engineers, to whom were owed the railways, power installations, water companies, and transport systems, had begun to undermine the British dominance.

"We are on the way out," said Sir Anthony. "The conversion from grasslands to farms, made possible by fencing and the railroad, in turn demanding a great influx of labour, has created political parties that are being urged to eliminate us. The public utilities we made are being taken over by the Government, at its own price. Something of our legacy will remain, of course. They play football, golf and tennis. Via our army in India we've even improved the polo! It's something that when the Argentine wants to pledge his word he says *palabra Inglés*, and when he wants to promise you that he will turn up in time, and not an hour late, he says *hora Inglés*—a sort of Greenwich time for him! It's the fashion now for the politicians to play us down, or exploit us, forgetting that with their *mañana* and corruption they would have got nowhere— for even their beautiful Buenos Aires has been created by the beef off all the British *estancias*, carried to the ports by our railways, and conveyed overseas by our refrigerator ships. A new race of Argentines is growing up, with a great future in its hands, away from the warring nations of Europe. They know less and less of the legacy we have given them. Perhaps they have an inkling when they buy their suits and shirts in

Harrods store on the Calle Florida, and because their offices close on Saturday afternoon—the *Sábado Inglés*. Meanwhile, we are holding on. My father spent his life here. He got his baronetcy for his pioneer work here. I was born here, I would like to die here—English nevertheless!"

There was a note of sadness in his voice. As he spoke he looked out across the waving plain of alfalfa grass, to a large herd on the horizon. In another direction, away to the right, there was a silhouette of men and horses ploughing the land. The long line looked like a cavalry regiment on the march.

"Young Cordell would be shocked by that," he said, pointing with his whip. "He'd have twenty Ford tractors doing it in a tenth of the time. I haven't the inclination or the money. I like to see horses at the plough driven by men who've broken them in and grown up with them. It would mean a change in labour, too. *Peons* are no good with machinery, are they Carson?" he asked, turning to his manager.

"We'd have to put in more Italians," answered Carson.

"Yes, Italians! We think of them as opera singers, full of Verdi and Rossini, but they're born mechanics. They can do anything with a machine. The electric light plant's run by Giovanni. Before we got him we broke down twice a week. And what road-makers they are! There are years of that sort of work before them here—the new gauchos taming the pampa with roads!"

Behind them at a distance rode Juan and three of his gauchos. They were riding to an ostrich round-up. The birds had been reported beyond Platt's Barn, a small granary two miles away. When they reached a scrub-like plateau they reined up. Mr. Carson surveyed the plain with field-glasses.

"There they are! Can you drive them past us here?" he added, turning to Juan.

"*Si, señor!*"

The gauchos, as Sir Anthony still called them, though they

carried few traces of their wild forebears, not even the mustach-
ios that once drooped from the face of every old gaucho, had
halted and took from their saddles long ropes.

"Juan, show the *señorita* your *bola*," called Sir Anthony.

Juan dismounted and walked up to them. He had a long thin
rope in his hand. It was in Y form, each strand ending in a
small round weight.

"It's an Indian lasso—a *boleadoro*. When the boys get
within a dozen yards of the ostrich they swing the *bola* and let
fly. The weights wrap the cords around the bird's neck and
legs, and down it comes," explained Sir Anthony. "Off you
go—drive down here!" he commanded, dismissing Juan and
his assistants.

They set off in the direction of the ostriches, making a great
detour.

"We only keep these birds as a sort of ranch decoration,"
said Mr. Carson. "Their feathers aren't much good. We make
brushes of them. They're rheas, not real ostriches, but they are
native to the pampa and fast runners."

"We'd better dismount—they'll see us and sheer off," said
Sir Anthony, slipping down from his saddle.

They waited. In about a quarter of an hour they saw the
ostriches moving, long necks and heads erect, coming rapidly
towards them, the horsemen in pursuit making cries. There
were about forty birds. Nearer and nearer they came. Their
pace seemed tremendous. As they drew abreast the horsemen
suddenly increased their speed. Juan was on the near side. He
was about twenty yards behind a quartette of fleeing birds
that had broken away a little from the flock, when he raised
his hand high above his head, whirled the *bola*, and let it fly.
The rope, free, horizontally propelled by its weights, flew in a
level line towards one of the birds. In a flash of the eye the
weighted fingers of the small lasso had wrapped themselves
round the long thin throat and legs of the ostrich. The bird

in full flight was flung violently down to the ground where it began kicking furiously, with wildly beating wings. In a trice Juan had vaulted from his running horse and was on the bird. Wary of the powerful legs, he trussed it rapidly. His two companions had captured their birds almost simultaneously.

Sir Anthony, Amelia and Mr. Carson mounted and rode over to the gauchos and the three trussed birds. They were rather bedraggled creatures from their struggle in the dust. Tethered and loosely trussed, they were allowed to regain their feet. There was a look of intense indignation in their baleful eyes.

"Watch," said Sir Anthony, dismounting and taking out his cigar case. "They like tobacco!"

He pulled out a cigar and offered it to one of the ostriches. It looked disdainfully for a moment and then snatched it instantly, chewed rapidly, and swallowed.

The other two ostriches began to squawk.

"Oh no, no! I'm not wasting good cigars on you girls," said Sir Anthony.

"What are you going to do with them?" asked Amelia.

"Release them. They're no good as a roast," replied Sir Anthony. He turned to the grinning Juan. "Pluck a feather for the *señorita*," he commanded.

Two gauchos held the bird, roped. The operation was swift. The bird protested against this last indignity. Juan wiped the quill on his denims and offered the feather, without speaking, to Amelia. Then the three ostriches were released, a wary process. Free, they went off at a tremendous speed over the pampa.

CHAPTER TEN

I

THE weeks slipped by. Sir Anthony was a liberal host. He liked to fill his house every week-end throughout the spring, summer and autumn. He had ten suites, each with a bathroom. There was a billiard room, a swimming pool, a large alley way for the playing of *bochas*, a favourite game of the ranch hands, played on the stamped earth with small wooden balls, a kind of rough bowls which created great excitement. In the stables there were thirty superb horses. Sir Anthony rode a three-thousand-guinea thoroughbred, imported from Newmarket, but his rough estate riding was done on a *criollo*. "They are as native to the country as you can get them, and very tough," explained Sir Anthony, as he walked through the stables one morning with Amelia.

They went from stall to stall. The horses lived like aristocrats, each with its name on the arch over the stall, in letters of silver. Sir Anthony called them by name and each horse lifted and shook its head, pleased by the sound of its master's voice.

"Ten of these *criollos* have been to Europe and back with me," said Sir Anthony, running his hand over a muzzle, "and I've paced them down the *avenidas* at the Seville *Fiera*, each with a pretty *señorita* riding them and covering their haunches with their flounced skirts. A proud day for a Pampa *criollo*! Well, it was an easy trip for them, by boat to Cadiz and then truck to Seville. A *de luxe* outing for them! Tomorrow I have a very old friend of mine coming to us who rode a couple of *criollos*, as the Argentines call them, from here to Washington, ten thousand miles, over the plains and the mountains! A terrific journey. He's written a book about it."

"You mean A. F. Tschiffely? I found his book in your library and read it," said Amelia.

"That's the fellow. He used to be a schoolteacher in Buenos Aires, but he didn't like that. He was mad about horses. One day he got the idea of making this ride, to prove what a *criollo* could do. Everybody thought him crazy, including myself, but, by God, he did it! It's made him famous. He chose the *criollos* himself from the El Cardel *estancia*. They were a wild pair that had belonged to a Patagonian Indian chief. They almost broke the *domadores* who broke them. But Tschiffely can ride anything, and he took them across South and North America, via the Panama Isthmus, the jungles, ten-thousand-foot ranges, scorching sands, gullies, torrents, despite ice, blizzards, pests, foul fodder—nothing stopped them, until he rode down Fifth Avenue in New York on them, dressed as a gaucho to tickle the Yanks. He was received by Mayor Jimmy Walker. They called him the Christopher Columbus of horseflesh. President Coolidge invited him to the White House. What a fellow! We'll try and get him talking about that two-and-a-half year's journey, but he's as shy as a jenny wren."

Sir Anthony slapped the neck of the *criollo* he was standing by.

"*Verdadero criollo!*" he said. "It's a virtue to have Creole blood today, horse or man. I'm always amused by my Argentine friends. You'll hear the *políticos* boasting of their ancient Creole blood and that they've made Argentina! It's quite a gambit now, with all this emphasis on national pride. It's all nonsense of course, which the new hotchpotch middle-class town-squatter believes. Actually Argentina's been made by the immigrants out of Europe, half a dozen different races, English,

Irish, Spanish, Italian and Hungarian. It's descendants of their blood who are the Argentines of today. The Creole *peon* would have gone on massacring the herds or sat on his haunches all day and watched his women work. Even now a lot of the work at harvest time is done by swallows."

"Swallows?" queried Amelia.

"That's our name for the *golondrinas*, the harvest labourers who ship in from Europe. Every autumn there's thousands of them cross the Atlantic, Italians mostly, attracted by the high wages. You see, as our seasons are reversed, they can work one harvest in Europe and another here. So we call 'em *golondrinas* —swallows."

"Do they all go home?" asked Amelia.

"No—unswallow-like they don't. Some of them stay. Very wisely the authorities don't make any fuss. They give us even more than they get, with their traditional skills. Look how they farm! Wonderful workers, raising flax, corn, wheat, grapes, sugar-cane and tobacco. They treat this rich soil with reverence, and I like to see them get on, possess their own small-holdings, and breed their children. There's a singular fact about them here. If you go to New York and Chicago and other towns, you find colonies of Italians all bunched together, speaking Italian, reading Italian papers, eating Italian food, Italian to the second and third generations, mostly dreaming of making enough to go back to their native land. Here they get assimilated. They're not Italian-Argentines. They're just Argentines. They even drop their language and speak Spanish. We British, well-settled here, tenaciously keep our dual nationality. When our friend Bishop blows up, about being squeezed out, he forgets that fact. The Argentines naturally don't like it, and they want to own the place themselves. One day they will—the *estancias*, docks, works, railways, electric plants, banks—all the things we've created. They'll be corrupt and seethe with revolutions, and dictators exploiting the country—but it'll be their own land in their own hands. Even so, just as my father's buried here, so I wish it. I shan't feel I'm in foreign soil, English as I am."

On the Saturday morning six guests arrived in time for lunch. Among them were Doña Lucia and Tschiffely, the hero of the great ride. He was a tallish lean fellow of about forty. Amelia complimented him on his book. He was a reluctant talker but little by little she induced him to release his horse-wisdom. His ponies were still alive, pensioned off on an *estancia*. They were sixteen-year-olds when he took them, sturdy creatures about thirteen hands high. One he rode, the other he used for a packhorse. He had started off from Buenos Aires one April day in 1925.

"The beginning wasn't too good. We'd twelve days solid rain in Rosario," he said.

"Weren't you desperately lonely—all through those prairie deserts and mountain ranges?" asked Amelia.

"My dear young lady, you don't begin a journey like that if you must have people to talk to! I read a bit sometimes," he added whimsically.

"Read—but how, did you take books?"

"One."

"What was it?"

"*Pickwick Papers*," he replied, laughing. "How's that for your Mr. Dickens? He's probably giving entertainment now. I left it with a priest in a Panamanian village. He knew English. I wonder what he made of it. Tell me—how's Don Antonio?" he asked, changing the subject abruptly. The house party was riding to an *asado* that had been arranged. A bullock would be killed and roasted in the open at a gathering of gauchos who were having a rodeo. Sir Anthony with Doña Lucia and some of the guests were riding ahead.

"Sir Anthony? He's quite well. Why do you ask?" said Amelia surprised by the question.

"I've not been here for two years. I notice a change in him, he's gone very thin," observed Tschiffely.

"I thought he was always thin?"

"Yes—but not like now. How long have you known him?"

"I've been at Tabara about a year," answered Amelia.

"Here all the time?"

"No—we go into Buenos Aires sometimes."

"You must forgive me—I never hear names when I'm introduced. Are you Don Antonio's secretary?"

"Yes."

"Miss Macreary?" he asked, smiling slightly.

"Yes," she replied, a little puzzled by his manner and questions.

"Your red hair and green eyes gave me a clue."

"To what?" asked Amelia.

"Two months ago I was in Cairo, dining at the British Embassy. A young Frenchman, from their Embassy, was a fellow guest. When he learned who I was he asked if I knew Don Antonio. I told him I should be his guest soon at Tabara. He said 'Then you'll meet there the loveliest young woman in South America with red hair and green eyes, named Macreary.' I don't disagree with him," said Tschiffely, smiling.

He saw the colour of her cheeks brighten, she appeared confused.

"I hope you don't mind the compliment?" he asked.

"Oh, no—thank you!" replied Amelia. "The Frenchman— was his name Etienne de Lérin?"

"Yes."

Amelia said nothing, and rode on.

"He gave me a message for you. It's rather cryptic but he

said you would understand. I was to ask you if the rain had come," said Tschiffely. "Does it make sense?"

"Yes," replied Amelia, and in a voice strictly controlled added, "He taught me a poem about the rain, which we both liked very much."

He was about to ask her whether she could recite it to him, and then he thought he had better not. Instead, he remarked— "It's a little world, isn't it, even here on the pampa."

III

The night after the guests had departed she sat up late in the small office off the library, in which she did her work. She was behind with some of the estate accounts. The night was warm. There was not a sound, the household had gone to bed. It was near midnight. As she wrote at her desk, her task almost finished, she heard the soft strumming of a guitar come in through the window. Her heart gave a quick beat. She knew at once who was playing out in the patio, somewhere by the giant eucalyptus. She stopped writing and sat, pen in hand, motionless. Her first impulse was to rise and close the french window, but she did not move. The soft seductive music seemed to fill the night. Presently a voice began to sing a Spanish lyric, very softly and slowly. She knew the voice, velvety and modulated. It was Juan's, the same as on that night preceding the hailstorm. When the lyric ended there was a deep silence. She glanced sideways looking out of the window but the night was moonless, and in the darkness of the patio nothing could be distinguished. She waited, hoping the singer had gone, yet hoping he had not, so exquisite was that guitar-playing and the low rich voice.

She closed the ledger and was about to rise when again the music of the guitar came in from the night and again the low voice sang to a pianissimo accompaniment: this time she could hear the words. It was the *Canción del Husar*—the *Song of the Lost Hussar*—*Oh Pepe mío, que hermoso eras cuando* . . . . "Oh, Pepe, how beautiful you were . . ." The lament had a piercing quality. It ended, and with scarcely a pause there followed the gay lilt of a Spanish dance. Every gaucho carried his guitar but here was a supreme artist. The dance ended. Again the deep silence of the night: but in that silence her heart seemed to be beating fiercely, and fear mingled with the ecstasy the music had evoked.

Amelia quietly put away the ledger. Something impelled her to switch off the desk lamp so that she was engulfed in the darkness of the room. She did not want to be seen from the outside world, sentient and watchful it seemed to her. She had moved, feeling her way towards the window, when the music began again. This time it was much nearer, it seemed to come from the flagged terrace of the patio. She withdrew into a recess between the windows, her breath coming quickly. She felt like an animal conscious of an unseen pursuer. He was singing again, every word now audible. She stood very still resisting the hypnotic music. It was an Andalusian love song, low, passionate, that once upon a time had been heard in old Spain. It was sung very slowly, very quietly until it died on the air like a sigh.

There was silence again. Inside the room, her heart beat strongly with the drama of the night, the pervading maleness of the voice, the knowledge of him somewhere near in the darkness, unseen but felt. She was acutely aware of his lithe body, his soft leopard-like movement, either sitting superbly upon his *criollo*, or moving noiselessly in the espadrilles on his bare feet; always a poem of movement, masterful, with a repressed insolence. He evoked a fear of herself, stirring an instinct so deep that she felt victimised and bound by emotions she could not define.

How long she stood there, in the dark recess of the window,

listening for some sound of a movement that never came, she knew not. A deep silence reigned. Nothing. He had departed and the knowledge that he had gone, left her at once relieved and regretful. There prevailed an awareness of him, of his slow appraisal of her when his dark eyes rested on her face, of a movement of him, of his brown hand on the reins, of his taut thighs in the saddle, the thrust of a foot in the stirrup, the swing of his flat shoulders as he turned his horse—in a dozen gestures a latent hypnotism pervaded her senses, try as she would to affirm her indifference. She felt encompassed by his possessive instinct. He embodied in every line of his body the mating instinct of the primeval pampa.

What folly in her to be so weak, so conscious of this *peon*! She resented the unrest he evoked in her, the consciousness of him that overlay her senses and made real a deep unsatisfied instinct. *Le jour où la pluie viendra.* Like a parched soil she awaited the generating rain, yet desperate to be so prone to folly. This fertile pampa, the rich grass, the herds in movement, the vast shining dome of the sky, all sang the hymn of Life.

She could not stand there forever in that dark room. Impelled by curiosity, she moved towards the window, seeking confirmation of the gaucho's absence. She put up a hand to close the casement and then stood transfixed. Before her, scarcely a yard distant, was Juan.

"*Señorita!*" he cried, in a low voice.

He was clad in a white shirt, open to the navel, revealing his brown firm chest with its thin gold chain and crucifix. The roll of the collar set off his powerful throat and the strong line of the wide jaw. The black hair hung loosely over his brow, a shining crown of his virile youth. He had pushed the guitar aside and its thin green ribbon lay across his muscled torso. His eyes, liquid and dark with their Indian inheritance, shone in the dim light, soft and tranquil, as they met her own. She was aware of a brown hand resting on the waist-band of his trousers. The usual leather belt had been discarded. A simple red sash was drawn tight above the hips. His other hand lay upon the guitar. His lips, slightly open, revealed the level line of his strong white teeth.

Amelia, in that moment compounded of fear and pleasure, was aware of a nobility of line in the face and figure before her. His features had a fineness uncommon in the *peon* stock. It was not only his youth that carried a grace of line and posture, there was also something at once aristocratic and arrogant that crowned his physical beauty. No wonder he had found his conquests so easy. Here was Don Juan again, reigning in the pampa.

Rooted in surprise, she made no response to his call. The passion in the word, the light in his eyes, the easy smile upon his dark face were unified in this prelude of desire. For a time, silent, they looked at each other. They were so near, her red hair and green eyes with the slender white throat and bosom, his black hair and smiling velvet eyes above the strong young throat, that they seemed like two flames the wind of passion would commingle. Noiselessly he took a step forward to cross the threshold, out of the faint light into the darkness of the room. Instantly, seized with panic, she closed the window upon him, so violently that it made a sharp sound in the still night.

He stood there for a moment, looking in through the window at the woman who had thwarted his approach. Whatever emotion possessed him, he gave no sign but stood looking through the closed window into the dark room. Then, in a gesture that mingled resignation with a certain satirical air, he raised a brown hand with singular grace, turned, and departed soft-footed into the darkness.

Amelia stood breathing hard, feeling the thud of her heart, her hand still on the latch of the french window. She watched him move, and go out of her vision with a calm dignity that stabbed her with contrition. Her sharp repulse had been born of panic, not against his intent, but against the weakness she felt within herself, the weakness of the flesh that half-yielded to a call heard in the flow of her blood. He was beautiful and urgent, a primeval creature that expressed a magic in the lines of his youthful body, in the unspoken demand in his eyes. It was not a sudden discovery, this potency of his body drawing her towards him. She had been observed, and observing, in a dozen modes and places where they had had physical awareness of each other. They were young together in this bright pulsing landscape of wide horizons singing a threnody of life. In the city there had been easier refuge from a committal of passion. Her near-surrender and withdrawal from Etienne, for all the poetry and subtlety of his approach, had been on a plane of sophistication whereon she had manoeuvred without disaster. The ultimate triumph of the flesh had been thwarted by a waywardness of the spirit he could not bend to his purpose. But this man out of the darkness, with the prelude of his music, had no sophistication in which to dress his passion. He was supremely male, uninhibited in his desire, and accustomed to command surrender. And she knew, this time, that she wanted to surrender. His urgent hands upon her would have found her wax. Only the window, shut in panic, had saved her. She was a woman with a woman's need, as urgent and simple as his.

Standing there, conscious of something lost that might have been hers for no asking, but which, in acceptance, had been the depth of folly, she became aware of the nature of the tragedy that had fallen upon this house. In all the months she had been here there had been no mention of Carmen Slowdon. There was probably no one left in the household who had known her. Thirty-five years had passed and the protagonists, excepting Sir Anthony, had all vanished from the scene, no shadow of them recalled. There were no portraits, no mementoes of the young wife, or of the child. Amelia would have known nothing of them except for Doña Lucia, whose youth had run with theirs, a friend of both families. From Doña Lucia came the portrait of the dark vivacious beauty the handsome young Antonio had married, at twenty-six newly the master of the Slowdon *estancia*. Young Roderick had been born within two years of marriage. Kurt Weninger was already the right-hand man at Tabara. The gentleman-gaucho had claimed her attention. "He was so handsome," said Doña Lucia, "that he caught the eye of every woman, with beautiful manners, and a splendid horseman, and an administrative gift that caused Sir Anthony to entrust to him more and more of his affairs in his absence. There must have been a mad infatuation for her to have sacrificed everything, her husband, her home, family, friends. She went without warning. What crazy creatures we women are!" exclaimed Doña Lucia.

Had there, then, been other nights when a figure had come out of the darkness of the eucalyptus tree, soft-slippered, low-voiced, a seducer of feminine frailty? The atmosphere had not changed in those thirty-five years, nor had human nature. Amelia began to understand how disaster had fallen upon Tabara. There were silences that were frightening, forces as of tides that swept in from the lonely pampa.

She reached her room. It was near midnight. A wind had begun to rise. There was always a wind, a *pampero*, haunting the plain, bringing voices out of the wilderness. It was possible that down in the patio he might be standing, watching the light that flooded her upper windows. The low seductive voice might cry, "*Señorita!*" How much of passion seemed to sound in that soft salute. She saw the smooth bronze chest, the potent loins, the confident smile.

"Absurd!" she said to herself. She crossed the room and almost violently drew the curtains. The sense of him out in the night still possessed her, in the form of his hand on the saddle, the line of his jaw above the chinstrap. And he was a *peon*, a gaucho of mixed Spanish and Indian blood, a mongrel!

She undressed slowly, got into bed, and put out the light. But she did not sleep. Her mind was disturbed, her body restless. Ought she to leave Tabara and put herself out of reach of temptation? She had a great admiration, indeed affection for Sir Anthony. He treated her with grave kindness and courtesy. Never for one moment was she given the impression that she was an employee here. The place had become a home. Now the nights drew in, she read to him, they played backgammon and billiards. All through the spring, summer and autumn, Tabara was full of guests staying for the long week-ends. The food was lavish. There was an excellent Italian cook. Two boys in livery, white coats with green facings, black trousers and shoes, white-gloved and well-groomed, waited at table under Pepe, the majordomo. It might have been a house in Paris or London in the old-style days.

There was an impression of great wealth but it was deceptive, Amelia discovered. For years Sir Anthony had lived up to the hilt. There had been successive disasters on the *estancia*, storms, plagues of locusts, cattle disease, and worse, a sudden fall in grain and meat prices. Wages were more generous than elsewhere, the workmen were well-housed, there was a hospital for the estate children. Again and again Mr. Carson had sounded a warning. Sir Anthony gave up his house in Buenos Aires, but he travelled regally. He took Carlos his valet, and two grooms with six or eight horses when he went to the *Fiera* at Seville, the guest of his old friend the Duke of Alba. After one crisis there was a mortgage on the *estancia* to finance a bank loan during a disastrous slump in a glutted grain market.

Amelia, keen in her detection of the strained finances, had long conferences with Mr. Carson. "Well, you try talking to Don Antonio. I can't make him face realities," he said one day. Amelia tried. Sir Anthony waved her figures aside. "My dear child, you've been listening to our gloomy Carson. He's been prophesying doom the last thirty years. He's never understood the resilience of the *estancia*. Next year we shall have a large profit. Meat prices are good, our shipments are up. The harvest is excellent. Tabara is very sound, my dear Amelia. Carson is an excellent manager but he's an inveterate pessimist. I am not at all worried!"

It was no use, Amelia discovered. He had lived like a millionaire. He would continue to live like a millionaire. Last year he had come home from the Automobile Salon with a new Rolls-Royce. "I can't keep on fetching the guests from the station in that old Mercedes," he said. "Utterly unsuitable for these roads!" was Carson's verdict when they looked at the elegant addition in the garage, standing with its six companions. "And I have to fight to get a new tractor because he hates machinery!"

Wildly extravagant, generous, vain, lovable, Amelia found in him all these qualities. But with them ran a hard grain in his character. He was an autocrat, he would brook no opposition. He was reticent and could pull down a shutter of steel on his affairs if he suspected an inquisition. Never had Amelia dared to make reference to the dead wife or the son in Austria shut out of his recognition. "The baronetcy, he can't alienate that? And what will he do with Tabara on his death?" Amelia asked Doña Lucia.

"None of us knows. He will not discuss his personal affairs," she replied.

All this Amelia had learned in a year on the *estancia*. She liked the life here but she found herself being isolated from any communal existence, except during visits to Buenos Aires. She met no young people of her own age, no young men to pay her homage. Her youth was passing, the growing need of a healthy womanhood went unsatisfied. There was the psychological jargon about being 'sexually starved'. She had thought it ridiculous and morbid when she first heard the phrase. Now, she realised how true it was. It could lead to reckless, unpredictable conduct, to sheer physical obsessions. It could lead to the embodied maleness of a Juan waiting in the dark night.

Fear seized her. She could not go on here, isolated, starved, tempted. An aura of disaster hung about the place. It had happened once. It could happen again. In the morning she would tell Sir Anthony she could not continue here. She would find some excuse. It would require much courage but she would do it. There could be no peace for her here. She was sorry for Sir Anthony, she was angry with herself, with her own frailty. It was the first break in her self-confidence. Believing that will-power was everything, she had never foreseen this frailty.

For a while, perturbed in mind, she listened to the wind testing the house with its invisible hands. Then she slept.

IV

It was a morning given from heaven. The vast dome of the sky was cloudless. The wind had gone, leaving a swept landscape, crystal clear. Rising and dressing, Amelia heard the familiar sound of the lowing of cattle. They were rounding in a herd towards the railroad docks, from which they would go up the branch line to the junction and then towards Rosario, the slaughterhouses, and the refrigerator ships docked and waiting for their cargo. The knowledge of the vast traffic of slaughter had depressed Amelia at first. This endless transition from the open grassy pampa to the fetid blood-drenched slaughterhouse, had greatly depressed her when she first came to the *estancia* and was made aware of the grim finality awaiting the milling livestock.

"It's rapid, a thousand times better than the lingering death Nature would give them on the pampa," said one of the overseers when Amelia expressed her feelings. He was an Englishman, educated, who had forsaken a Buenos Aires bank for the free life of the pampa. "I'll tell you something, Miss Macreary," he said, slapping the back of a young bullock he had led up to the fence where she sat on her pony. "Last year I took a holiday and went to England for three months. I stayed with an old aunt. She was living in one of those hotels dotted all around South Kensington—they call them all 'Courts' to disguise the fact they're old mansions knocked together. They were once the little palaces of Queen Victoria's industrial tycoons. Their descendants have been driven by taxes into genteel poverty. There they all are, hundreds and hundreds of impoverished old ladies, who can't die because of penicillin, and who amble around on sticks, like birds with broken wings. They're widows mostly, with sad memories of former happiness, waiting for Sunday when their sons or daughters come to take them out to have lunch with the grandchildren. Then back they go again, to their pigeon-cotes, an egg with tea and toast for breakfast, a shilling extra if they have it on a tray in the bedroom, their rheumatism being very bad that morning; the television room, after dining at one of fifty little tables, and bed at ten o'clock. 'Lift up your hearts' says the radio at eight o'clock in the morning. Morning after morning the poor old things try to lift up their hearts despite the weekly bills that have risen five shillings, the underground fare by fourpence, while the War Loan of a swizzling Government sinks to a new low. 'We want Mary, we want George!' scream the yahoos at Buckingham Palace railings, but all that those old ladies want, if they faced it, penned-up down the Cromwell Road, is oblivion. They're kept from that by the latest antibiotics, which enable their hearts to flutter a little longer, their bellows to wheeze, while their poor old bodies sink lower and lower in the well of loneliness. Among all these gentle old birds, a few males, like plucked turkeys, stumble around. My God, spare me that death-in-life! Wouldn't it be better if, like these cattle, they could get a sudden knock on the head and be free of it all, no burden to themselves, their relatives, or the State? No, Miss Macreary, don't you waste any sympathy over these cattle. Unlike us, they go out at the top of their form, their eyesight and legs good, their skins shining! And after death they don't clutter up the heavens as angels, they provide a feast on British dinner tables!"

"I think you're a little ruthless. Some of us are rather fond of our poor lonely old folks! We'll join them ourselves one day," said Amelia.

He gave a hearty laugh, and slapped the back of the bullock. "For my own sake I hope not. I want to go with a bang when my day's done. I expect you'll call me a pagan! I am!" he said, jubilantly. "Good morning, miss!"

He led off the bullock.

She recalled the ex-bank clerk's homily as she heard the cattle lowing happily, oblivious of their fate. In this bright morning how far off the panic and nightmare of last night now seemed! All because a young man had played a guitar in the darkness and offered her, doubtless, an erotic adventure. She must keep things in proportion and herself in hand.

When she descended to breakfast her overnight resolution to leave Tabara had weakened. She found five of the guests at breakfast.

"Did you hear that guitar being played last night, and someone singing? Just ravishing!" said Mrs. Finkelbaum, French-born, married to a New York stockbroker, his third wife. "I got up and looked out. And there was a man standing near a window in the patio. What a glorious creature! He looked like a sleek panther. And what a voice! I wonder who he was, singing there in a Romeo rôle!"

"I didn't know Romeo added a guitar to his other inducements," said old Señor Domecq, mordantly.

"He was our *peon* Juan. He fetched you from the station yesterday," answered Amelia.

"Oh, that gorgeous young chaffeur? I noticed him!" exclaimed the imperturbable Mrs. Finkelbaum, pushing back a dyed lock. "*Peon* or no *peon*, he's a menace to susceptible girls. I shall speak to Don Antonio. He shouldn't equip his Mercury with a guitar!"

They all laughed. Sir Anthony had not come down to breakfast. The riding party was not starting until ten o'clock.

V

Amelia was in her office when Pepe came in.

"Sir Anthony's not coming down, *señorita*. He's not well. We've sent for the doctor."

"Not well, what is it, Pepe?"

"He had a heart attack while in the bath. Carlo found him there. He'd fainted. We got him to bed. He seems all right now. He would like to see you, *señorita*, in about half an hour."

"Thank you, Pepe. I'll go up to him."

She found Sir Anthony sitting up in bed, clad in a red Chinese silk dressing-gown patterned with gold dragons. She was amused to see he wore red silk gloves to match. They made him look like a Cardinal.

"It's nothing," he said, when she greeted him. "Very silly of me. I had the bath water too hot, and fainted. Might have drowned, of course. Not a bad end!"

"Now, Sir Anthony, you know you've no intention of coming to an end yet. It wouldn't be Tabara without you," said Amelia.

There could be no thought now of leaving the *estancia*, but her overnight resolve was half dead anyhow. She must take control of herself. It seemed as if Sir Anthony had divined something of her unrest for he said to her, "I wanted to tell you that this coming winter I intend to rent a furnished house in Buenos Aires, and take Pepe and the servants. You can live at your apartment if you wish, but I'd feel happier if you were at hand and could be in the house. I want to do some entertaining. I'm sure it gets a little monotonous for you here. After all, you're young. I've been offered the Domecq house, they're summering in Paris. I hope this is agreeable to you?"

"I can't tell you how agreeable, Sir Anthony!" exclaimed Amelia. "You must be a thought reader!"

"No—I had a hint from Doña Lucia. She thought you should see more of some agreeable young men and not so much of this old one. I too want a little life. I know the doctor won't agree. He'll tell me I'm to keep quiet and will want to put me in cottonwool. He's been trying to bury me for the last ten years with his warnings to go slow. Well, I'm not going to tell him a word of my plans. Now, my dear, will you ask Mr. Carson to come and see me. When the doctor's been we'll do the letters. Tell my guests I'm very sorry to be hors-de-combat, and I want everything to be done that's arranged for them. But I don't want to see them—except Doña Lucia, of course."

Amelia left the room and closed the door softly. The winter in town! Her old friends, the theatres, cinemas, dances, shops. She had never let herself admit how much she missed them despite the fascination of this life in the pampa. She would stay with Sir Anthony, but her own little place would be accessible. She would hear music, but not the guitar of Juan played in the darkness, nor his low voice calling 'Señorita!'

As predicted the doctor ordered Sir Anthony to stay in bed for a week. And as foreseen, Sir Anthony was out riding over the *estancia* within three days, his eyes observing everything.

CHAPTER ELEVEN

I

FOR several days Juan saw nothing of Señorita Macreary. Then he was sent away for two days' cattle-branding. His mind returned repeatedly to the red-haired girl with the green eyes. He knew she was conscious of him by her manner, by her abruptness when she gave him an order, or by turning away when she knew he was watching her. The beauty of her, the fairness of that skin, which seemed to take a glow from the rich red hair that crowned her, the slender line of her limbs in the jodhpurs, the firm breasts moving under the wind-pressed silk of her blouse as she leaned forward in the saddle, the green eyes that met his only momentarily, yet betrayed her awareness of him—he held each detail of her, fuel to the flame of his desire. If on that night he had acted more swiftly when he had called to her by the open window, he might have gained his purpose, but for the first time in his life he felt uncertainty. It was one thing to make conquest of the women on the *estancia*, he played a sure hand there. It was another thing to take this young Englishwoman, of another class, another world. Intoxicated with the unusual beauty of her, he had lost his assurance. He should have said nothing, have stepped in from the patio. Well, there would be another occasion. He felt her interest in him. He must be patient.

Almost a week had passed when, stacking fodder in the large stable, he saw her come in and go towards the saddle-room, papers in her hand. He swiftly moved across the stable. He was half-naked and perspiring from his labour, a white kerchief bound round his brow as a sweatbreak. In his soft rope-slippers he gained the door of the saddle-room. By the fading light of the afternoon he saw she was writing in chalk on the order board, consulting the papers in the other hand. For a moment he watched her, unseen. She was hatless, in a tight brown tweed skirt that moulded her waist and slender hips. Then swiftly, noiselessly, he went and stood in the doorway. She had not heard him. In silence he waited.

The writing finished, she turned and saw him, smiling, with naked torso, bound brow, his thumbs hooked in each pocket of his baggy *bombachos*. He made a splendid figure of masculine virility, poised, a smile on his handsome dark face. She looked at him for a long moment.

"Yes?" she asked, in a controlled voice, her hand putting down the piece of chalk with which she had been writing the order.

"Is there anything you want, *señorita*?" he asked in his low voice, taking one hand out of a pocket, and leaning on the doorpost.

Amelia observed the ripple of muscles as he raised his arm, the bronze torso with its square pectorals, the flat smooth stomach. His brown shoulders shone with the sweat still on him.

"No, nothing," she said after a pause.

A bead of sweat ran from his brow down his cheek, halted on the strong jaw, and fell on his chest. Somewhere behind her mind ran a remembered line—*and there where your heart is, leave a little spot of rain, limpid, pearly* . . .

They stood looking at each other. It was a fraction of time but in its deep consciousness it seemed immeasurable. His eyes drank in the beauty of the delicate woman before him, the incredible milky rose-flushed skin, the exquisite mouth and throat, the channel of the breasts, the aureole of red hair, its fire contrasting with the cool translucent green of her eyes. He looked at her, carried almost beyond physical desire to a nameless wonder. It was perhaps this adoration that she found in his intense dark eyes, for something dissolved her anger and fear. The rhythm of his youthful body, as his hand had moved to rest on the door frame, had the transcendency of poetry, visible in the warm hue of his flesh. The moment was pregnant with the sensuous power emanating from him.

She withdrew her eyes from his, and found words to break the spell of silence.

"Nothing, thank you, Juan," she repeated, and moved towards the door.

He hesitated. For a moment it seemed as if he intended to block her way. She stepped firmly forward, ignoring him. He swung aside, his strong hand still resting on the doorpost. Suddenly, as she came near him, he slipped to his knees. Stopping her, he seized her hand, crying, "*Señorita*, you are beautiful, beautiful!" and, holding it between his own, covered it with passionate kisses.

She looked down on the smooth dark head, the golden shoulders above the groove of his muscular back, and catching her breath disengaged her hand from his impassioned grasp. His upturned face and quivering mouth turned her anger. It was a child kneeling there.

"Stand up, Juan—and don't be so—foolish!" she cried. The word 'impertinent' had been on her lips but she changed it.

He found his feet. Without a word or a glance Amelia walked on out of the shed, expressing a cool self-possession that was but a thin façade to the tumult within her.

She gained her office, shut the door and sat at her desk, motionless. Her heart was still hammering. She leaned back and closed her eyes. His sheer male beauty was still about her, an instrument of passion beyond compare. The power was physical, wholly an expression of nature which sought to perpetuate itself. She was aware of this, and angry with herself in this awareness. She felt guilty because of the mildness of her reproach. A *peon*, an employee on the estate, it had been an act of arrogance. She should have left him in no doubt of her resentment. She had failed to maintain her position. The cause of her failure had not to be sought.

How fortunate it was that they were moving to Buenos Aires! She could not have stayed here now, despite many attractions. The winter, with its shorter days and longer nights, its absence of guests bringing movement from the larger world, would have preyed upon her. She had hesitated in her decision to leave because of inconveniencing Sir Anthony, and the thought of not being with him troubled her. A feeling of attachment had grown in her. She never ceased to take delight in his strong though odd personality. He cast a spell of distinction on everything he did. He was handsome to the eye, and inspiring to the mind. The aristocratic quality that marked him in every mood and action invoked something akin to hero-worship in her. There was also his mysterious aloofness in some matters, the sense of steel under his amiable, smooth character. It enabled her to comprehend those courtly Spanish conquistadors whose fine civilisation was accompanied by such relentless passion in the quest of their fortunes.

It was hard to reconcile Sir Anthony's delicate comprehension, his response to all that was honourable and just, with that sealed phase of his past. Had there been no mercy for the erring woman, whom he had loved deeply? His rejection of her, his adamant silence through all the years, his inhuman indifference to the child of their loins, suggested a cruelty foreign to his nature. Doña Lucia had once remarked "You will never quite know our Don Antonio. After forty years of friendship I am still in the outer corral."

As Amelia sat there, waiting for the turbulence evoked by Juan's behaviour in the stable to subside, she found herself thinking about the dead woman who had once reigned as mistress at Tabara. What had been the nature of her temptation? What kind of a man had been that gentleman-gaucho? Another Juan, one of Nature's highly endowed lechers, a transatlantic Casanova who had poisoned the air of this Eden?

The telephone ringing broke her speculation. It was Sir Anthony.

"There's been a murder at El Quintero," he said.

"A murder!"

"Yes—the usual thing, a knife fight of two of our gauchos over a girl. The police are there, an awful commotion. Carson and I are riding over at once. Don't wait dinner for me."

El Quintero was a settlement six miles up the *estancia*. Well, it was not Juan who was involved, though his reputed adventures might have induced a dozen fights. She was glad it was not him. She would not like him to end, murdered, or as a murderer. There was an odd gentleness in his audacious masculinity. He could play a guitar, as well as tame a bronco.

II

Sir Anthony was back in time for dinner. He found his doctor had called and was waiting to see him.

"Now, you're not to scold me! You'll find I'm perfectly all right!" he said, as soon as he entered the house. "Miss Macreary will tell you I am eating and sleeping well, and taking things easy."

"Do you call riding six miles and back to a murder taking things easy?" asked Dr. Garcia. "I forbade you rides of more than half an hour."

"This is an exceptional circumstance. We don't have a murder every day," said Sir Anthony, gaily, filling his doctor's glass with a Mendoza wine, as they sat down to dinner.

"What happened—have they got the murderer?" asked Amelia.

"I libelled our gauchos, my dear. It was an affair *à la*

163

Pagliacci. One of our Sicilian workers was having an affair with the wife of another Sicilian. The enraged husband attacked the lover. They had a knife duel. The husband was killed but the other man was so badly wounded that he died soon after the police arrived. So it solved itself. You see, you don't have to go to the Opera Colón to get Italian drama! We have all the actors on the estate. When I was a youth there was a drama here that surpassed anything that has ever happened since. My father brought over some Hungarians from the Puszta to work as herdsmen. They are the finest horse-men alive. We have the breed here still but most of them have turned to farming instead of ranching. Well, it seemed that two of the youths quarrelled over a *peon* mistress, and they settled it in the Puszta fashion. They rode out on to the pampa, naked to the waist on their horses, and began a duel with twenty-feet long leather whips with which they were expert. A frightened *peon* saw them flaying one another alive, until one of them fell from his horse unconscious. The other fellow rode over and over him until there was nothing left but a pulp! Then he made off, all bloody, to the hut where the girl was. He picked her up and disappeared in the direction of the Andes. There was nothing seen or heard of him again. The telegraph in those days didn't run beyond Mendoza. Thank God, we've very little crime to contend with these days. The pampa has been civilised. There are plenty of love affairs if you can call these animal matings by that name—you know that well enough, doctor! Women have a pretty low rating among the gauchos. As in many Latin countries, where the family is the unit, the grandmother is enthroned as the matriarch, while the daughters are expendable in the conservation of the family's wealth. Outside of this, every man has his mistress in his *gar-connière* round the corner. Our little Father Martinez, who comes here, must have pretty tough ears from all he hears in the confessional! Only very occasionally do the affairs run to violence as at El Quintero today, and then it's mostly in the foreign element. As you know, my dear doctor, we've Don Juans on the *estancia* but we look the other way."

The servants changed the plates for the next course.

"I hope my little story hasn't put you off the cook's excellent Hungarian goulash," said Sir Anthony, smiling at them.

CHAPTER TWELVE

I

THE winter in Buenos Aires was very gay. There were theatres, operas, balls, cinemas and dinner parties. The Domecq house in the fashionable Barrio Norte district was ideal for entertaining. It had a small ballroom, four magnificently decorated reception rooms and was well staffed by some of the Domecq servants left behind, as well as by those brought from Tabara.

The doctor's orders that Sir Anthony should lead a quiet life were wholly defied. He entertained constantly, he went everywhere. Amelia found herself working harder than in Tabara for she now became something of a social secretary. Sir Anthony would not let her leave his side, with the result that she saw very little of her own apartment. In the midst of so much social activity her own circle of acquaintances grew. She had three constant attendants, young James Fayne, young Richard Cordell who seemed to divide his time between his *estancia* and his aunt's town house, and lastly, still in a state of calf love, young Emile Daudet, a constant bearer of flowers and a willing equerry for all messages or small errands she requested. She had made a new friend, Mitzi Tamare, the bright little Austrian wife of a young Argentine lawyer. They were frequently guests in the house. Amelia saw here a chance to pursue her passion for languages. She now sought to add German to her Spanish and French. She was aware that by some inexplicable quirk of heredity she was a born linguist. It was very odd, considering that there was not a drop of foreign blood in her veins and that she had had to make her escape from a frightful native accent. In Mitzi Tamare she found a ready tutor. Within three months they were reading the poems of Heine together; and at last, largely to please Doña Lucia and Sir Anthony, Amelia took bridge lessons. Alas, unlike her foreign languages, she had little card sense. Her progress was slow and fatiguing, but little by little she became a modest player.

Once a month she wrote a long letter recording her activities to her mother in Glasgow, but in these she made no mention of cards. In the Macreary household they were regarded as the weapons of the devil. There was not a pack in the house. The report that she had learned French had not been regarded favourably at Abernethy Villas. French was the language spoken in Paris, and Paris was the haunt of wickedness.

How far away that house in Glasgow now seemed! Far more than the eight thousand miles on the map, far more than the year 1934; it belonged to another age, almost another planet. And yet, at odd moments her mind travelled back to the deserted home, and in the back kitchen she saw her father in his stockinged feet, warming his toes on the steel fender. How it had irritated her once; now, how it evoked a tenderness towards the recalcitrant culprit who refused to be 'refined', as he put it, when meeting her remonstrances. Sometimes to her face her new friends called her 'the bonnie Scots lassie'. She now accepted the compliment. And something she began to realise brought sadness to her thoughts. She knew now that she could never go back home. To visit it, yes. To stay there, no. She had entered another world, with its social graces, its international atmosphere, its widened outlook, its movement, colour and wealth. She moved easily in places and among people that no longer made her apprehensive. Her enjoyment was without restraint. She recalled how her first sight of Sir Anthony on the boat, aloof, aristocratic, had impressed her. He still impressed her, but in place of awe she felt affection and gratitude.

He treated her with the same high courtesy as that shown to the proudest of the *señoras* in the best society of Buenos Aires. She felt she had his confidence, except in that phase of his life to which he never alluded.

Perversely, it was this silence that worried her. It expressed a contradiction in his nature that obsessed her mind. Did he never think of the son, the heir to the baronetcy, somewhere in Austria according to Doña Lucia. He must now be a man of about forty-four. Had there been no communication between father and son? None, said Doña Lucia. After the death of Carmen Slowdon and the Great War, even the tenuous links between Carmen's relations had been broken. The Debrett she had found at Tabara was an old one, dated 1920. It recorded Roderick's birth in 1892, and the death of Lady Slowdon in 1914. At the British Consulate, in whose library she had consulted a later Debrett, dated 1934, there was no addition to the record.

Amelia made no further enquiries. If it had come to the notice of Sir Anthony that she was pursuing enquiries her position might be jeopardized.

"Leave it alone. After all it's none of our business," warned Doña Lucia. "Not even I have dared to ask him anything about Roderick. It's touching dynamite."

One thing was very clear. Sir Anthony refused to recognise Roderick as his son. "It's a mad obsession. But for that he might have married again," said Doña Lucia.

"Might have married again?" repeated Amelia. "I don't understand—why shouldn't Sir Anthony have married again after his wife's death? He was only fifty when she died."

"I believe he did not marry because he knew that any son he might have by a second marriage could not succeed to the baronetcy while Roderick lived. That is not only my guess but my husband's," said Doña Lucia. "You may think that our Don Antonio's a vindictive old man. We both know he's not.

He's a most sensitive, considerate man—but on this one question of poor Carmen's infatuation and Roderick's legitimacy he is quite mad!"

"That bears out what my father always says," commented Amelia. "There's a screw loose in every brain. It explains two things, genius and madness, and some folks say they're the same thing."

They had come to the last month of their tenancy of the Domecq house. Every week of their sojourn in Buenos Aires had been enchanted, and now before them loomed the delights of spring at Tabara, and the intoxication of the pampa. They would ride their beloved horses again over the lush prairie grass, there would be that pervading cow-music, the lowing of cattle in movement, there would be the *domadas*, and on warm summer nights those alfresco feasts in the meadows, the *asadas*, when a whole ox was roasted and gauchos played their guitars. There would be the glorious wide-winged sunsets. There would be Juan again with his feline movement, his proud seat in the saddle, his folksongs to the guitar. She could think of him now without apprehension. She had a firm control of herself again.

Throughout the winter months young Richard Cordell had come in from his *estancia* on many occasions. He was quiet in speech and manner, a man of strong character, with much enterprise in directing on the most modern lines the vast *estancia* owned by the Cordell family. His father was crippled with arthritis and lived mostly in Buenos Aires now. Oddly, he was a fine Italian scholar and spent his time making a new translation of Dante's *Comedia*. He had another hobby. In a large book he had kept a record of how long, in spring, summer, autumn and winter, it took the sun to touch the rim of the horizon through six inches of space measured on the western window of his study in both homes. This he checked with a sunset time-table. He had carried on a long correspondence with Greenwich Observatory and the American one on Mt. Wilson. "My old man's fallen in love with you!" said Richard Cordell one evening as they were dancing. "But he's not an original in that—everybody does!" He looked down at her and danced a few steps before adding quietly—"Including me!"

She smiled up at him. "You're very sweet," she said. "At first I was rather afraid of you!"

"Afraid of me—why?"

"Oh—strong, silent man—you know!" she replied, mischievously.

He gave her a little hug, but said nothing.

That night when he drove her back to the Domecq house he did not get out to open the door for her. He switched off the engine and sat in the car. He held her hand as she thanked him for the pleasant evening, then, releasing it, he lifted the white fur that had slipped from her shoulders. The light of the street lamp fell on her face and he had a fresh vision of the beauty of her, the white skin, the aureole of her red hair, the green eyes under the sweeping lashes, and the perfect throat bound by a necklace of brilliants. As his hand left her shoulder it came down to her own, holding a purse in her lap, and gently covered it.

He looked at her, steadily, and then in a low voice said—"I have never kissed you. May I?"

It was so shyly said that the words seemed to be wrapped round with silence. She turned her face to his, making no reply but he found assent in her smile. He bent forward, their lips met, then slowly, gently, they withdrew from each other. After a silence he half-turned and sought for her hands. Holding them in his own, he said, very quietly.

"The strong silent man wants to break silence a little. Amelia, you don't know me yet but I'll chance my luck. I love you. Could you think of marrying me? The assets aren't much, I know!"

He tried to laugh but his eyes resisted the attempt. He held her hands and became silent.

Amelia looked at him closely, and smiled.

"Richard, you don't know me! But it's very dear of you. I'm rather bewildered. Doesn't one say 'This is so sudden!'—something hackneyed like that? But it is a surprise, and I can't make you any answer yet."

"I'll wait. I know I've rushed the fence. Think it over. Tell me as soon as you can if it's 'yes' or 'no'."

He raised her hand and kissed it. Then, after a pause, got out of the car, opened the door and escorted her to the house. When the butler came they shook hands formally.

"Good-night, Amelia."

"Good-night, Richard," she said. "Thank you!"

The door closed. Amelia ascended the wide staircase with the ornate gilt-iron balustrade.

In her own room, she switched on the lights. The maid had drawn the rose-silk curtains, turned down the bed and put on it her white nightdress. Pink and white slippers stood by the *fauteuil*.

She threw her fur down on the bed and went over to the wide glass-topped dressing-table with its gilt side-mirrors. She sat on the low stool before this Empire table and looked at herself in the large mirror flanked by rose-shaded candles. She noticed in that soft light how red was her hair, how white her throat and bosom. She put a thin hand to her face and pushed back a strayed curl.

Well, here she was. For a second time a man had offered her marriage. What different men they were! Etienne, debonair, polished, light as thistledown, so that his courtship seemed a wind-tossed thing, a game that, lost or won, could carry no hurt. And now Richard Cordell, serious and a little ponderous, given to silences and slow speech but very admirable, a rock compared with a floating buoy. Duller? Yes, duller, but as a travelling companion more durable.

And then it occurred to her that this was not how one considered a proposal from a man who loved. Here she was again, attracted, flattered, moved, but not overwhelmed, not really in love as she imagined being in love should be. Oh dear, oh dear.

She pushed back her hair a little wearily, took off her necklace, looked at herself critically. What was the matter with her? Richard Cordell was well-bred, good-looking, affluent. She could not imagine a nicer man. And Etienne, with looks, position, volatile but interesting always, had offered her so much. Her luck could not run forever, and, for a woman, time was a weighty factor. The fading rose went unpicked.

She shook her head at herself in the mirror. Without red hair, green eyes, a rose-leaf complexion, where would Amelia Macreary be? Here, possibly, at her typewriter, and always at her typewriter. So far she had been incredibly lucky, falling in with Tabara, and its wonderful life. But Sir Anthony would not live for ever. Then the typewriter and some Señor Diaz again. What a prospect!

She got up and prepared for bed. In bed that consideration went on. No, she was not in love with Richard. She was not in love as, so easily, insanely, she could be with that *peon*, the guitar-player, Juan. If he were not a *peon*, if—but he was a *peon*, he was married, with two children and probably more. He was a rake, a no-good! Preposterous! It didn't make sense to be ready to throw oneself away for a mere body, for muscles in a silky brown skin, a panther in the prairie grass!

She turned out the light. She turned on the light. She changed over the pillow to make it cooler to her cheek. But she was still hot and restless. She got out of bed, took off her night-

dress and slipped naked between the sheets seeking coolness.
Richard–Etienne–Juan. Juan–Etienne–Richard.

It was past two o'clock when she fell asleep.

I I I

The next morning she went out with Sir Anthony to a gun-
shop and afterwards to Harrods, where she helped him to select
a wedding present for a young couple he knew. They drove
about in his very ancient barouche which he had brought up
from Tabara. It had bright yellow wheels and was lined with
a plum-coloured velvet-buttoned corduroy. With its pair of
horses wearing crested gilt bridles, and the coachman attired
in a yellow-faced livery on the box, it was the smartest turnout
seen along the *avenidas* and drew all eyes.

The morning was sunny but sharp. They had a black vicuna
rug over their knees. Sir Anthony wore a tightly buttoned-up
overcoat, a brown Derby, and brown gloves. Amelia wore a
light green skirt and coat. It matched her eyes. She liked
driving with Sir Anthony, but often protested for it held up
her work in the little office she had created in the small room
overlooking the garden. More and more work, connected with
the *estancia*, came into her hands. She was bringing order into
the administration at last. In consultation with Mr. Carson she
had effected some economies. When she reported these to Sir
Anthony he always said, "Splendid, splendid, my dear! What
should I do without you!" but she noticed that he never really
observed what these economies were. "Yes, yes," he would
say, as she turned over the sheets explaining the details. "I am
sure Carson approves. All my life he has been the bogieman
threatening me with bankruptcy!" When Amelia consulted
Mr. Carson he, too, would not seem very impressed, and would
say "Yes, very good, I quite agree." One day when she was
really proud of a considerable saving she had made on the

domestic side, by cutting down the outrageous food bills at Tabara—clearly several families were being fed from the back door—Mr. Carson said, a little satirically, "You know, Miss Macreary, anything you save will only encourage Don Antonio to purchase something quite useless. Don't let him know there's anything in hand. He was offered a horse out of the Zuloago stables the other day—thirty thousand dollars, a wonderful pedigree, it's true—but the very idea, thirty thousand dollars, and in the red at the bank!"

How much they were 'in the red' at the bank had come to Amelia's notice only two days later. There a rather ominous note with the quarterly account, asking whether Sir Anthony could see his way to reduce the overdraft. It stood at two hundred and twenty thousand dollars, on which he was paying seven per cent. Despite this he had rented the Domecq house for five months for five thousand dollars. Amelia was staggered by the entertaining bills. Just now, in Harrods, he had spent two hundred dollars on a wedding present. "Put it on the account," he said. Amelia made a note to look at that account. She had overlooked it in her last monthly survey.

"Don't you think we ought to employ a good firm of accountants?" said Amelia to Mr. Carson. "You can suggest it, my dear Miss Macreary—he'll tell you what he told me when I suggested it. 'Accountants are prophets of doom, they make me miserable. We've a good lawyer, it's his business!' he said. And that was the end of the suggestion."

"But it isn't the lawyer's business!" said Amelia.

"Well, where would you begin? The estate accounts are in pretty good order—it's Sir Anthony who cracks them. If you can get him in order, I'd be much relieved."

She knew now she could not get Sir Anthony in order. The habits of a lifetime were too ingrown. Last New Year's Day he had given her a present of a thousand dollars. She had protested. It was one quarter of her yearly salary. "You're badly paid, my dear. Let me ease my conscience," he had replied.

"Wedding presents are an awful business," said Sir Anthony, ruminating on his purchase at Harrods. "That alarm clock we've bought. They'll probably have twenty alarm clocks. So I've told them on my card to trade it in if they wish."

He gave a little laugh and then, looking sharply at Amelia, said, "You're rather pale. Were you out late last night?"

"Not very late—but I am rather tired," Amelia replied.

"Then we'll go home. I've only one more call," he said. Raising his ebony stick he poked the coachman gently in the back.

"Drive to Lederer's!"

"Si, señor!"

Lederer's was a shop for electric things. When they drew up Sir Anthony tried to rise. He could not. He sank back on the seat, a spasm of pain crossing his face.

"Cramp!" he said, as Amelia turned to him, alarmed. "There's a little packet for me in the shop—will you get it for me, my dear?"

She left him, the groom watchful, and went into the shop.

"I've called for a parcel for Sir Anthony Slowdon," said Amelia to the assistant.

"Yes, señora. I believe they are ready," replied the assistant. He walked away down the shop.

What are 'they' thought Amelia.

The assistant returned with something in his hand.

"Yes, señora, here they are," he said, reaching for a piece of wrapping paper. 'They' were a pair of electric curling irons, very compact, that had been repaired.

"How much?" she asked, taking the parcel.

"Fifty pesos, please."

She paid the assistant, repressing a smile. The delightful vanity of Sir Anthony! 'They' explained the beautifully curled beard and moustache that added so much to his seig-neurial air.

The opening of her handbag to take out a purse gave her a slight shock. In it reposed a stamped letter she carried for mailing.

When she emerged from the shop to rejoin Sir Anthony it seemed as if Fate abetted her intention. There was a mail box in the wall by the entrance. She stopped, opened her bag and took out the addressed letter. As it fell in the box her heart thumped. She had made the decision and dared Fate. The letter was addressed to Richard Cordell. It told him that, deeply appreciative and touched by his offer of marriage, she felt that she must decline the honour. But she hoped their friendship would continue.

She crossed the pavement to the carriage in a kind of trance. She heard Sir Anthony thank her for the parcel, and the carriage move on.

"Now home. You look very tired, my dear. You must rest—and no more late nights."

She tried to smile but what he saw in her face made him wonder. He also saw her hand tremble as it pulled over her knees the vicuna rug. What could have upset her so, she was always so tranquil, he wondered.

CHAPTER THIRTEEN

I

THEY had begun the last month of their tenancy of the Domecq house when the household was thrown into a state of alarm. One evening soon after dinner, when the ladies had gone into the drawing-room, as he was selecting a cigar, Sir Anthony collapsed. They picked him up from the floor and carried him to his bedroom where he lay insensible. A terrible half-hour passed before the doctor could be reached. When he came out of the bedroom, with Pepe and Carlos in attendance, Amelia knew at once that he had grave news.

"It's a coronary thrombosis. I must get in a colleague and a nurse. Meanwhile, he must not be left," he said. "May I use the telephone?"

"It isn't fatal, doctor?" asked Amelia, standing with their dinner guests.

The doctor raised his hands, but made no reply.

"I will go and sit with him," she said, excusing herself to the startled guests. She gave orders for Doña Lucia to be informed, and also Mr. Carson at Tabara.

She relieved the housekeeper in the bedroom, and sat by Sir Anthony, who was breathing audibly. Presently the doctor joined her.

"I don't think we should move him to hospital yet—my colleague will be here in a few minutes," said the doctor.

They quietly discussed Sir Anthony who was still unconscious.

"I am not very surprised, he would not heed my repeated warnings," said the doctor. "I was dismayed when he came here for the season. But you know how intractable Don Antonio can be."

Within half an hour the colleague arrived. Amelia left the room and found Doña Lucia had just entered the hall. Amelia informed her of what had happened. They went upstairs together to await the verdict of the doctors.

Sir Anthony recovered consciousness the next morning. He also seemed to recover something of his old spirit. He absolutely refused to be moved to a nursing home. He hated nursing homes. The doctor was in despair. Day and night nurses were engaged. His speech was a little difficult, but his mind appeared to have lost none of its acuteness. "I believe you think I'm dying," he said to the day nurse. "You'll say 'No', of course —they train you to say 'No' in any event."

On the fifth day he told Carson he wanted to see the British Consul-General. In vain Carson remonstrated. He was in no fit state to conduct business.

"You are not suggesting my mind's impaired?" he asked Carson sharply.

"Not for a moment—but you were to be kept quiet."

"Tell the Consul-General I want to see him. You needn't inform the doctor."

That evening Sir Anthony took a violent dislike to the day nurse. "I don't like her lower lip, she's a sourpuss. Send her away!" he cried.

"But the doctor——" began Amelia.

"I don't care whether she's the doctor's fiancée or mistress, send her away! I want you to stay with me."

The doctor, consulted, withdrew the nurse. Amelia took on her duties. "Quiet, keep him quiet—that's all that matters," he said.

The next day Sir Anthony seemed much better. In the afternoon the Consul-General came to see him. They were closeted together for about half an hour. As soon as Amelia had entered the room, after his departure, he asked her to sit down at the side of the bed.

"Tell me, my dear, have you a birth certificate?" he asked. "I mean, here, with you."

She looked at him in surprise. "Well, yes," she answered after a pause. "I keep it with my passport and my insurance policy."

"I've always known you were a sensible girl!" exclaimed Sir Anthony. "Sit down and give me your hand."

She put her hand on the bedcover. He took it in his, ungloved, veined these days.

"It is very unlikely I shall last long—I don't want to live on in this condition. I want to thank you for all your help and devotion. You have made this last year one of the happiest of my life. I am now going to make a request of you. When I die there will be death duties on my estate. It's already much encumbered, as you know, but there should be a fairly large residue. If I had a wife she would automatically, under our laws, receive one half of my residuary estate, no matter what heirs might appear. It is because of this that I am going to make a request to you, which I hope you will grant me. The fact is, my dear child, I want to marry you."

He looked at her kindly, a pressure on her hand in his own frail one. Before she could recover from the shock and find any words, he continued to speak.

"It cannot be for very long. It would also give me great pleasure. I have an unbounded admiration for your character. Well, my dear?"

His eyes rested on hers. He saw how shaken she was, and how speechless. He waited, holding her hand, a faint smile on his face.

"But Sir Anthony—it's—oh, I am quite bewildered! I—I —Oh, I must have time to think, please!" she cried.

"My dear, there's very little time. And the more you think the more bewildered you will be. And then, myself, I can't face any prolonged uncertainty," he said, gravely. "I want your assent now."

"But what will everybody think? What will they say?" exclaimed Amelia.

"What they will say I shall be beyond caring. I have never cared about what they say. And you, I know, have character enough to sustain your own actions. Amelia, I must not talk too long. Tell me now that you agree."

She looked down. With her free hand she covered her face. There was absolute silence for a few moments, then very softly, taking her hand from her face, she said, "Very well, I will marry you."

He smoothed the hand beneath his own, and spoke to her. "It's all very simple. The Consul-General will expedite matters and marry us, here—though I could wish it was at Tabara."

As he spoke he saw she had begun to cry quietly.

"Don't cry, my dear. You have made me happy," he said. "Bless you. Will you ask Carson to come to me."

She stood up, then, stooping, she touched his brow with her lips. A tear fell on his cheek. He smiled, lightly caressed her hair, and followed her with his eyes until the door closed.

Stunned, she sat in her room, deeply agitated. A hundred fears assailed her. What would Doña Lucia think? There would be talk of her having snatched a dying old man. She remembered what friends had said when she was considering going to work at Tabara. 'Perhaps the old boy will leave you something. He can't live for ever.' 'It wouldn't be the first time nursey-nursey's swallowed the lot.' It was horrible to think how they would gossip and leer. She didn't want Sir Anthony to die, she didn't want his money. A little legacy perhaps. But Tabara, or only part of it? The thought was frightening.

After a time, more composed, she decided to see Doña Lucia. She had complete faith in Sir Anthony's oldest friend. She took up the telephone and to her great relief Doña Lucia answered at once.

"Something's happened, something very important. Can I see you, please, now? Can I come to you!" asked Amelia.

"Certainly, come along at once. I'll give you tea," replied Doña Lucia.

How calm, how reliable the old lady was! She was the only person in Buenos Aires to whom she could talk freely, whose advice she would not hesitate to accept.

In half an hour she was shown into Doña Lucia's drawing-room. Her friend rose to greet her, took her by the hand and made her sit down by her. She saw at once that Amelia was greatly agitated. The tea tray was before her. She poured out the tea, and handed a cup to Amelia.

"Now, what has happened?" she asked, smiling.

Amelia told her, her sentences disjointed in her emotion.

"Although I've told him I would, I can't, can I? Everyone would call me an adventuress!"

"Not everyone. I shouldn't," replied Doña Lucia, very calmly. "You told Anthony you would marry him?"

"Yes. It was so extraordinary, so overwhelming, he almost compelled me!"

"Have you considered the effect on him if you were to tell him you won't marry him?"

"But Doña Lucia—what is my position?"

"Your position, my dear, is excellent—you can give our poor Anthony a little happiness in the last few weeks or more of life. The doctor has very little hope."

Amelia twisted the handkerchief in her hands.

"There's something else," she said. "There's his son Roderick, I should be stealing Tabara from him."

"It's not as simple as that."

"Simple?" queried Amelia.

"We none of us know whether Roderick is alive. No one has heard anything since his mother died, over twenty years ago. Anthony has no intention of letting him inherit more than he can help. On the subject of Roderick we must recognise Anthony is not a sane man. He is mad and vindictive to the very end, I am sorry to say. If you marry him you might be in a position to make some retribution."

"Retribution? How? I don't understand!" exclaimed Amelia.

Doña Lucia put down her cup, and looked steadily at the anxious young face before her.

"I've a confession to make, my dear. I knew about Anthony's proposal before you. He told me what he had in mind almost a week ago."

"You knew!" cried Amelia, wide-eyed in astonishment.

"I knew and I agreed to his plan," replied Doña Lucia. "It is very clear to me that he wishes to pursue his insane resentment against Carmen and Roderick to the very last. Owing to our laws he cannot disinherit Roderick, as he would like to, but he can halve his inheritance by marrying you, since by law you would be entitled to half of the estate. That is what Anthony has in his mind. It's ridiculous, but on the subject of his son he's been ridiculous for over thirty-five years. We cannot change him. You can, of course, decline to marry him and that would defeat his purpose. This would, of course, give him great distress, moreover, I cannot see why you should penalise yourself. I don't know how large his estate will be when it is all wound up but there must be quite a sum involved. He has made legacies, I know, to Mr. Carson who has managed his affairs for so long, and to some others who deserve to be remembered. As you must be aware, with this one exception concerning Roderick, he is a generous-minded and in many ways a most lovable man. Now, if your conscience troubles you in this matter, you could, if you wished, give to Roderick as much of your inheritance as you thought proper, but I don't think you should be quixotic. We are assuming, of course, that Roderick is alive, somewhere. You have it in your power to make Anthony happy in his last days. I really feel, my dear, that you should keep your promise to marry him. I know his mind is set on this."

Amelia was silent for some time, while Doña Lucia watched the anxious young face.

"I find what you say rather perturbing—I know now the motive behind Sir Anthony's proposal," said Amelia. "It's not very flattering to me, is it?"

"Let us be fair to Anthony. The motive certainly exists. On the other hand I know he has a very great admiration for you. I think you should do this for him. And, my dear child, without seeming too worldly, it does give you a position!"

"Very well, I will keep my promise. But what a strange thing to happen to me!" exclaimed Amelia. "I used to laugh at my father who was so fond of saying 'Position in life is everything' though I never knew quite what he meant!"

"Not everything, but a very great deal. It's a very strange world, my dear. I long ago ceased to be surprised by anything!" observed Doña Lucia.

I I

The marriage of Sir Anthony Slowdon to his young red-haired, green-eyed secretary was a brief sensation in Buenos Aires and among the *estancia* owners. The explanation was very simple. The silly old man, already on his death-bed, and not responsible for his actions, had been caught by an audacious young woman who had nothing but her figure, her red hair and green eyes as assets.

The ceremony was performed by the Consul-General in Sir

183

Anthony's bedroom. He was already sitting up. He began to talk of going to Tabara. In this he was opposed by his doctors. As usual he got his way. The journey was made in an ambulance car. He arrived at the *estancia* no worse for the journey. The Domecq house was released on the due date of the lease.

The life of Sir Anthony at Tabara was that of an invalid. The whole establishment was muted to conform with his delicate state. He was now allowed to sit up daily in his room. Here Amelia read to him. He saw Carson and a few of the overseers but it was really to humour him with a pretence of business rather than to transact it. And there was a daily performance that had a note of pathos. Aware that he might never ride again, he had his favourite horses paraded in the patio. Every morning at eleven o'clock he sat in a chair by his open bedroom window and looked down at his beloved animals slowly ridden or walked round the flagged courtyard. In charge of this cavalcade came Juan, solemn, soft-voiced and deferential. Sometimes Sir Anthony talked to him about the horses.

There was the warmth of spring in the air. The birds were nesting, even the little daylight owls that sat on the wire fences in pairs, calm observers of the life around them, were amorous. One warm night, at Sir Anthony's request, he had Juan play his guitar and sing. He asked for the old *estancia* songs, *Adios, Pampa Mia*, and other favourites. He heard them, sitting at the window while Juan took up his favourite place under the eucalyptus tree. When he had finished singing he came on to the patio, dark and graceful as ever. They thanked him. He looked up, smiling and bowing. Then, calling *Buenos noches, Señor Don! Buenos noches, Señora Doña!* he withdrew noiselessly into the darkness.

There were no guests, no week-end parties. A lawyer came often to transact business. Doña Lucia came and sat with Don Antonio in his room. He walked a little now, on her arm, or on Amelia's or on the nurse's. He was as sharp as ever with Carlos about his clothes, his shoes. He wore gloves again. His Buenos Aires doctor visited him weekly, and conferred over their patient with Dr. Garcia.

"Look! I've had enough of this! Tomorrow I'm going downstairs! Do you realise I've been up here in this damn room for over a month?" he said, while the specialist held his stethoscope over his heart. "Is it going on—or stopping?" he demanded, irritably.

The doctor smiled at Amelia and the nurse. "Don Antonio has no gratitude to us for keeping him alive," he said. Then turning to Sir Anthony, "Perhaps in another week we will let you go downstairs."

"Another week! My dear doctor, I'd sooner be dead than be trussed up like this. I expected to be gone a month ago."

"You are a very ungrateful man, Don Antonio. Here's Lady Slowdon, your nurse, Dr. Garcia, and myself all doing our best to get you into the corral again—and you bellow at us! One week more and then you can go downstairs."

When they had left Don Antonio, the doctors conferred. Then they went to the manager's office. Mr. Carson was in.

"Well?" he asked.

Dr. Guzman shook his head. "This, very confidentially. We don't think he can last more than a week. The heart has deteriorated badly."

Carson made no reply. He stood, and made a circle with the end of a ruler. Then he looked at them.

"A week? You mean there's no hope—he'll never be able to ride round the *estancia* again?"

"Never."

"Do you think he knows?"

"Yes," said Dr. Guzman. "I think he knew since that accident in his bath. He's put up a wonderful façade."

"I've known Don Antonio for almost forty years," said

Carson slowly, setting down the ruler. "All that time he's put up a wonderful façade. No one's ever got behind it."

Two days later, in the morning at half-past seven, Amelia, who slept in a room adjoining Sir Anthony's, was awakened by a tapping on the door. She rose, put on a dressing-gown, and opened the door. Carlos stood there, very agitated.

"*Señora*, Don Antonio's missing!"

"Missing!" echoed Amelia.

"He's not in his bedroom. He's not in the bathroom! He didn't call me at half-past six, as he always does. I waited until a quarter-past seven. Then I went to his room, rather worried. He's not there!"

"We'll look together—come in," said Amelia. She opened the communicating door and stepped into Sir Anthony's room. The blinds were still down. The bed had been slept in. The room was empty. Sir Anthony was not in the adjoining bathroom.

They stared at each other in bewilderment.

"Call Pepe, call all the servants," commanded Amelia. "We must search the whole house."

For half an hour the house was searched, upstairs, downstairs, in the two great wings. There was no sign of Sir Anthony.

"Do you think he's gone to the stables? Call Juan, have them searched. I must dress," said Amelia to the butler.

She dressed rapidly. As she went down Juan came into the hall. Don Antonio was nowhere in the stables. Distracted, Amelia sent for Mr. Carson. She could not touch the breakfast her maid had brought on a tray. In five minutes Mr. Carson came in. He spoke very calmly to her, and organised a thorough search. Three-quarters of an hour passed, then she saw the manager coming down the staircase, followed by Pepe.

He crossed to where Amelia stood before the large painting of an old gaucho chief in a great red poncho that Sir Anthony had commissioned from Bernaldo de Quirós, a famous folk painter.

"We have found him," said Carson.

Something in his face told her the worst.

"Dead?" she asked, in a whisper.

"Yes—seated in a chair."

"In a chair! Where?" asked Amelia.

"It is very singular. We found him in the old nursery, on the upper landing, which has been locked up for years. He must have had the key and gone along there. He was seated in an armchair by an old rocking-horse. He must have died, sitting there, he had slumped in it."

"The nursery was Roderick's room?"

"Yes."

They looked at each other. Neither said anything.

"Is he there now?" asked Amelia after a silence.

"No—we have taken him to his room."

"I'll go up," she said.

Carson followed her up the staircase.

Later, he took her aside. "I have something to tell you. We found this in his hand—he must have taken it out of a drawer that was open."

Carson took out of his pocket an old photograph. It was of a small boy, riding a pony, with a gaucho in attendance. The boy had a beautiful face, delicate in feature, fair.

"Roderick?" asked Amelia, as she stared at the yellowing photograph.

"Yes—round about 1900, I should think."

Amelia said nothing for some time, then very quietly asked a question.

"Do you think Sir Anthony was troubled in his mind at the end, about Roderick? There must have been something to make him get up and go along to that room. He had to go up a flight of stairs to get there?"

"Yes, I'm afraid that's what finished him. As for Roderick, you may be right. We shall never know, I fear. Do you realise the search now begins? Roderick's the third baronet."

"He's in Austria?"

"Doña Lucia thinks so—but no one seems to have heard of him since his mother's death during the Great War."

"And if Roderick's dead?"

"If he is—the baronetcy will go to a cousin, if there is one. There's one possibility we haven't taken into consideration. He might have married and have had children. If there was a boy, then he'd be in direct succession of the title. You see, it's an extraordinary situation. I wonder what the Will will tell us—Sir Anthony made a new one in Buenos Aires."

IV

In the month that followed, the swift passage of events left Amelia exhausted and bewildered. Happily Mr. Carson, for all his years, was a tower of strength. He was wise, calm, capable. No detail of the *estancia* escaped him.

Sir Anthony was buried in the Slowdon mausoleum, as he had wished. It was in the shape of a small Doric temple, of imported white marble. Amelia had seen it one day when out with him. It stood in a small Protestant cemetery next to the Catholic one, at the western extremity of the *estancia*, whose employees were buried there.

An old Anglo-Argentine firm of solicitors, Mayne, Gonzalos and Gomez, dealt with the Will. Amelia went to Buenos Aires after the funeral and saw them. A white-haired old gentleman,

Mr. Howard Mayne, received her in his office. She had met him when he had come to the Domecq house last winter. He might have stepped out of a lawyer's office in King's Bench Walk. He wore a black coat, pin-stripe trousers, a double-breasted waistcoat with a thin gold chain, and a small pearl pin in his grey tie. He had known Sir Anthony before his marriage. He read the Will to Amelia and Mr. Carson, whom she asked to go with her. The Will had many clauses. There was a long list of legacies to employees. Sir Anthony left Mr. Carson one hundred thousand dollars. Pepe and ten servants had legacies. Doña Lucia was remembered. Two remarkable facts emerged. There was not one relative, Amelia apart, mentioned in the Will. There was a legacy "to Juan Miguel Toloso, my stable overseer," a farm of five hundred acres, house, and all equipment *in situ* at El Miro. It was too early to give a firm estimate of Amelia's inheritance. There was a mortgage on Tabara, and a bank overdraft.

"Sir Anthony always lived up to the hilt, I fear," said the lawyer. "We were never successful in restraining him, as Mr. Carson will confirm. If Tabara is sold—we already have three offers for it—we estimate, after allowing for legacies and taxes, there should be an estate of about three hundred thousand dollars falling to you, Lady Slowdon, contingent on Roderick being alive and claiming; more, of course, if there are no heirs. Our estimates are provisional. To keep Tabara intact would be impossible, I fear, should you wish to retain it."

"No, I want it sold. I shall not live there. But I want Mr. Carson to have every consideration," said Amelia, turning from her lawyer to her manager.

"I have received that, Lady Slowdon. Sir Anthony knew that I wished to retire. He has been very generous," said Carson.

"There is one thing you have not mentioned, Mr. Mayne.

There is no legacy, no provision for Sir Anthony's son?" asked Amelia.

"None. Sir Anthony was adamant when I raised the point. As we all know, he had a conviction we could not shake. He was aware, of course, that under Argentine law, Roderick had an inalienable right to one half of his estate."

"Is my own inheritance unconditional and unencumbered?"

"Absolutely. It is freely at your disposition."

"Roderick or Sir Roderick as he now is—is there no clue of any kind as to where he is?" asked Amelia. "Surely there must be some trace of him?"

Mr. Mayne picked up a dossier and opened it.

"We have made several enquiries. We have written to the British Embassy in Vienna, and to the Editor of Debrett's *Peerage and Baronetage*. We have just had their replies. The Embassy say they have no trace of Roderick Slowdon. They lost many of their records in the 1914–18 War. The Editor of Debrett has made a singular revelation. On the 1900 edition proof-form Roderick was given as the heir to the baronetcy. On the 1901 form Roderick was struck out. Debrett's wrote to enquire the date of Roderick's death, and the name of the heir apparent. To this enquiry they received no reply. Nor were any subsequent proofs ever returned. They continued to give Roderick as the heir. The position is singular. We are now writing to the Lord Chamberlain's Office, and to the secretary of the Standing Council of the Baronetage, in London, in the hope that they may have a clue to Roderick. It may be we shall have to send someone to Austria, as the Will cannot be settled until we have satisfied ourselves regarding Roderick's existence or his death. What is quite extraordinary is that by some means Debrett, since 1920, has recorded the death of the first Lady Slowdon, in 1914. This, we knew, took place in Vienna in 1914. It is all very complicated and puzzling. However, you can rest assured, Lady Slowdon, that your rights are not in any way involved."

Back at Tabara, Amelia had another shock. Discussing the legacies, she said to Mr. Carson, "I suppose we can inform Juan about his farm?"

"The solicitors will do that, but there's no reason why he should not know now," agreed Carson.

There was a pause. They looked at each other.

"I expect you are surprised at the size of the legacy," said Mr. Carson. "It will set him up for life."

"Yes, it does seem rather generous—but Sir Anthony was very fond of Juan. He always had him near him."

"Yes."

"You say 'Yes' as if you were withholding something," said Amelia, watching Mr. Carson's face.

There was a silence again.

"Lady Slowdon, I see no reason why you should not know," said Mr. Carson, quietly. "Juan Toloso is Sir Anthony's son."

"What!" exclaimed Amelia. "But it's not possible! He's a *peon*!"

"Not wholly. Sir Anthony had an affair with a gaucho's daughter, on a small *estancia* in Santa Fé Province. It happened some years after his wife's flight. He told me about it one day. The mother had died, and the child had only an old hag of a grandmother. He brought the boy to Tabara, and placed him with a family, saying he was an orphan. I thought the whole proceeding very unwise—but Sir Anthony wanted it that way. The boy grew up here. As you've seen, there's something more than the *peon* in him."

"Yes—I've been puzzled by him—it explains so much, his manners, a show of arrogance at times," said Amelia. "Does he know?"

"I think not. There's been talk, doubtless. There will be more now when this legacy comes out."

"Will it go to his head?"

"I don't think so. He's as shrewd as he's—promiscuous!" answered Mr. Carson, with a smile. "If he has any inkling of his relationship to Sir Anthony, for whom he has a great loyalty, he certainly has not shown it. Arrogant yes, but never presuming."

"If you don't mind, I'd like you to tell him about the legacy. My position is rather fantastic—I suppose I'm a sort of step-mother to him!" said Amelia. "Altogether, I don't quite know where I am!"

For a considerable time Amelia was not quite sure where she was, or what she was. The Scots lassie, the adventurous typist who had projected herself out of Abernethy Villas three years ago had had her ambition fulfilled in the most astonishing manner. She was a baronet's widow, titled, with a fortune of some sixty thousand pounds. She could not quite realise this violent turn of the wheel of fortune. She envisaged the sensation in Abernethy Villas, in the gloomy office of her old employers. On informing her people of her marriage she had said, "When you write to me address the envelope to 'Lady Slowdon'." Even now when she saw her name on the envelopes she had to overcome a hesitancy in opening them, they seemed the property of someone else.

Two months passed. The enquiries about Roderick were still being pursued. They were without any definite news. The *estancia* had been sold but the transaction would not be completed for a year, and until then she retained the occupancy. The sale involved another shock. It was bought by a syndicate formed by Richard Cordell. He came over to visit her. He was as charming as ever but restrained. There was no allusion to her rejection of his proposal. Just before he left, the business concluded, she said to him, with a directness that surprised him, "I would like to say something, Richard. I must say it in justice to myself. Believe it or not, when you honoured me with your proposal there was nothing in my mind about marrying Sir Anthony. That developed afterwards, during his illness—at his urgent request. I respected him deeply, but I was not in love with him."

He looked at her, his solemn eyes steadily meeting her. She felt then how very attractive he was, how honourable, reliable, handsome. Had he asked her at that moment to marry her, she might have said 'Yes'. She was feeling very much alone. But he made no offer.

"I'm quite sure, Amelia, you did what you thought was right. You must have made the old boy's last days very happy."

When he had departed Amelia thought she had been foolish in recalling what was passed. She felt, despite his words and manner, he had not believed her.

One day, at their request, she went to the office of Mayne, Gonzalos and Gomez. She had conceived a great liking for Mr. Mayne, with his fatherly understanding manner. When she had signed some papers she looked up and smiled at him. He saw before him an exceedingly beautiful red-haired, green-eyed young woman of much character, for whom his admiration had steadily developed through the weeks of their cooperation. His first impulse had been to remain coldly proper towards a young adventuress who had played her cards adroitly and gained a title and a fortune. He had changed his view. Her youth and beauty apart, she shone with honesty. Her character revealed a strength based on a singular candour and sensibility. To this she added a very great capability, shown in every step of a complicated business.

"Mr. Mayne, I've decided to do something that may surprise you. I've discussed it with Doña Lucia and Mr. Carson. I am troubled in my mind about Roderick Slowdon. I have decided to go to Austria, to search for him. If I find him, I shall divide my legacy with him. I feel I have no right to such a large sum of money. I must do something to put right the injustice he has suffered."

Mr. Mayne listened, motionless at his desk. He did not reply at once, meditating. Then he spoke in his calm, fatherly manner.

"Lady Slowdon, your proposal does you great credit. It is almost quixotically honourable. May I make just one observation? I think that in marrying you, Sir Anthony not only paid you the tribute he wished, and indeed you brought him great happiness, but pursued his vendetta against his wife and the boy. In one matter I considered him completely insane—his determination to regard Roderick as Kurt Weninger's son, and to repudiate and disinherit him as far as the laws of inheritance would permit. He was a man of very deep passion, complex, very honourable in many ways. Nevertheless, there is one point, arising from your generous spirit. If you fulfil your mission, are you aware that you are subverting the intention of your husband? I imply no criticism of your proposal, indeed I admire it. Nevertheless I make the point."

His fine old face, tranquil, watched her, while he spoke in measured words. Amelia sat thoughtful for a while and then smiled at him.

"I'm glad you have made the point, Mr. Mayne. It is a sound one," she said. "It has been in my mind. My decision has been strengthened by what happened in the last few minutes of Sir Anthony's life. We shall never know what impelled him to get out of his bed and struggle up to that deserted nursery, to take out of a drawer, after many years, a photograph of young Roderick. I should like to think that, because of some intuition of death, he had an overwhelming desire to undo the wrong he had committed. Whether that is so or not, I feel I must act according to my own conscience in the matter."

194

Mr. Mayne listened. At the conclusion he smiled paternally.

"My dear Lady Slowdon! I greatly admire your attitude in this strange business. I feel you are right. I am also very pleased by your decision to go to Austria. You can render us great help. We seem to be getting nowhere in regard to the important matter of Roderick's existence and whereabouts. We must satisfy ourselves as to whether he is living or dead. It is holding up the settlement of Sir Anthony's estate. I have a feeling that we should start investigations from the point where we last knew that Roderick was alive, namely in Vienna. It would be of the greatest service if you personally would go there. We could employ someone but no one would have your precise qualifications, or your ability. How soon do you feel you could go?"

"At once. I shall go to visit my people in England first."

"Very well, do so. We shall, of course, place ample funds at your disposal, an interim payment of your inheritance. And I wish you a happy journey and every success."

CHAPTER FOURTEEN

I

FROM the heat of summer Amelia sailed into the winter of Europe. She went to England first. How different was her return journey. No elegant aloof *hidalgo*, Sir Anthony, in the deck chair. No effusive, noisy *diva* adjacent, no quick-witted, debonair Etienne. Amelia was amused inwardly when her stewardess addressed her, this time without error, as "M'lady". How far that *petite gamine*, a baronet's widow now, had travelled in so brief a time, and how quickly she had become adjusted to her new circumstances. She sat at the Captain's table, in that distinctive selection of 'somebodies' that is part of a purser's business. She was bowed in and out of the dining saloon by the Chief Steward. All the ladies were very affable, the gentlemen deferential.

She arrived in Glasgow in a snowstorm, a week before Christmas. She enjoyed the forgotten phenomenon. It had no violent onslaught like a Tabara hailstorm. There was a large group of her family waiting on the platform to receive her. The brothers, sisters, brothers-in-law, sisters-in-law had taken the day off from their duties. On the journey to Abernethy Villas they filled three taxis. Windows down the grim, grimy street framed inquisitive watchers. She was amused by a large card that hung from the front door knocker, inscribed in large letters, with the legend "Welcome to Lady Amelia Slowdon— The neighbours." Poor dears, they did not know that only peers' daughters carried the Christian name with the surname: she was Lady Slowdon. But no matter.

At home she discovered that her family's speech and

manners no longer irritated her. She knew she could escape at will from their hearty little world. She even enjoyed seeing her father resting his stockinged feet on the fender, complaining of chilblains. She suppressed any protest that came to mind. She was careful to show no sign of arrogance or superiority. She visited the neighbours, she received the Presbyterian and Episcopal parsons who called. She visited her old employers at her father's office, and heard the report "Your Amelia's a real leddie." She took the family to the theatre, and to dinner at the Central Hotel. She bought her mother a fur coat, her father a gold wristwatch. There were presents for every one of the family. In all, it was a most successful visit. When she departed on the express sleeper for London the family saw her off. There was unanimous agreement on the verdict of Alec's wife, once very critical of Amelia, "I must say she's greatly improved, and carries it off marvellously."

II

It was Amelia's first visit to the Continent and she elected to travel to Vienna via Paris. France was the home of the French language and she felt a kind of proprietory interest. Etienne had told her a great deal about his student life there. She had spent a week in London seeking clues to Roderick Slowdon. She had gone down to a little office of the Standing Council of the Baronetage, grandiloquently named but modestly housed, in Telegraph Street in the City. They could tell her nothing. She had got nowhere, but she obtained letters of introduction to several persons in Vienna who might prove useful to her. She was warned that the capital was in a state of turmoil. Hitler, encouraged by the Austrian Nazis, who had murdered Chancellor Dollfuss, was increasingly hostile and threatening an invasion. The Chancellor, Schuschnigg, was making a desperate fight for independence. All Europe was watching the struggle.

Amelia stayed a week in Paris, at the Ritz Hotel in the Place Vendòme. She went to the theatres, and was enchanted with a performance of *Le Bourgeois Gentilhomme* at the Comedie Française. She made tiring excursions to the Louvre, suffering bitter disappointment in the *Mona Lisa* by Leonardo da Vinci but overwhelmed by the *Winged Victory of Samothrace*. She shopped with near delirium along the ravishing *boutiques* in the Rue de Faubourg St. Honoré and in the Avenue de l'Opéra. She treated herself to meals at famous restaurants, whose names occurred in the novels she had read. She was thrilled to walk the Rue de Bac, the Rue de Varenne, and other quarters known to Proust's crowded gallery of characters. More and more she thought of Etienne de Lérin who had made her aware of the French scene. If only he had been with her. Unhappily she was quite alone, conscious that a pleasure shared is a pleasure doubled.

Somewhat exhausted by her discoveries, she travelled on to Vienna in the Orient Express. She arrived there on a January day to find the capital under a pall of snow, but it was sharp, dry and sunny. She had booked a room, on advice, at the Hotel Sacher. It was possible from this famous hostelry to walk across to the Opera House. To her delight they were playing Mozart's *Don Giovanni*, and at the Hofburg Theater a Chekov play. She obtained seats for both.

The hotel was deliciously warm. Off the salon she found a little room lined with photographs of the famous beauties of the Emperor Franz-Joseph era, all dead, mostly forgotten. What a Vienna they had known! Now it was under a heavy threat. Hitler was at the gates. The ruins of buildings, bombarded during a Socialist revolution, were still visible. There were few signs of the famous Viennese gaiety, the *gamütlichkeit* of its tuneful light operas. The spirit of Strauss and Lehar had deserted Vienna. Perhaps it returned when the lime trees flowered on the Ring and in the Prater. There was still gay music in the restaurants and the cafés.

She began her quest. They were cooperative at the Embassy, and at the British Consulate-General, but so many records had vanished in the Great War. To go back to 1900 was like investigating prehistoric times. At last, by an odd chance, the Consulate produced a 1913 telephone directory. No Slowdon appeared in it but they found, among a list of Weningers, three Kurts. One of them lived in Neubaugasse.

Amelia took a taxi and went to the house in Neubaugasse. There were shops on the ground floor. The apartments above had been converted into offices after the War. Amelia became aware how in the course of twenty years almost one half of a city's population had changed, its citizens vanished or dead. In that period a devastating war had decimated the population.

After three weeks of enquiries she faced a blank. Where had they buried Carmen Slowdon in November, 1914? She found an intelligent young University student and employed him to search the obituary notices in the Vienna newspapers. Nothing. She inserted advertisements asking anyone who had known Carmen Slowdon, Roderick Slowdon or Kurt Weninger, to communicate with her. At the end of one month she felt defeated.

Meanwhile the charm of this anxiety-stricken city enveloped her. She could imagine its beauty and allure in the summer, when the band played in the Hofgarten and the outdoor cafés spread their gay umbrellas and awnings and put out their tables. The opera and the ballet were still excellent. She went to the theatres, handicapped by her small knowledge of German, but delighting in the stage sets, the people in the foyer.

One morning when she was in her room, the telephone rang. It was the reception desk, which informed her that a gentleman, Professor Heinrich Hofmeyer, was in the hall and desired to see her. What was his business? They did not know. She said she would be down in a few minutes. Possibly a tout trying to sell her something.

When she went down the reception clerk pointed to a very old gentleman sitting in a corner of the lounge. He was white-haired, distinguished-looking, very feeble and old. He rose as she approached and bowed.

"Lady Slowdon?" he asked.

"Yes."

"My name is Hofmeyer—Professor Heinrich Hofmeyer," he said, speaking good English. "I saw an advertisement in the *Tageblatt* asking for any information concerning Roderick Slowdon."

"Yes, that was my advertisement. Can you tell me anything about him?" asked Amelia, surprised. Then, seeing how frail was this old gentleman, she said, "Do please sit down!"

"Thank you. I am a retired professor of art. Some years ago, about 1931 there was a youth named Slowdon who attended my classes. He was a very clever boy."

"Boy? I'm afraid it cannot be the Roderick Slowdon I seek—he would be a man of over forty. What was his Christian name?"

"Toni."

"Anthony?" repeated Amelia.

"Yes—a very nice youth, madam."

"Do you know anything about his family. Was he English?"

"He was, I understand, partly English. He told me his mother was Austrian, his father English."

"Did he live in Neubaugasse?"

"That I cannot say, *gnädige Gräfin*. He came from Graz."

"Was his father named Roderick?" asked Amelia, her voice trembling with excitement.

"I never heard his name."

"This is most extraordinary. My husband by his first marriage had a wife, of Spanish origin. They had a son, Roderick, born to them in Argentina. The mother left Argentina in 1900, and came to live here, bringing her young son. I believe she assumed the name of Weninger. She died in 1914, just after the war broke out. It is Roderick, her son, I am trying to trace."

The professor twisted a frayed hat in his frail hands. His cuffs were threadbare. Genteel poverty was written over him.

"It is curious you mention Argentina, *gnädige Gräfin*," said the professor, after a few moments of meditation. "I remember that one day we had a stuffed ostrich as a model. He told me that his father, who was dead, had a child's picture album that came from Argentina, and in it was a picture of some ostriches, called rheas, standing on a prairie."

"That is remarkable!" exclaimed Amelia. "I have been living in the Argentine and have seen these ostriches on the pampa! You never remembered him saying his father was named Roderick?"

"No—but I do recollect that he was an orphan. He had a grandmother with whom he lived, both his parents being dead. Later, he went back to Graz, and he told me he was entering a military academy there, to do his military service."

"But wasn't he English?"

"He spoke English very well, but he was born in Graz, and, I believe, is an Austrian. It would explain the military service. I was sorry to see him go. He was one of my brightest pupils."

"What did he look like?" asked Amelia.

"He was tall and fair—in appearance *hochgeboren*, we say, aristocratic."

"He went back to Graz—did you ever hear from him?"

"Indeed. My hopes for him have been fulfilled. Only last week I had a card from him announcing an exhibition of his landscape paintings."

"Here—or in Graz?"

"No, in Kitzbühel. I have the card with me."

The professor picked up a worn leather portfolio and took out a printed card. It announced an exhibition of landscape paintings by Franz Slowdon.

"But this says Franz Slowdon," said Amelia after reading the card.

"He is Toni Franz Slowdon. He signs his work Franz. I am very proud of him!" said the old professor smiling. "Two years ago he visited Vienna for a few days. He called to see me. He was then living in Graz. He had left the military academy. He did not wish to become an officer."

Amelia glanced at the clock.

"All this is extremely interesting. I want to talk to you. Will you not have some lunch with me?" she asked.

"That would be a great pleasure, *gnädige Gräfin*," he replied.

They rose and went into the dining-room.

It was half-past two when Professor Hofmeyer left. Amelia went up to her room. She sat in a chair by the window, overlooking the back of the Opera House. They were sweeping up the dirty melted snow. She was hardly aware of what she saw, her mind restless with excitement. Here was a development they had never given thought to. If Toni Franz was the son of Roderick, and Roderick was dead, then this boy was Sir Anthony Slowdon, the third baronet. Boy. He was not a boy any longer. He must now be a young man.

She must go to Kitzbühel. The Professor said it was about seven hours' journey from Vienna, and famed as a ski-ing resort. It was now the height of the season. She had asked the Professor if he would accompany her to Kitzbühel. He assented readily.

She picked up the telephone and asked for the desk. She wanted two rooms reserved for next Tuesday at a good hotel in Kitzbühel.

"It is the height of the season, my lady, but we will see what we can do," replied the clerk.

When she came in at six o'clock a note in her box informed her that two rooms had been reserved at Schloss Kaps.

III

They journeyed to the little town of Kitzbühel in the Austrian Tyrol. It was a region of mountains covered with snow. A rack and pinion railway and a ski-lift ran to the famed ski-ing slopes. Amelia was enchanted with the little town, with its old tower gate at one end of the Hohestrasse and the church at the other. The long street with its overhanging gables was lined with shops and cafés. There was great activity up and down this street in the evenings, the restaurants crammed with skiers of all nationalities, zither music sounding in the snug stove-warm cafés. By day the town was deserted, everyone being up on the ski-ing slopes.

Schloss Kaps spread itself on a knoll just outside the town. It had been for centuries the stronghold of an old family of Austrian counts that had produced a cardinal, an ambassador, and numerous court officials. The 1914–18 War had brought it to ruin. The Gräfin, with a rising family, had converted the Schloss into a pension, filling its thirty rooms with guests. Amelia occupied a corner room that had its own roofed balcony commanding a view of the town and the foothills dotted with chalets. They dined in a long heavily raftered room hung with family portraits, senators and soldiers in their robes and uniforms, each picture carrying the family arms in one corner. They formed a curious gallery of dour, lecherous, debonair, handsome counts who had ruled their little domain through four hundred years. The living youngest representative of the line was a good-looking laughing lad in the typical Tyrolean costume of leather shorts, green jacket and white stockings.

His sister wore the flowered 'dirndl' and a gay knitted wool bodice. They bowed and curtsied to the guests. The entrance to the Schloss was up a drive that led into a gravel courtyard. The entrance door in the stone façade was heavily studded. Above it, in an entablature, was the Austrian eagle of the family coat of arms.

The morning after their arrival Amelia and the old professor sought the gallery in which Anthony Slowdon was exhibiting his paintings. It was in a back room of a stationer's shop in the Hohestrasse. They were the only visitors. There was not even a caretaker present. The Professor proudly showed Amelia the work of his former pupil. The paintings were fresh in their colours and vigorously executed. They covered various Austrian scenes including some delightful views of Vienna in summer sunshine. There were also half-a-dozen excellent portraits.

"They are good, yes?" commented Professor Hofmeyer. "But he is, essentially, a landscape artist."

Little red discs on the frames indicated that six of the twenty-one exhibits had been sold.

They spent half an hour in the gallery. No one came.

"I'll go and ask in the shop where Toni is," said Professor Hofmeyer. He returned in a few minutes. "They say he comes in usually in the evenings—he goes ski-ing in the daytime! These young men don't attend to their business like we did. Perhaps they are right. Where is my youth now, and what did my industry bring me?" He shrugged his shoulders and smiled wanly. "I learn Toni lives in a small chalet he has taken. It's just up behind the Schloss. We might return that way and arrange to see him. How surprised he will be to see me!"

They were equipped with snowshoes, the morning was crisp and sunny. The town, white-robed, smiled in its mountain valley. They climbed a little way and came to a crossroad, marked by a wayside shrine, a crucifix under a wooden canopy, vases of flowers at its base. They turned right and traversed a level road above the town, bordered with small pensions, a few bearing the legend *Zimmerfrei* in their windows. There was a sound of running water. Distant, rose the snowy wall of the mountains.

"Here it is!" exclaimed the Professor.

They halted before a newly built wooden chalet, with a covered balcony that ran round two sides, hanging over the valley. The door was reached across a little wooden bridge. The chalet, above the fir-clad valley, had a delightful fairy-tale air.

The Professor pulled the chain of an iron bell. There was a sound of footsteps. The door was opened by a pleasant round-faced young woman, in an open-necked, short-sleeved dirndl costume, her plaited hair coiled over her head.

"Does Herr Toni Slowdon live here?" asked the Professor.

"*Ya*, but the Herr Slowdon is not here. He's out on the Hahnenkamm. He comes back at four o'clock," said the young woman.

"Oh, this lady and I desired to see him."

"Ask her if she can give him a message to call on us this evening at Schloss Kaps," said Amelia, who had been able to follow the conversation. "Is she his wife do you think?"

"Are you Frau Toni Slowdon?" asked the Professor.

"*Nein! Nein!*" replied the young woman laughing and blushing. "I come to keep the Herr's house and cook for him."

"He is alone?"

"*Ya*—but he is always out, ski-ing, lunching, dining—and the gallery."

"Not much painting?" asked Amelia attempting her German.

"Not much. He is so popular. Herr Toni *ist sehr gemütlich*."

"I believe the girl's in love with him," said the Professor in English to Amelia, beaming.

"Then please will you ask Herr Toni when he returns if he will call to see us at Schloss Kaps. Say Professor Hofmeyer called. He knows my name," said the Professor.

"*Ya*," replied the young woman.

"*Danke. Aufwiedersehn!*"

"*Aufwiedersehn*, Herr Professor."

Smiling the apple-cheeked young woman closed the door.

Around half-past five a servant tapped on the door of Amelia's sitting-room where she was talking with Professor Hofmeyer. He went to the door.

"Herr Schlowdon is in the hall to see you, Herr Professor," said the maid.

The Professor looked at Amelia.

"Ask her to bring him up," said Amelia.

She got up from her chair, and went to the window overlooking the distant town below. Her heart was beating more quickly. She felt apprehensive. Was she really going to see Anthony's grandson, was this the end of the quest? It was so surprising. She had never thought of the possibility of finding, not Roderick, but Roderick's son, a young man.

There were footsteps. The Professor went to the door. She did not see, keeping her back to the room, the meeting between the Professor and his pupil but she heard the boisterous greeting between them. Then she turned. She saw before her a blond giant, quite six foot, made larger by the long woollen pullover and the blue ski-ing trousers tucked into heavy boots. He was ruddy, grey-eyed, his head covered with a close cluster of chestnut curls. But in that first moment she knew he was Sir Anthony's grandson. There were the same fine features, the well-shaped head, broad brow, slightly aquiline nose. Her mouth opened involuntarily in a little gasp of surprise.

"This lady has come from Vienna to see you!" said the Professor.

The young giant looked at her, surprised.

"I am Lady Slowdon," she said, holding out her hand, which he took in a large firm grasp. "Are you the son of Roderick Slowdon who was born in the Argentine?"

"Yes—he was my father," replied the young man somewhat astonished.

"Sir Anthony Slowdon was his father?"

"Yes. I'm called after him. He lives on an *estancia* in Argentina. But my father quarrelled with him, I was told. I never knew my father. He died when I was a baby—in a concentration camp. You see, he was British."

He paused. He seemed a little bewildered.

"You will pardon me—did you say you were Lady Slowdon?" he asked.

"Yes—I am the widow of Sir Anthony Slowdon, your grandfather."

"But he must have been a very old man! And you—and—oh, I'm sorry," he said, awkwardly.

"Yes, he was an old man, he was seventy-three. I married him only a short time before he died. I was his secretary before that. Won't you sit down?"

The young man sat down. She noticed the breadth of his shoulders, the strong neck revealed by the open shirt. She saw at a glance, as he rested them on his trousers, that he had the fine Slowdon hands. Two of the fingers were nicotine-stained. Presently, in a conscious silence that had fallen, he put up a hand and eased his shirt with a finger. Then their eyes meeting, they smiled. He could see her now, the aureole of red hair, the lovely clear green eyes and marvellous complexion, the neat figure and small feet. Her legs were exquisitely shaped. Their eyes met, and he gave a low laugh, rubbing his hands on his long thighs.

"This is very strange!" he said, addressing the Professor.

"Lady Slowdon has been trying to find you for many weeks. Then I saw her advertisement," said Hofmeyer.

"Advertisement?"

"I put an advertisement in the Vienna papers asking if anyone could give me news of Roderick Slowdon," said Amelia. "And the Professor brought me news of you."

"But why should you want to find me? My grandmother told me——"

"Your grandmother?" repeated Amelia.

"Yes, my mother's mother. She brought me up in Graz, where she lives—and I live mostly. My grandmother said there had been a great quarrel, my other grandmother, my father's mother, had run away from my grandfather with another man —after that the family broke up. My father, I heard, was very bitter about the old man in Argentina."

"Then you know the story of your grandmother, Carmen Slowdon, and Kurt Weninger?" asked Amelia.

"Yes. My grandmother told me that my father was very fond of Kurt Weninger, who left him a small legacy."

"The Professor tells me you are an orphan?"

"Yes, my mother died when I was thirteen. We had lived with my grandmother at Graz since my father's death."

"You speak of two grandmothers. Do you realise you have a third? I am your step-grandmother?" asked Amelia, smiling.

He laughed loudly and slapped his thighs with his hands.

"You? But that's ridiculous!" he exclaimed.

"I agree. But as I married your grandfather I suppose I am your step-grandmother—however much you may dislike the fact!"

"Oh—oh no! I don't dislike it. I think it's great fun! What do you say, Professor? Fancy having a grandmother like— like——"

He hesitated, met her eyes, and collapsed in laughter, giving the Professor a thump on the back.

"Forgive me, Lady Slowdon, it's all a bit staggering!" he cried, his merry eyes dancing.

"Won't you call me Amelia?"

"Yes—I'd love to, grandma! Oh, I say! What a funny state

of things! You must call me Toni—everybody does, and a grandmama must!"

"I don't think I like the grandmama business," said Amelia.

"Of course not, it's ridiculous, but you started it! Have you come all the way from Argentina to find me?"

"Well—to find your father, thinking he was alive."

"It's jolly nice of you. Did the old boy ask you to?"

"No," said Amelia. "On the contrary. He never spoke of your father. It would greatly surprise him if he could know I was here. It is entirely my idea," said Amelia. "The lawyers also want information."

"Well, it's nice of you, to come all this way. Isn't it, Professor?" he asked.

"It is very extraordinary—I am happy to have been of service," said the Professor.

Toni Slowdon got up, and shook himself, puppy-like. He was so very young despite his big frame. He rubbed a hand through his curls. "You know, I am rather dizzy! Let's go down to the bar and have a drink."

"And afterwards, won't you stay to dinner?" asked Amelia, rising.

"I'd love to, grandm—— Amelia," he replied eagerly.

"There's something you don't seem to have realised yet," said Amelia, quietly.

"No?"

"You are now Sir Anthony Slowdon, the third baronet."

He stared at her for a long moment; then he looked from her to the Professor and then back at her.

"Well, I'm damned! I am Sir Anthony Slowdon, third baronet? Why, so I am! I say, we must have a drink on that!"

He went to the door and opened it for them.

CHAPTER FIFTEEN

I

A VISIT planned for a few days became a visit of three weeks. One evening, as they were dining in a restaurant off the Hohestrasse, a local tavern of character, with an elaborate iron-work sign of a reindeer hanging outside to denote its name, and with wooden 'pews' inside, their tables lit by thick white candles in iron sconces, Toni said to Amelia, "Why don't you let me teach you to ski? You'd love it!"

So she began to learn. He spent his mornings with her on the nursery slopes. He was delighted with her progress. "You really are an extraordinary person!" he exclaimed.

"Why do you think so?"

"Well, I've been watching you. In the first place, I've never known a girl to pick it up so quickly and I've good reason for knowing. The last three seasons I've been giving ski-ing lessons in the morning, to help out, and painting lessons in the evening. You're the quickest pupil I've ever had."

"Do you think you could teach me to paint?" she asked, laughing at him.

"I'll bet I could. Look, I've been watching you at your German—you're gabbling away like a native!"

"I hope the accent's all right, not too native?"

"No—it's quite good. And look how you talk French—I've heard you in the bar at the Schloss with those Paris honey-mooners. Then, of course you've Spanish—and I expect you ride like a jockey, after living on the pampa. Can you sing?"

"No, I can't sing."

"Thank goodness! You've been giving me an inferiority complex!"

"May I now make my contribution to this Mutual Admiration Society? I know, of course, that you are a marvellous skier, twice runner-up in the local championships. You are a very clever painter. According to the Professor, you're his most brilliant pupil . . . I assume you can swim?"

"Pretty good," he agreed. "Ride, run, box, dance, shake a cocktail, play the guitar, and play the fool, all pretty good. A rotten soldier, slovenly——"

"Have you tried soldiering?" asked Amelia surprised.

"Yes, I did my military service. I was in the cadet school at Graz."

"But are you Austrian or English?"

"Both. My father, I'm told, insisted on having me registered as English. He married my mother in the British-Consulate at Vienna."

"Your mother was Austrian?"

"Half. You see, my grandfather, at Graz, was English. He was born in England, and went to Buda-Pest to manage one of the Royal Stables. So you see I'm a bit of a mongrel!"

"I never met anyone so English in my life!" commented Amelia.

"The authorities here insisted I was Austrian. They called me up, so I went to the Academy at Graz. That's what worries me a little. Austria's going Nazi—you'd be surprised at the number of Austrians who like to shout 'Heil Hitler', even after they murdered poor little Dollfuss. He'll start a war one day. Then where am I? I'm damned if I'll fight against England for the Nazis. I'm thinking of moving to Paris. You'll find me with a beard, in corduroys, living on the Left Bank and keeping a trollop."

"I don't see that. I see you in a Guards regiment, if it comes to that, going all stiff when they play the National Anthem."

"You're Scots. Wouldn't you prefer me in a kilt?" he asked playfully, his hand on hers.

"I should love you in a kilt!" she replied.

The little orchestra had begun to thump and whine. *"Ich tanz mit dir in . . ."* moaned the curvous crooner at the microphone.

"Let's dance," he said, pulling her up.

Six-foot-one he towered over her. He danced well. There was a great deal she did not know about him, after three weeks. But one thing she knew. She was in love with him.

I I

The news became increasingly perturbing. In February the Austrian Chancellor had been bullied by Hitler. Vienna was undermined with the Nazi plotters. The Government tried hard to fight its internal and external enemies. In a desperate effort to maintain its independence a plebiscite was to be held on the thirteenth of March, so that the whole country could proclaim its support of the Republic.

The tension mounted daily. The visitors to the winter sports began to leave, apprehensive of future events. Professor Hofmeyer had been back two weeks, and wrote one day to say that he had wonderful news. He had arranged for one of the leading art dealers in Vienna to give an exhibition of Toni Slowdon's paintings at the end of March. Elated, Toni began to arrange for the transport of his canvases. He had a friend with a studio in Vienna with whom he would stay.

"You must come to my show," he said to Amelia, when he had shown her Professor Hofmeyer's letter. "It's a most charming little gallery. I shall give a cocktail party for the opening. Now say you'll be there!"

"I should like to, but——" She hesitated.

"But what?"

"Do you think there'll be trouble—the news is very ominous. A lot of people think Hitler will grab Austria."

"I hope not! We all believe that old Schuschnigg's too clever to let those Nazis swallow us. You'll see, the plebiscite will give a thumping 'No!' to the Hitler gang."

She did not share his confidence and decided to return to Vienna. She had not completed her mission, and felt increasingly disturbed by her task. Nothing had been said about the Slowdon properties in Argentina. He showed no curiosity. Twice she had tried to approach the subject but she had failed. One day some transfer deeds arrived that required signing in the presence of the Argentine Consul-General in Vienna. She mentioned the deeds and said she would have to go to the Argentine Embassy in Vienna, on the instructions of her solicitors in Buenos Aires.

"Splendid. Now you've got to be in Vienna! Something to do with the Will?" he asked lightly.

"Yes—with the sale of Tabara."

She had told him much about life at Tabara.

"I hope you've got it. We're all disinherited, I'm quite sure. And I wouldn't touch a penny of the old devil's money anyhow, not after the way he behaved to my father and grandmother. It's no business of mine but I hope you're comfortable?"

"Very. Your grandfather left me half of his estate. But Toni dear, it is business of yours! This is a serious matter. You will be getting a letter from Sir Anthony's solicitors. By Argentine law one half of the estate comes to me, as his widow, the other half goes to Roderick, and since your father's dead, and he was the only child, it comes to you."

"To me? You mean the old bastard—oh, I'm sorry— couldn't disinherit us? I'm to get half?"

"Yes, Toni dear, he wasn't an old bastard, as you put it. Something happened at the end that makes me think he regretted his conduct towards your grandmother and your father. He got out of his bed and climbed the stairs to the old nursery. The effort killed him. We found him sitting there with your father's photograph, as a young boy, in his hand. We shall never know what went through his mind in those last minutes of his life but it seems pretty clear. As for what I've received under the Will, I'm not happy about it. How can I be? You must see my point of view. I was his wife for less than a year, and I inherit a large sum of money. I'm not an adventuress."

"Adventuress! Good Lord, what an idea!" exclaimed Toni.

"But I shall feel one if I have all that money to which I don't feel entitled. Toni, please, I want you to take half of it. It's yours, really."

"What! On top of all that I'm going to have! Preposterous! Enjoy it, if the old devil wanted you to have half, he wanted you to have half. I'm not touching a penny of it. Just how much shall I inherit since he couldn't help it?"

"About three hundred thousand dollars."

"Good God! It makes me dizzy! You see, my dear little lady, I don't really want money! I have my father's little estate, I manage to float comfortably. I've been quite lucky at my job. The only thing I want to do in this world is to paint. All my artist friends haven't a bean, well, not many beans, let me say, but you can't believe how we enjoy ourselves!"

"But Toni, you must have money to live!" protested Amelia. "You'll want to travel—to marry one day and have a family, to——"

"Listen! Two of my best artist friends are married and have five kids between them. They're the happiest lot you ever saw.

> The girl who marries a man for money
> Often finds sand in her pot of honey.
> The man who marries a girl for 'dough'
> Just buys himself a packet of woe.

215

Ever heard that American ditty? Beware of honey and 'dough'! It attracts parasites."

He laughed, and then saw something in Amelia's face that checked his mirth. There was a wave of emotion troubling it.

"I say, have I been very rude about grandfather Anthony? I'm sorry! I wouldn't do anything in the world to hurt your feelings. And dearest Amelia, I'm just overcome by your generosity—but I couldn't, I really couldn't touch a penny of your money. It seems as if I've got too much already. Good Lord, who would have thought it! And on top of all—a lovely step-grandmother! I'm feeling almost grateful to that old—to dear grandfather Anthony!"

They laughed together but he saw she was near to tears.

"Now, powder your pretty face, dear little lady. We are due at the Café Hirsch," he said, glancing at his wristwatch. "Let's be going!"

III

They arrived back in a Vienna seething with rumours. Faces were grave. On the Austro-German frontier there were a million Nazi soldiers. The Chancellor stood firm. He had made a clever move in declaring a plebiscite for the thirteenth. It had adroitly cut out all the young hotheads screaming "Heil Hitler!" for voting was restricted to those over twenty years of age.

Amelia went back to the Hotel Sacher. It was almost empty. The Opera House was also half-empty. People spoke in whispers, like conspirators. There were stories of young Austrians slipping over the frontier to join the Nazi troops. There was a bloody pitched battle at the University between young students and Nazis. There were rumours of desertion in the police force.

Toni Slowdon laboured to get his exhibition ready. It was to open on the twentieth of March. He sent out cards for the Private View. Every day he called at the hotel and took Amelia out, showing her things in Vienna she might have missed, the Imperial Vaults with the tomb of the young Duke of Reichstadt, Napoleon's ill-fated son, the little King of Rome, and of the Crown Prince Rudolf, evoking the suicide pact at Mayerling. He showed her the open-air pulpit in the little Platz behind the St. Stephanskirche where, overnight, in the snow, Mozart's coffin had lain, preceding the pauper funeral, because there was no money to pay for a bier inside the cathedral. They went out to Grinzing, and to Heiligenstadt, to see the alley where Beethoven had taken his evening walk. They dined in one of the Weinstubes, hot and noisy, with zither music and singing of Austrians drowning their anxiety in wine. He took her to Franz Lehar's house by the Danube and showed her the desk on which he had written *The Merry Widow*, and a half-dozen other world-famous musical comedies.

There was a day of warm sunshine and blue skies when they went out to Schönbrunn. They visited the vast palace, and then walked up the long avenue, tree-bordered, to the Gloriette on its commanding hill, whence they looked down on the gardens, parterres, fountains and geometrical paths that led the eye to the long white façade of the favourite palace of old Emperor Franz Josef where, in a plain iron bed, in grief and austerity, he had died just in time to miss the resounding crash of the Austrian Empire. Over all this beauty and the memorials of a long, proud history, brooded the heavy clouds coming up from Hitlerian Germany. But for a time they forgot the troubled world. They were young, they were happy, the sun shone, and they were in *Wien, Wien, die Schöne Stadt*.

They had raced down an avenue and come to rest by the ornamental water where Diana the Huntress stood with her virgins and hounds. A jet of water glistened and trembled while the goldfish swam in and out among the water lilies. The sharp air had brought a crimson flush to Amelia, and as she stood there, a little breathless, her red hair flamboyant under the green hat that matched her eyes, Toni piercingly realised her utter beauty, the redness of her lips, her shining teeth, the thin arched eyebrows, and the pink conch-like delicacy of her ears.

He held out his hand to her. She took it and he led her towards a baroque alcove, fern-embowered. Water cascaded over a laughing faun. Suddenly in a wave of delirious youth he pulled her to him, and wordless, purposeful, crushed her in his arms, his mouth on hers, and held her thus in a long water-tremulous silence.

He raised his face and looked down at her, soft, surrendered, lifted on a wave of ecstasy. They could not speak. The glory of the morning lay about them, then the world came tiding in again upon their consciousness. He released her, and linking an arm in hers began to walk down the long tree-arched avenue.

IV

The evening of the tenth, Toni and Amelia were dining at Sacher's. On their way to the restaurant there was a warning call over the radio. Everyone stood still and listened to the announcer. Chancellor Schuschnigg was going to speak to the people of Austria. There was a pause and then another voice, even in tone, deliberate, came on the air. It was the Chancellor. The effort to remain independent had failed. Hitler had forbidden the plebiscite to be held on the thirteenth. It was useless to continue the struggle. He absolved them all from their vows to the Austrian Republic which in its present form had ceased to exist. Tomorrow morning the German Army Corps were crossing the Austrian frontier. Austria was no longer independent. It was incorporated with Germany.

When he had finished there was absolute silence. In the hotel foyer no one spoke but looked from one to the other with strained faces. Suddenly, from a lounge in one corner, a thick-set spectacled little man jumped up, thrust out his right arm and shouted in a rough voice, "Heil Hitler!"

No one heiled Hitler. He looked round and then, stiff-necked, strutted angrily out of the foyer. Slowly but still word-less, people began to move.

"Hitler wasn't going to risk that plebiscite," said Toni, in a low voice. "Let's go and eat." They went into the restaurant. It was early for Vienna to dine. The room was almost empty. White-faced waiters stood around. The head waiter came with a professional smile, gave them the large *Carte de Menu*, and waited for their order.

They ordered. When the waiter had gone Toni put out his hand and took Amelia's, lying on the table.

"You're not nervous?" he asked, gently.

"Yes, I am, very! What's going to happen now? Will there be fighting?"

"No—there won't be even a struggle. Austria is a corpse. But we must be careful what we say."

"Your Exhibition?"

"I shall hold it just the same. I don't know about the studio."

"The studio where you live?"

"Yes—the friend who's lent it to me, Oscar Neumann, is a Jew. I'm afraid they're going to have a bad time, like those poor devils in Germany. Thank God, he's away. I wonder now if he saw what was coming and he's bolted. Many of them have. Well, we shall see."

They did not have to wait long. The next morning, at seven o'clock, in the breaking dawn, Amelia was awakened by a loud droning overhead. She sat up. Planes. The heavens shook, filled with them. She got out of bed, putting on a dressing-gown, went to the window, drew the blind and looked into the street. She stood transfixed. In the half-light, in the space before the Opera House, stood half-a-dozen tanks, huge, menacing. There were soldiers in uniform around them. The noise of the planes overhead increased.

Amelia lowered the blind again, turned on the light and rang the bell. After a time a maid tapped and entered. The chambermaid was a middle-aged woman, deadly pale. She spoke English.

"They've come?" asked Amelia.

"No, madam, only the advance troops. The army marches in at eleven. We are all to be on the streets to welcome them. They're already putting up arches and flags. There's a rumour they've arrested the Chancellor."

"What do you think is going to happen? Will there be fighting?"

"I don't think so, madam, but there's no peace here any more. My husband's a Social Democrat, our son's a Nazi—we have terrible scenes at home. Everybody's gone mad," she said, despairingly.

"Can I have coffee and rolls?"

"Certainly, madam."

"In twenty minutes. I'll take my bath."

"Very good, madam."

The chambermaid went into the bathroom to run the water. The drone of the planes overhead was continuous. It was like a long growl of thunder preluding the storm.

Amelia turned off the light, went to the window, drew the blinds and looked out. The tanks were still there, grey, with their sinister long guns, the swastika painted on their sides. A small crowd stood gaping at them.

As Amelia sat at her breakfast she reviewed the position. Ought she to leave Vienna? Leaving Vienna meant leaving

Anthony. This had been the happiest two months of her life. The thought of not seeing him was unbearable. She knew beyond any possible doubt that she was in love with him. All her hesitations were a thing of the past, her rejection of Etienne de Lérin, of James Fayne, of Richard Cordell, events which had perturbed her so, had faded into the past. They had all offered her very much, security, position, pleasant companionship but they had not been able to evoke that deep certainty which made her ready to surrender everything. For the first time she now felt no hesitation. She loved Anthony Slowdon. She was completely, happily, captive. What a singular end to her quest of the missing heir!

She thought of old Sir Anthony. If he had seen this young giant, his grandson, so unmistakably a Slowdon, would he not have buried his preposterous antagonism? A strange man, how austere and wilful he was, how handsome in presence, the *hidalgo* in perfection. She remembered warmly his exquisite courtesy, his gentleness, the pleasure of her life at Tabara. Tabara, how far off, how utterly different, with the pampa, the vast lonely plain, the white tufted cottony grass waving under the wind, the cow-music of the moving herds, the little owls sitting paired on the wire fences, the wide-winged level sunrises and sunsets, the gauchos with their bright scarves, baggy trousers, rope shoes, Juan the *domador*, with his dark, arrogant, male confidence—how utterly different, how far away from this frenzied, war-threatened Europe it all was!

And the next step? Where was her life to be spent? She missed Tabara deeply but even had it been possible to keep it, it was not a woman's life, certainly not a lonely woman's. The death of Sir Anthony had engulfed her in so great a change that she had not yet been able to foresee her future course. Now, here in Austria, with the finding of Anthony, a new vista opened. If he asked her she would place her life in his hands unhesitatingly, though she really knew so little of him. And how little he knew of her! In the past enchanted weeks, in Kitzbühel, on the ski-ing slopes, in his chalet-studio, and now in Vienna, with its daily excursions to galleries, palaces, theatres, snow-laden woods, the warm gaiety of the inns at Grinzing, in the restaurants and cafés of a Vienna no longer so gay but still so *gemütlich*, she had come to know him more and more. All that she saw of him deepened the spell upon her.

Gradually she had learned the details of his life, of the father he had never known, who had married at twenty-one and died of pneumonia in a concentration camp at twenty-five. Anthony had told her of his young mother, heart-broken, who had taken him to her old home at Graz, where his childhood had been so happy. Then he had lost his mother, consumptive, undermined in health by the near-starvation of the war years. He knew a little about his Spanish grandmother and the liaison with Kurt Weninger from whom, through his father, had come a legacy that provided a small income.

Amelia was dismayed by Anthony's fierce independence. He utterly refused to consider the offer of half her fortune. "No, my dear, you enjoy your money—the old boy wanted you to have it. I don't mind telling you that whatever will come to me will stink. He hated my father. He hated all of us."

In vain she had emphasised the probable change in Sir Anthony in those last hours at Tabara, when some stirring of remorse had driven him out of his room up to the closed nursery where they had found him.

"It's no use, Amelia, you can't make me love that vindictive old man," said Anthony, firmly.

She had informed Mr. Mayne in Buenos Aires of Roderick's death, and forwarded the details given her by Anthony, his only child and male heir. What was the position now?

Little by little she had learned from Anthony of his boyhood in Graz, of the old grandmother he adored. "I'm going to take you to Graz to see her," he said. "Guess what her name is— Smith! You couldn't have anything more English than that! She's Frau Schönborn-Smith, and very proud of the Schön-born connection. They're a very old mediatized family."

"What's that?" asked Amelia.

"Families that still rank as princes although they have lost their sovereignty. The Schönborns have a palace here but the war crippled them."

"So you're blue-blooded!" exclaimed Amelia, and he laughed.

"I'm supposed to be the son of a bastard, aren't I?" he said.

"And I'm a *gamine*," replied Amelia.

"A what?"

"A *gamine*—a saucy baggage."

"Good Lord! You! Where do you get that from?"

"A very nice young Frenchman I knew in Buenos Aires." She quoted the poem to him.

"What nonsense! There are no raindrops on you, my dear little red-head—you're *poil-de-carotte*!"

They laughed as he hugged her and swept her hair with his mouth. She tried to tell him about her own origin, the back street in Glasgow, her commonplace family, the brothers, the sisters. He began to sing a tune—

"Oh, tell me, pretty maiden, are there any more at home like you?
There are a few, kind sir, just one or two.

Grossmütter Schönborn-Smith sings that. Are they all green-eyed?"

"No—except with envy. They're not at all bad, really."

"One day you'll take me to see them. I've never been in England."

"Scotland," said Amelia, correcting him. "We are a superior race, we're Clydesiders."

So she had hidden nothing from him, her Abernethy Villas-typist origin. Indeed, he seemed to admire her all the more.

"What a girl!" he had exclaimed. "You frighten me a little! No wonder the old *hidalgo* got unhorsed!"

"I suppose you think I hooked Sir Anthony?" she asked.

"Not at all—he just lassoed you, and who wouldn't!" he retorted.

Now as she ate her breakfast in the hotel bedroom, with the steady beat and drone of the aeroplanes over this doomed capital, she wondered what would happen next. He seemed very much in love with her, in his laughing boisterous way. But he had not asked her to marry him. "Oh you know *him?* Isn't he gorgeous, *der Damenheld!*" she had heard a girl in a café say to her friend, who had seen Anthony coming in. Amelia asked him what a *Damenheld* was.

"Lady-killer," he had replied. "Why?"

"The girl over there called you that."

"What nonsense. She's a *kokette!*"

Of course women ran after him. How serious was he? He had tremendous charm, gusto, looks, and at odd moments the imperiousness of his grandfather. She would soon have to leave Vienna. Then it occurred to her that she did not have to leave. She did not have to leave anywhere, or go anywhere. No one waited for her. It was rather a frightening thought.

She had almost finished breakfast when the telephone rang. It was Anthony.

"Have I woken you up?" he asked.

"Oh, no. I'm breakfasting. These planes! There are tanks outside."

"Yes—they're coming in. Look, everybody's told the big in-vasion comes on at eleven. They all have to be on the Ring, waving flags, 'heiling' the conquering heroes. They will be!

I'm not saying anything over the telephone—it's tapped. At ten o'clock I'm coming to fetch you. You'll have a fine view of the march-in from this studio. Will you be ready?"

"Yes."

"Good, at ten then," he said, and rang off.

She was down in the hall when he came. There was an air of tense excitement everywhere.

"I've got a taxi, we'll have to make a detour. They've closed the Ring."

The crowds were massed along the Opernring and the Kärntnerring. Swastika flags were everywhere. There was the sound of a band playing.

"You'd imagine it was a public holiday instead of a funeral. *Gott erhalte, hoch der Führer*, the song-theme. The idiots! They've all forgotten Sarajevo and the shot that rang round the world!"

They stopped the taxi in a back street, and made their way, pushing through the mob on the Kärntnerring where the entrance to the studio was. It was on the top floor. A corner window commanded a vista of the Ring, packed on each pavement with spectators and seething with excitement. The planes overhead kept up a steady patrol. The façades of the tall buildings were covered with fluttering red and white swastika flags and streamers.

"I wonder what they've done with Schuschnigg—he's lucky if he's alive," said Anthony.

They stood at the window waiting. It was a cold grey March morning, the sky full of fleecy clouds. The trees of the Ring were not yet in leaf. The minutes marched on to the zero hour. At five minutes to eleven there was a deafening roar in the upper air. A hundred warplanes in massed formation were flying over the city. The air pulsated with them. Vienna lifted its face skywards. Then, since this was the prelude, there was the sound, distant, down the Ring, of massed bands and the earsplitting bombardment of a great phalanx of military motor cycles, followed by armoured cars and churning tanks. They came steadily on down the Ring, a wall of moving steel. Behind these followed the helmeted troops, first the renegade Austrians, after them the Hitlerian storm-troopers. The crowds broke into delirious acclamation. Flags fluttered, the cheering was half-drowned in the rattle of tanks and artillery, the tramp of feet, the high drone of planes, the bursts of music from intermittent brass bands. And then came a line of cars, flanked by motor cycles, and, standing up in one of them, was a little man wearing a scrub moustache, grim-faced, with arm upraised. He was greeted by thousands of Austrians, flags waving and voices screaming *Heil Hitler!*

The length and power of this invasion of armed might were staggering. The tanks, guns, armoured cars, marching troops and massed regimental flags never seemed to end. It was noon when they had passed. From somewhere a salute of guns barked over the city.

Amelia and Anthony came in from the window.

"It's terrifying!" said Amelia. "What happens now?"

"The local Nazi hooligans will run amok, there's nothing to stop them. The Jews will be the first to suffer, the pattern's been set in Germany."

Four days later Anthony's prophecy was fulfilled. The Jews were rounded up. They were compelled to wear a yellow star upon their sleeves. Their shops carried across the windows large posters 'Forbidden to Aryans'. Some of the windows had been smashed, some looted. A Rothschild had been arrested, a philanthropic old man, much respected. There came stories of hooligans who had entered cafés, taken outside Jewish customers, and beaten them. Anti-Nazis were beaten with rubberjacks, *Gummiknuppel*, but *Stahlruten*, steel whips, were used on the Jews. They lacerated their faces and shoulders. Some of them died after a visit from the Nazis.

One afternoon, after shopping in the Kärntnerring, Amelia saw four Nazis, mere boys in their uniforms and high boots, marching an old Jew along. At a point in the street they stopped and forced their victim on to his knees. They violently thrust his face down until it struck a *Kruckenkreuz* painted on the pavement, a symbol of the Patriotic Front. A soldier appeared with a bucket and brush. They made the old man scrub out the symbol of Austrian resistance, beating him over the head whenever he stopped. For half an hour a jeering crowd watched the performance. Shocked and sickened, Amelia hurried back to her hotel.

She felt she must get out of Vienna. Every day there was a fresh violation of human decency. The affable young clerk at the reception desk had disappeared. When Amelia asked where he was she was told he had gone. They were not allowed to employ Jews. At Elizabeth Arden's the same thing happened, her hairdresser, a delicate, refined young man was missing. Schuschnigg was not dead. He was a prisoner, as were all the leaders of the Fatherland Front. The elation of the triumphant Austrian Nazis had vanished. There was an atmosphere of suspense, suspicion, espionage, a feeling that everything was in the grip of a ruthless vindictive authority. The radio poured out a stream of abuse of the old regime. There was inflammatory propaganda against Czechoslovakia over the Sudetenland, ridicule of Chamberlain and Daladier. Gradually the sense of something evil, proliferating in the community, weighed heavily on Amelia. She communicated her apprehension to Anthony. They had gone out in his car to a small restaurant in the Wienerwald, high up over the city.

"Yes, Vienna is a prison. Now my exhibition is over I feel I want to get out. Next Thursday Oscar Neumann, who owns the studio, is returning from his people near Innsbruck. I think he's foolish, he should keep in the country away from Vienna. I've written him so but he insists on returning."

He paused, took out his pipe and lit it. He drew at it in silence for some time, then, taking it out of his mouth, spoke with an unusual gravity.

"Amelia, I've something I want to say to you. I feel you shouldn't stay here, but I feel also that I don't want to lose you. I love you, will you marry me? Let us go away from here, anywhere out of Austria. If a war should break out, as an

Austrian, an ex-cadet, I should be called up. If I refused to serve, as I should, then either I would be shot or sent to a concentration camp, where I might die like my father. At present I can get out. I believe I can get a British passport. My father registered me at the British Consulate at birth—thank God, I've got that paper. I'd like to go to England although I'm a complete stranger there. If I'm going to die in battle, I'll die British. Only two things worry me, losing my old grandmother—and you."

"You don't have to lose me. I'll come with you. Let us be married in England, we belong there," replied Amelia.

He said nothing, his eyes meeting hers. Then, taking her hand across the table, he raised it to his lips, holding it there briefly. The gesture was an Austrian one but it conveyed to her all that she longed for. Separation from him had become an unbearable thought. Now, she was no longer alone in the world. A slight smile lit her eyes.

"Darling, you are thinking something—what is it?" he asked.

"A rather singular thing, Anthony. I shan't have to change my name," she replied.

CHAPTER SIXTEEN

I

ANTHONY'S friend returned on Thursday. The next day they came to lunch with Amelia. Oscar Neumann was a dark delicate-looking young man with a sensitive face. He talked nervously, was highly intelligent and well-read. He was taken into their confidence, and congratulated them. They told him they were leaving for Paris en route for England in a week's time. The business of the Exhibition was settled. Contrary to expectation it had been a success. He had sold eighteen of his twenty-four canvases. He was leaving that evening for Graz to say farewell to his grandmother. On Monday, he would be back, preparing for his journey.

"Why don't you come with us?" Anthony asked his friend.

"I can't. I have my people, my studio, my connections. What could I do in England? I can't imagine living anywhere but in Vienna," he replied.

"You should get out—while you can, at any cost," urged Anthony.

"They might not let me go. Besides we Austrians aren't Germans. You'll see, we'll soon damp down these Nazi firebrands."

"But you've heard what they're doing here to the Jews!" cried Anthony. "For God's sake, get out, Oscar!"

The young man shrugged his shoulders. *"Das Schicksal,"* he said quietly.

"Fate! No—don't let fate overtake you. Come with us, Oscar," urged Anthony.

The young man smiled gently. *"Ich habe mein Wien zu gerne,"* he said, half under his breath. He loved his Vienna.

On Monday Anthony was back. He rang from the studio to say that he would call at six o'clock, to go out with Amelia to dinner.

He had not called at half-past six. At seven o'clock as he was still absent, she called the studio. There was no reply. Possibly he was on his way. She waited an hour, wondering what could detain him so long. He was a punctual person. At a quarter-to-nine, having called the studio twice, she went down to dinner. The tables were always filled with Nazi officers these days. They dined well, long and noisily. One young officer, with a bullet head, at an opposite table, ogled her. Finally he came over, clicked his heels, bowed and announced his name. She stood up and left the table. Half-a-dozen officers at another table, seeing his rebuff, burst into loud laughter.

Flushed, angry, Amelia went back to her room. She tried to read but she was too worried to concentrate. She rang the studio again. No one answered. Was it possible that he had forgotten their engagement? At eleven o'clock she went to bed, and slept uneasily.

She rose at eight, breakfasted and waited for a call. He must have some explanation. No call came. At nine o'clock she asked the operator to ring the studio. A few minutes later she was told there was no connection. She was now greatly alarmed. Had there been an accident? She considered calling a taxi and going to the studio, and then she thought of Professor Hofmeyer. She asked the operator to call him. In a couple of minutes she was speaking to him, saying she would like to see him at once. She refrained from giving any reason. She was now in a state of foreboding.

"I will come at once, *gnädige Gräfin*," he said.

In half an hour he was shown into her sitting-room. She told him the reason she had sent for him. "It is very strange. Toni is always so punctual—and where is Herr Neumann, who also lives there? No one answers," she said.

"We will go and see what has happened," replied the Professor.

In a few minutes they reached the door of the block of flats. There was no lift. They ascended the stairs to the fifth floor. The Professor knocked on the door. No answer. He knocked again, and then tried the door. It was locked. At that moment he saw something that made his blood run cold. He said nothing to his companion.

"I think we should go. There's no one in," he said, calmly.

They had reached the floor below when two men, coming up, intercepted them.

"A moment, *mein Herr*," said one of them. "Who are you —what do you want?"

"Who are you?" demanded the Professor.

The man who had spoken opened his coat. On the inside pocket was a badge. He was from the Police Bureau.

"We have come to call on Herr Slowdon, our friend," said the Professor. "I am Professor Heinrich Hofmeyer, late Director of Art in the Rothschild Academy."

"And you?" said the officer brusquely, turning to Amelia.

"This lady is the Gräfin Slowdon, visiting Vienna, staying at the Hotel Sacher. She is a relation of Herr Slowdon who is staying with Herr Neumann, the owner of the studio above."

"We must ask you to come with us to the Police Bureau," said the officer curtly. His companion did not speak.

"Very well. Has anything happened here?" asked the Professor.

The officer made no reply. He turned and began to go down

the stairs. His companion waited until the Professor and Amelia had passed him, and then followed behind.

At the door there was a police car. They were ushered into it.

"But this is an outrage! I insist on calling the British Embassy!" cried Amelia in English.

The officers made no reply. They knew no English. The chauffeur started the car.

"It is better to say nothing, *gnädige Gräfin*, at the moment," said the Professor in a low voice.

The car roared through the streets, turned in at a great archway past two armed sentries and drew up at a door in the corner of the courtyard. They got out, went up to the first floor and were conducted down a long corridor to a room. It was bare except for a table and four chairs. The officers left them, the door closed.

"Whatever is it all about?" asked Amelia. "This is really outrageous! Cannot we telephone the Embassy?"

"They will not let us telephone. We shall be questioned. Say you know nothing."

They waited in silence. Presently an officer returned. He asked the Professor to follow him. The door closed. She was alone.

A quarter of an hour elapsed. She got up and went to the door. It was locked. Fear and indignation possessed her. She picked up a chair and began to beat it against the door. Nothing happened. She sat down again, trembling. In a little while the lock turned. The same officer opened the door, another one stayed in the corridor. The officer said something she did not understand, and indicated she was to follow him. They went down the long corridor to another room, the second man following behind. Amelia was shown into a room where an officer sat at a desk. He rose when she entered. The door closed leaving them alone in the room. The officer motioned her to a chair before seating himself. He was young and good-looking. He wore the insignia of a captain. He spoke to her, calm and well-mannered.

"I do not speak German," said Amelia firmly. She thought it wise to conceal any knowledge of the language.

"*Ach! Parlez-vous français, madame?*"

"*Oui!*"

"Will you please give me your name and address," he said, picking up a pen.

"Why should I give you my name and address? Why am I brought here in this outrageous manner?" cried Amelia, indignantly.

The young officer smiled faintly.

"Madame, we have our duty to do. Your name and address, please."

"I am Lady Slowdon. I am staying at the Hotel Sacher. I am British."

"Thank you. You were found visiting the studio of Oscar Neumann. Why were you visiting him?"

"I refuse absolutely to answer any questions! I demand to be put in touch with my Embassy!" said Amelia firmly.

He looked at the young woman in front of him. She was unbelievably beautiful with her red hair and green eyes. The flush of anger enhanced her complexion.

"I am sorry, madame, that you will not help us in some enquiries we wish to make."

"I am not answering any questions except in the presence of an Embassy official," said Amelia firmly.

"In that case, we may have to detain you for a considerable time."

"Then detain me," retorted Amelia.

There was a pause. Their eyes met. He saw a little flame of anger in her incredible eyes. She did not flinch.

He picked up a telephone and said something so quickly in

German that she could not follow. He replaced the telephone. Then he took out of his breast pocket a gold cigarette case, opened it and offered her a cigarette. She noticed his nails were manicured. She suspected his blond hair was artificially waved.

"*Merci, non!*" she said.

He smiled slightly, took out a cigarette, replaced his case, and produced a lighter.

"*Pardonnez-moi,*" he said, with a slightly mocking air, and lit the cigarette.

There was silence in the room. He sat back and drew at his cigarette, watching her with an air of supercilious admiration. She returned his survey with icy composure.

The door opened, the officer had returned. The captain addressed some words to him and moved from his desk towards the door. She rose. The officer opened the door, the second man was waiting there. As she went out the captain, standing by the door, bowed slightly.

"*Aufwiedersehn, gnädige Gräfin,*" he said.

She walked past him, her head up, as if he were not there. Her gaolers led her down the long corridor, then down the stairs up which she had come. The same car was at the door, they ushered her into it. Where were they taking her now? To a prison? The car left the courtyard, and swiftly threaded the streets. She was surprised to see suddenly the back of the Opera House. In a few moments the car stopped by the pavement. The officer jumped out and held the door for her. She got out. She was back at Sacher's! The officer raised his soft Homberg hat, and smiled satirically. She walked with stiff dignity into the hotel.

When she had gained her room she almost collapsed. A great anxiety possessed her, for Anthony, for the Professor. After a few minutes, more composed, she took up the telephone and called the Professor's house. A woman's voice answered.

"Are you Frau Professor Hofmeyer?"

"Yes?"

"This is the Gräfin Slowdon speaking. Is Professor Hofmeyer in?"

"No, *gnädige Gräfin*. He went out about an hour ago."

"Will you please ask him to call me as soon as he comes in? Thank you."

She replaced the telephone. She had refrained from alarming the poor woman. She sat back and contemplated what next to do. She felt she should go to the Embassy and tell them what had happened, that Anthony had disappeared.

Towards noon the telephone rang. It was the reception desk, informing her that Professor Hofmeyer was below. She told them to send him up. A great relief came over her.

"I have been terribly worried about you," said Amelia as she met him at the door.

"*Gnädige Gräfin*—how worried I have been about you!" replied Professor Hofmeyer, his hand shaking. "What did they do to you?"

"Nothing. I absolutely refused to reply to any of their questions, so they brought me back here—and you?"

"They severely cross-questioned me. They wanted to know when and where I had last seen Herr Neumann and Herr Slowdon. I told them I had never in my life met Herr Neumann, or been to his studio until this morning, that I was there because I had offered to accompany you as you were very worried that your relative, Herr Slowdon, had not kept an appointment for dinner yesterday evening, and you had been unable to make any contact by telephone. They tried very hard to make me say more, to contradict myself. They could not, as I was speaking the truth. They asked how I came to be with you. I told them. They bullied me, then they let me go, saying they might want me again. I asked them why we had been arrested in this manner and could they tell me what had happened to the gentlemen. They refused. Ah, what have we come to Lady Slowdon, with these scoundrels in power. My poor country!"

The old Professor pulled out a handkerchief and wiped his brow with a shaking hand. He was nervously perspiring. "But how happy I am to see you safe," he said. "I was so full of fear for you."

"Have you any idea what it is all about? What has become of Anthony and Herr Neumann?"

"Yes. I have much of the story—it is a terrible one. You may remember, *gnädige Gräfin*, that there are shops on the ground floor of the apartments? It happens that at one of these shops a young woman works who is a neighbour of ours. So that when we were being hustled into that police car she knew me. She was so upset that she decided to go home and inform my wife. She could not leave the shop at once. Happily I had arrived home before she came, or my wife would have been terribly upset. She has told me what happened upstairs. I knew, of course, there had been violence——"

"You knew—how?" asked Amelia.

"When I knocked on the studio door I noticed some brown stains on the floor. They were dried blood, and the trail came out from under the door. I did not tell you, and then the police came. It seems, according to my young neighbour, that yesterday afternoon two police officers, in mufti—she knew them because of the automobile, drew up and entered the building. Curious, she watched. After a while the two men came down with Neumann and another man—Toni, we assume. They were forced into the car. She was shocked to see that Neumann was covered in blood and in a state of collapse. Obviously he had been badly beaten up. She had no chance to see Toni. They were driven off. A little later another police car arrived. Two men got out. They went into the shop next door and asked where the caretaker lived. He lived in the basement. They found him and they went up to the studio. The caretaker told her, after they had gone, that the studio was in a terrible state, the furniture was smashed, chairs upturned, and blood all over everything, on a mirror, on a canvas, and on the floor, still wet. They searched through all the drawers and broke open a chest and took away a file of letters. Then they ordered the caretaker to lock up the studio with his duplicate key, which they took away with them."

"But why—what was it all about?" asked Amelia.

"My neighbour does not know for certain, but she has an idea. Neumann, whom she knows and likes, used to buy things in her shop—it is a stationer's. He told her one day that he refused to wear the yellow star all Jews have now to wear. She said she thought he was risking a great deal, but he insisted that he would not be humiliated in that way. She has an idea also that he had not registered. That may be the reason for all this. The police may have come to arrest him and there was a fight in which Toni was involved. What terrible times we live in! *Gnädige Gräfin*, you will leave Austria?"

"No! Not until I know what has happened to Anthony. I shall go to the British Embassy. We must find out what has happened to them both," she said. Then, glancing at her watch, "It's one o'clock. Let us go down and eat."

After lunch, when the Professor had gone, Amelia called the Embassy. She gave them her name and said she wished to see the Ambassador personally. Her call was transferred several times and finally she reached the Ambassador's secretary. Amelia insisted that it was a matter of great urgency. No, she would not state what it was. The secretary said he would call Lady Slowdon when he had seen the Ambassador, who was very busy.

"Will you please tell him that, however busy he is, this is a matter of life and death," said Amelia firmly.

In ten minutes the telephone rang. The Ambassador would

be pleased to see her at a quarter to six. In the taxi on the way to the Embassy Amelia reflected that had she been a Mrs. Slowdon, staying at a second-class hotel, she would never have got anywhere near the Ambassador. Titles had their uses, however cheapened by prolification these days.

She was received by the Ambassador soon after her arrival. He seemed a little surprised when she was shown into his room.

"You are Lady Slowdon?" he asked, shaking her hand.

"Yes—of Tabara, Buenos Aires."

He offered her a seat. She told him her story. He listened gravely, and then asked her questions. "I would like one of my assistants to hear this," he said. He picked up the telephone and asked for Major Cripps to come in. A middle-aged man appeared. He was introduced to Amelia. The Ambassador gave him a résumé of her story.

"What can we do? We have no right, of course, to concern ourselves over Neumann, an Austrian subject; but Mr. Slowdon is a British subject, resident here," said the Ambassador. "Can you ask the Police Bureau for information about him? We should be entitled to see him, and know why he was arrested."

"We can ask them but we shall probably have an evasive reply. They are very obdurate these days and all the people in the Bureau have changed. They're arrogant Nazis. But we'll try. I'm not quite clear about how Mr. Slowdon came to be in the studio of this Oscar Neumann," said Major Cripps.

"Mr. Slowdon lives in Graz. He borrowed the studio from Herr Neumann while he was having an exhibition of his work here," explained Amelia.

"He is a British subject, resident in Austria?" asked the Ambassador.

"His father, Roderick, was British. Anthony was born here.

He was registered at the British Consulate at birth by his father."

"Has he a British passport?"

"I don't think so. A few days ago he talked to me of getting one. We had planned to be married in England," said Amelia.

"Ah, that's a complication if he has no passport. I fear it greatly weakens our position, eh, Cripps?" asked the Ambassador.

"Very much so," agreed the Major. "They may claim we have no jurisdiction."

"Lady Slowdon, I'm a little in the dark. Would you mind me asking you a personal question?" said the Ambassador, agreeably.

"Not at all," responded Amelia.

"You are Lady Slowdon, wife of Sir Anthony Slowdon, baronet, of Tabara, Buenos Aires? We thought that Lady Slowdon died in 1914."

Amelia smiled. "I see you have been looking me up in Debrett! You found the first Lady Slowdon. I married Sir Anthony, the second baronet, last year. He died soon after, so Debrett hasn't caught up with us yet. Mr. Anthony Slowdon, about whom we are talking, is actually now Sir Anthony Slowdon, the third baronet. He is the son of Roderick who was the former Lady Slowdon's son—he died during the last war in a concentration camp here in Austria. So Anthony Slowdon is my late husband's grandson, and I'm his step-grandmother, although we're about the same age. We are engaged to be married. I'm afraid it sounds awfully complicated!"

"It sounds very romantic to me," said Major Cripps, looking at the vivacious red-haired young woman appreciatively.

"Well, Lady Slowdon, we'll do what we can. As you see, it is difficult with these people newly in power, and his not holding a British passport. You will be staying in Vienna for a while?" asked the Ambassador.

"Yes—until I know what has happened to Sir Anthony."

"Then I hope you'll come and dine one evening. You are at Sacher's?" asked the Ambassador.

"Yes, thank you, I should love to!"

They escorted her to the door. When she had gone they looked at each other.

"What an extraordinary young woman!" commented the Ambassador. "If she married Sir Anthony last year and he died last year, he must have been about seventy-three. Debrett says he was born in 1864."

"The old boy was a jolly good picker, sir! Did you ever see such eyes and hair!"

"And figure—yes, yes," said the Ambassador. "It's very odd though, isn't it, all those Slowdons living here—the first Lady Slowdon, the son Roderick, and his son, this Anthony. The boy was registered here at birth—do you think you can find the record?"

"I doubt it. All our records up to 1918 were lost. We'll look."

"H'm—that makes things difficult. Anyway, let's do our best." He pulled a copy of Debrett towards him and opened it at a marker.

"The first Lady Slowdon died in 1914—Spanish, Carmen Juanita Beaumont y Cardenas, born Seville, 1866, married 1890, Sir Anthony Slowdon, second baronet. One son, Roderick, born 1892. That must be the father of our Anthony. Strange there's nothing here about Roderick's marriage, nor of his death, nor of the birth of a son. Yet I feel Lady Slowdon's telling the truth."

He closed the Debrett and pushed it away. "Well, see what can be done, Cripps."

"I will, sir, but it's going to be difficult. Those Nazis in the Police Bureau are arrogant devils to deal with."

He left the room. Three-quarters of an hour later he came back to the Ambassador's room.

"I've got a little bit of news for you, sir, but not concerning the missing Sir Anthony. Young Thomas, when I called him in to start our enquiry at the Police Bureau was agog with excitement. It seems that Lady Slowdon showed up here some weeks ago, trying to find some trace of Roderick Slowdon. She turned the department upside down. They just couldn't get over her—those green eyes and red hair! It seems that she also turned over the Consulate-General, and one of our fellow's been going to dine at Sacher's just to look at her when she comes into the dining-room! He saw her pestered by a young Nazi officer one evening. It seemed she froze him on the spot and made him look like a slapped puppy!"

"Well, you don't surprise me. I don't wonder that old Sir Anthony met his Waterloo. I'm asking her to dine one evening, and you must join us and bring Mrs. Cripps."

"Thank you, sir. That will be quite an event!"

III

Five days of frightful anxiety passed. The British Embassy got into contact with the Austrian authorities.

"The trouble is no one seems to be in absolute authority," said Major Cripps when Amelia called to see him, anxious for news. "It would appear, Lady Slowdon, that, as we feared, the military are in complete control, and all the civil authorities have been superseded. The military authorities are, of course, the German Nazis, who have taken over the country. They treat us with contempt. Our other difficulty is, as our people told you when you were making enquiries here, that we have no record whatsoever of Sir Anthony. It is most unfortunate that we lost all our records up to 1918 owing to the Great War, and some other records were lost in a fire during the street fighting in the Revolution later. I fear that the passport is going to be a great difficulty, but the Ambassador has instructed us to do all that we can, and I can assure you we shall try to get Sir Anthony a passport, somehow. So don't give up hope, Lady Slowdon."

Obsessed by the fate of Anthony and young Neumann, Amelia found she could not enjoy any of the pleasures of Vienna. The opera and the theatres were in full swing again, life began to assume its normal pace though there were more uniforms on the street. The military police were visible everywhere. There was a constant roar of their armoured cars down the streets. It began to be known what was happening to the unfortunate Jews. Most of their shops were burned, Jewish lawyers could no longer practise in the courts, there were raids on cafés where they congregated: they became a hunted community. Then rumours began of arrests by night, of Jews being swiftly taken away in trains to concentration camps in Germany. No one protested. A cowed population saw their fellow citizens of Jewish blood being insulted, harried, assaulted, arrested, and swiftly spirited away.

To occupy her mind during this ordeal of waiting for news, Amelia engaged Professor Hofmeyer to give her German lessons. It put money in his pocket, it gave her company. They visited the art galleries together, but all the time she thought of Anthony languishing in some gaol.

On Sunday morning they attended service in the Burg-Kapelle and heard the famous Vienna choir boys. After the service they went to the Spanish Riding School and saw a parade of the famous white Lippiza stallions. The Professor knew a captain of the riding school and after the performance they were invited into the stall of one of the horses. There were a small table and chairs. Sitting in the stall, they drank a glass of wine toasting the beautiful Lippiza horse that calmly looked on.

Amelia returned to the Hotel Sacher having said goodbye to her escort. After lunch she was writing letters when the telephone rang.

"Yes?" she asked.

"Amelia—I'm downstairs—Anthony!"

"Anthony! Come up at once."

"Very well."

Amelia replaced the receiver, her hand shaking. She waited. It seemed an interminable time before there was a tap on the door. She was there immediately and opened it. At once they were in each other's arms. Then she saw that his lip was cut, a bandage was round his head and one hand was bound up.

"Where have you come from? What happened?" asked Amelia, as he released her.

He said nothing for a moment or two, made a gesture, and sat down.

"I'll tell you, my dear," he said. "It's not a pretty story. When I called you on Monday on my return from Graz, I was at Oscar's studio. I was about to leave, a little before six, after I had been talking with Oscar, when there was a banging on the door. Oscar opened it. Two men stood there. Without a word they walked in. 'Oscar Neumann?' one of them said, 'you are under arrest. You will come with us.' Oscar asked why. 'We've nothing to say to you. We'll give you five minutes to pack a bag,' they said. Oscar again demanded to know who they were, why he was to be arrested. They told him they had come from the Police Bureau. He said he wouldn't go with them. He had his back to an easel and was deathly white. I got up from a chair by the stove to remonstrate with him. Before I could say a word those two brutes pulled out their steel whips and began to beat Oscar over the head and

244

shoulders. It was too much for me. I went for one of them. There was a free fight, all of us mixed up, the furniture crashing over. But they were too much for us, big powerful brutes armed with those *stahlruten*. One of them had poor Oscar on the floor and was mercilessly thrashing him. I struggled with the other brute and was knocked almost insensible with a blow on the head. Poor Oscar lay moaning in a pool of blood while the officer handcuffed him. I was bleeding badly too, and too stunned to know exactly what was happening. I can't remember anything clearly until I found myself at the foot of the stairs and being hustled out to a waiting car. I made an attempt to break away and got another blow from that steel whip. I was blinded with blood. They threw us into the car and carried us off to their barracks. I was put in a cell alone and kept there until ten o'clock at night. Then I was taken before three officers, still soaked in blood, put under a blinding arc-light, and interrogated. They wanted to know why I was in the studio, how long I had been associated with Oscar, where he had been and what he had been doing all the time he had been away. They asked for my registration papers. They examined them and when I said I was a British subject, they laughed and said, 'You're an Austrian—look at these papers.' They refused to let me communicate with the Embassy. Then they took me back to my cell. I had nothing to eat until the next morning. I didn't know what had happened to Oscar. I don't know now. I was questioned twice again, but of course they could get nothing out of me—there's nothing to get. They charged me with opposing the police, and violent assault. It seemed, I was glad to learn, I had broken the nose of the brute who tackled me. On Wednesday they sent a prison doctor to look at me. I asked him what had happened to Oscar. 'You'll not have to bother any more about him,' he said grimly. I don't know what's happened to the poor fellow. I fear the worst. About ten o'clock on Friday morning, they shifted me out of

245

the cell into an ordinary room. Another officer interrogated me, quite politely this time. This morning they sent for me again. At the end they asked me to sign a paper declaring I was not a Jew and that I had nothing to complain of in my treatment during arrest. I sensed that something was afoot. I signed, anything to get out of their clutches. At two o'clock they gave me back my papers and told me I could go. I've come straight here. I've been worried to death about you, my dear. You must have wondered what on earth had happened to me!"

"I knew!"

"You knew—but how? They wouldn't let me communicate with anyone," said Anthony.

"I've been in their hands also, I and the Professor." She told him her story.

"So that's why they released me! You got the Embassy moving! I felt something had happened with that signing of a paper to say I had nothing to complain of. Nothing to complain of!" repeated Anthony putting his hand up to his head. "I've a cut four inches long, and my hand is lacerated. But it's nothing to what they did to poor Oscar. I don't know what they've done with him, whether he's dead or alive. Darling, we must get out of here. This place has been turned into a hell. They are quite mad. One day Hitler will start a war—can't the British see that? They're out to conquer the world!"

Amelia went over to him and touched the bandage on his head.

"Shouldn't you see a doctor?" she asked.

"Perhaps, but first, I'm ravenously hungry—I've had nothing since seven this morning and then only a crust and awful coffee. Oh, those bloody swine! Sorry, Amelia!"

"Bloody swine is not a bit too strong," she said, picking up the telephone and ordering food to be sent up at once.

Anthony took her hands in his, held them a moment, then leaned forward and kissed her.

"Listen, darling—we've no time to lose. We must get out of this town as soon as possible. First I must have a British passport. When I've got that, there's something else. Have you your papers with you and your passport?"

"Yes. Everything, including a copy of your grandfather's Will and his death certificate—but why?"

"Because we'll need them—we're going to be married at the Consulate as soon as possible. And then goodbye Vienna!"

"But Anthony, darling, can we? Is it possible?"

"I hope so. We're going to try anyhow. That's what Consuls are for, among other things. And as soon as we're married we'll leave for Venice, it's the nearest place out of Austria."

"Venice? Venice?" repeated Amelia, dumbfounded.

"Yes—what's wrong with Venice?" he asked.

For the first time for days Amelia broke into laughter, and put her arms round his neck. "But it's almost ridiculous!" she cried.

"Ridiculous—why ridiculous, my girl?"

"Because, Anthony darling, it's so commonplace! All honeymooners go to Venice! And now a red-haired widow from Buenos Aires and a poor boy with a cracked skull just out of prison are joining the everlasting procession of brides and bridegrooms!" she cried, hugging him tightly.

She was laughing but he saw her eyes were brimming with tears.

IV

They found wonderful allies in their hour of need. Major Cripps produced a wife, the wife was a bosom friend of the Consul-General's wife. The Embassy and the Consulate joined forces to make their path smooth. But it took two weeks to get the necessary papers in order. There was a swift journey to Graz to collect a birth certificate, to draw some money out of the bank where Anthony kept an account, to get clothes, replacing those locked up in the studio.

Anthony insisted on taking Amelia with him to Graz. He wanted to show Grossmütter Schönborn-Smith his fiancée. There was great mirth when Anthony's grandmother and step-grandmother met. She was a witty sharp-worded old lady.

"The situation has a whiff of incest about it. Thank God you're a pair of immoral Protestants! I don't know what Holy Church would say about it! Your father," she said, addressing Anthony, "married my daughter after only two months courtship, and here you are marrying someone you've barely known three months! The Slowdons are fast workers—and good pickers."

There was a tearful parting from the old lady. She had two daughters to console her, aunts to Anthony, who had helped to bring up the orphaned child. Back in Vienna they completed their arrangements. They thought it wise to keep everything as secret as possible, the shadow of the Police Bureau being over them. They were married in an office carrying on its walls two portraits of King George VI and Queen Elizabeth, in a ceremony so brief that they wondered if they really were married.

For Amelia the ceremony had a curious echo. This was the second time she had been married by a British Consul-General, and to a husband named Slowdon. But there was no doubt about it. The marriage certificate was witnessed by Major Cripps, Mrs. Cripps and Professor Heinrich Hofmeyer. One shadow fell on that happy morning. There was no clue to the fate of Oscar Neumann. He had disappeared leaving not a trace.

The hours before they reached their sleeping-car, Venice-bound, were an ordeal. They were still apprehensive of the Police Bureau. The next morning at the frontier station they were again fearful. Their British passports were examined. All was well. The Austrian control officer politely saluted. The train went on over the frontier into Italy. Through the window of their wagon-lit they saw the jagged peaks of the Friulian Alps, rosy in the dawn. Italy, with no shadow of the Swastika yet upon it.

There followed, after their descent from the Alps, and the journey over the flat Venetian plain, the speechless wonder of the exit from the drab railway station on to the Grand Canal, with the first black gondola, the first high-arched marble bridge, the green lapping water, the commotion of boats, launches and steamers, the wide green waterway bordered by towering palaces.

Their hotel on the Grand Canal had a large garden from which, across the water, soared the vast façade and voluted dome of Santa Maria della Salute. On a warm April day it was possible to lunch in that garden with its superb vista. The manager of the hotel was a ski-ing pupil of Anthony's. He gave them a room with a balcony commanding the Grand Canal and its wide opening into the lagoon.

Through days of inexpressible happiness they explored the city of the Doges, by launch, by gondola, but mostly on foot, for as Anthony knew, having spent many student months in this maze of palaces, bridges, courts and canals, one could only discover the endless marvels by walking and loitering.

The days were sunny though sharp. Sudden gusty visitations of rain bestowed new riches, touching the reflective marble with varied lights and colours. Nor did they resist the commonplace. They bought corn and fed the pigeons in the Piazza and had themselves photographed in the act.

One week, two weeks, three weeks, and then, one morning, they had to make a decision. London or Buenos Aires? Letters from Messrs. Mayne, Gonzalos and Gomez ended their indecision. The discovery of Anthony had brought a new factor to the involved conditions of old Sir Anthony's Will. The grandson under Argentine law had a claim on the estate as the sole male heir. "We feel it is essential Sir Anthony should come to Buenos Aires to facilitate the necessary legal business," wrote the solicitors. "The transfer of Tabara cannot be completed for six months and you are entitled to stay there until the completion of the sale. We are writing Sir Anthony, pointing out how necessary it is that he should be here."

There was a letter also from Doña Lucia. Surely the bridegroom, Anthony's grandson, would be brought for inspection? "Do come. I long to see you both."

The discovery at the shipping office that a boat sailed in mid-May for Buenos Aires from Genoa sealed the matter. They booked a passage.

CHAPTER SEVENTEEN

ON an afternoon in July 1942, at the corner of Cromwell Road and Queen's Gate, London, a large house was demolished by a German bomb. Only a shattered shell remained of a mansion in which, through more than fifty years, there had been a succession of lunches, at homes, dinners and balls. Victorian security, Edwardian gaiety, and Georgian prosperity had lost their memorial. Windowless frames, like the sockets of a skull, bore witness to the visitation of violent death. Cats and rats haunted the large desolate basement, littered with bricks and charred beams where once a dozen servants had sat round the kitchen table. A broken Corinthian column was the sole witness of grandeur upstairs. Across the road, in an adjacent mews the trail of destruction had also spread.

On the morning after the bombing, in a flat on the second floor of a house in Queen's Gate, whose back windows overlooked this desolation, Lady Slowdon, who had miraculously survived, sat down to write a letter to her husband, Captain Sir Anthony Slowdon, now somewhere in North Africa. He had been gone two months, after a leave that had been heartbreakingly brief. Happily, Amelia had her work at the War Office, an antidote to brooding. The letter she had begun writing yesterday evening had been interrupted by air raid sirens and had been laid aside when, with the other occupants of the house, she had taken refuge in the capacious basement.

She now began the letter again, with its particular news, but was destined to be interrupted again. The telephone rang. Grateful that it was still intact, she picked up the receiver on the writing-desk, where it stood beside a large photograph of her husband in uniform.

"Yes?" she said, a little impatiently.

"Lady Slowdon?"

"Yes?"

"*Le jour où la pluie viendra——*" began a soft voice.

"Etienne!" exclaimed Amelia.

"*C'est moi!*"

"Where are you?"

"I am here in London via Bordeaux and a submarine! I'm on the staff of de Gaulle. When can we meet?"

"Are you free for lunch?" asked Amelia.

"Yes—that would be delightful!"

"Then, if you don't mind a snack lunch, come here, at half-past twelve. You'll find me covered with dust. We were bombed last night. I warn you it won't be a Brillat-Savarin lunch."

"A biscuit with you would be a banquet, *chère* Amelia."

"You haven't changed."

"Oh, yes I have. I am a most reformed character!"

"We'll see. At twelve-thirty, then."

"*Merci. A bientôt,*" he said.

Etienne de Lérin in London! She had often wondered what had happened to him in the world holocaust. Death stalked everywhere. From a cousin in New York came word of Professor Hofmeyer's death. Grossmütter Schönborn-Smith was gone. In five years there had been no news of the fate of Oscar Neumann. Mr. Carson had died. Her brother Henry had been lost at sea. Here, in London, amid the bombings, death had ceased to be a significant thing. It had become a commonplace of their lives.

Anthony, restless at Tabara, and certain a war was going to break, had booked a passage home from the Argentine. The timing was felicitous. They arrived one month before Hitler marched into Poland and opened the second World War. More British than the British, Anthony had joined up at once, after some fuss over his birthplace. He had been a year in England before being sent abroad. A friend had procured her a secretaryship in the War Office. Her work was a tranquilliser. Through blackouts and bombings she was seeing it out. Day and night her great anxiety, that of a million other women, was what might happen to one particular man in a place never quite defined. When Anthony returned on leave life was good again in their too brief reunion. And now here was Etienne, very much alive.

Amelia picked up her pen to continue the letter. There was a knock on the door. They were determined not to allow her to get on with the letter. She got up and went to the door.

"Yes?" said Amelia sharply, opening it. A white-faced girl confronted her. She knew her. She occupied one of the ten rooms in the converted apartment house.

"Oh, Lady Slowdon! I'm terribly sorry but something awful is happening upstairs!"

Considering what had happened overnight all around them the complaint had little force.

"What is happening upstairs?" asked Amelia.

"It's Miss Pears in Number Seven. She's just called me in—she's having a baby! She says the bombing's brought it on!"

"Aren't you a nurse?" asked Amelia. She had seen her in uniform.

"Yes—I'm at St. Mary's, but I'm not in the maternity ward. Please, can I use your telephone to call a doctor?"

"Yes. Come in!" said Amelia.

They dialled the doctor's number. There was no answer. After three attempts they called Operator. Operator curtly said, "The line's out of order—dozens of lines are out of order this morning!"

"You'd better go at once and get the doctor. I'll go up to Miss Pears," said Amelia.

She had no more experience with maternity cases than the white-faced hospital nurse, but she did not lose her head. While the doctor was sought she went upstairs to Number Seven, and sat with the groaning Miss Pears, a platinum blonde, who worked as a telephone operator at an Army hostel in the King's Road. Amelia did her best with the frightened girl.

The doctor arrived in the nick of time. Miss Pears was delivered of a boy.

"I warned her," said the nervous young nurse. "He was always spending the night here. I couldn't get into the landing bathroom while he was shaving!"

"Why should you want to?" asked Amelia.

"Oh, I don't mean that, Lady Slowdon! I meant he monopolised it!"

Back in her own flat, it was half-past eleven. The morning was lost. She had barely time to get the lunch ready. Thank heavens there was a bottle of wine, left over from Anthony's leave. You could not give a Frenchman lunch without wine, not even in war-time, and such a Frenchman.

She slipped the unfinished letter into a drawer, went into the tiny kitchen, put on an overall, and began to prepare the lunch. As she held a saucepan she broke into a smile. How long ago it seemed since, in a restaurant in Buenos Aires, Etienne, satirically listing her accomplishments, had asked her if she could cook, and she had told him she was not fond of the frying pan, the oven and the sink. Now here she was with them all. It was surprising how one changed.

She had just completed her toilet when the bell rang. She went down to the front door and opened it. There he stood, in a smart dark blue uniform, perhaps more debonair than ever.

"Etienne!"

"Amelia!"

"Come up—I'm on the first floor."

When he was in the sitting room he opened his arms and she went into them. They embraced each other.

"What fun! But a drink first, sherry or gin? The choice is poor these days," said Amelia.

"Sherry. Here you are, Lady Slowdon, twice over!" he said, his eyes twinkling. "And where's Sir Anthony?"

"Somewhere in Africa. And you—when did you get here and how did you find me?"

"I looked in the telephone book. There you were, or rather Sir Anthony. I'd heard you were married and in London."

"We've only just got in it—that was lucky. And what's brought you to London?" asked Amelia.

He told her. The account sounded very simple, Cairo, Paris, the Army, the Underground, a Free French submarine bringing him to Plymouth. But obviously there had been hair-raising moments. He had left his wife with his people in Provence.

"Your wife—you are married!" cried Amelia.

"Yes—two years. I'm a father! Look!"

He pulled out a wallet, opened it and eagerly showed her a photograph of a young woman holding a baby.

"Claudia and Robert," he said, beaming.

"Robert—a boy?"

"Yes—nine months old."

She returned the wallet. Their eyes met. They both smiled at the wonder of it.

"She looks nice—not a *petite gamine*," said Amelia mischievously.

"As nice as the nicest *gamine* I ever teased, *chère* Amelia!" he cried, catching her hand.

"And now—lunch," said Amelia, leading him to the small table she had set by the window overlooking the wide tree-lined avenue.

At half-past two, when Etienne reported to his headquarters, gay and charming as ever, she went to the small writing-table and took out the much interrupted letter. She read what she had written, a chronicle of little events saved for her weekly account.

". . . I have not been to the War Office since Monday. I have been feeling very tired, a little tense, but I am all right now. I went to our doctor. Tony dearest, you will be a father, I learned. Yesterday we were almost bombed out, but I am all right. Quite well, and very very happy . . ."

She finished the letter, addressed the envelope and then went downstairs to catch the four o'clock post. There was a pillar box standing on the corner, under the branches of a tree. It had survived the bombing. It was very old, possibly sixty years, for it still had V.R. on its bright red face. There it was, constant, cheerful, still performing its office while a war raged on the earth and in the heavens. Amelia put in her letter and speculated on how many missives it had received down the years. A very great number. But certainly it had never received a happier one than that she had just posted.